Praise for Kate Donovan

"Kate Donovan's *Parallel Lies* is so full of action
it will keep readers on the edge of their seats from
start to finish. Her characters are well-developed
and her dialogue and description are great."
—*Romantic Times BOOKclub*

"*Identity Crisis* is a terrific CIA suspense thriller
that never slows down until the final confrontation
between the Feds and the bad guys occurs."
—Harriet Klausner

* * *

*A rough voice reminded her of the
danger to an agent on an unsanctioned
op in a foreign land. "Freeze!"*

Miranda spun toward the voice, and as she did so,
the test tube of HeetSeek slipped from her grasp,
crashing to the floor at her feet.

She jumped back, certain that the lab would be
rocked by an explosion. When nothing happened,
she almost laughed with relief. Then she raised
her hands above her head, looked directly into the
angry eyes of the armed men in the doorway and
said with a cheerful smile, "I guess I'm busted.
And so is my loot."

Dear Reader,

Every once in a while when I'm writing a story, I fall in love with the wrong guy—a guy the heroine would *never* choose because he's so flawed. She rides off into the sunset with her chosen love, and I'm left with two choices—rehabilitate *my* guy so that he's hero material, or just keep him for myself.

At least, that's the way it used to be.

Enter Silhouette Bombshell, which gives me a third choice: find a heroine who loves my flawed guy, warts and all. Because in Bombshell, he really doesn't have to be a "hero" in the sense that he saves the day—the heroine takes care of that! He just has to be the right guy for her. And he has to be sexy.

Which brings us to fiery, tortured Ray Ortega. If you read *Identity Crisis,* you know how badly he screwed up. If you didn't read it, even better! This story tells you all you need to know about Ortega's shortcomings—*and* his impressive strengths.

But most of all, you'll be impressed by Miranda Cutler. She really does save the day—in ways you could never expect. I hope you agree they're an incendiary pair!

Best wishes,

Kate

Kate Donovan

EXIT STRATEGY

Silhouette®

BOMBSHELL™

Published by Silhouette Books

America's Publisher of Contemporary Romance

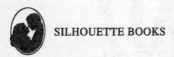

SILHOUETTE BOOKS

ISBN 0-373-51381-X

EXIT STRATEGY

www.SilhouetteBombshell.com

Printed in U.S.A.

Books by Kate Donovan

Silhouette Bombshell

KATE DONOVAN

is the author of more than a dozen novels and novellas, ranging from time travel and paranormal to historical romance, suspense and romantic comedy. An attorney, she draws on her criminal law background to create challenges worthy of her heroines, who crack safes, battle bad guys and always get their man. As for Kate, she *definitely* got her man and is living happily ever after with him and their two children in Elk Grove, California.

To Paul—writing this story was a breeze
because I had you to inspire it.
Love, Kate.

Chapter 1

"This is such an honor, Ms. Smith. Working with you and your team. You guys are legendary at Langley. Especially you." Twenty-six-year-old Miranda Cutler took a deep breath to stop herself from gushing. Then she adopted a more businesslike tone. "May I ask why I was chosen for this assignment?"

"You have all the necessary qualifications," Jane Smith explained, reaching across the kitchen table to finger a lock of Miranda's hair. "You live in a building with security cameras, and you have red hair. Or at least, almost red. If there was more time I'd make you lighten it, but this will have to do."

Miranda stared for a moment, certain that the older agent was joking. Then without pulling away she murmured, "I don't understand."

"Don't be misled. It's a compliment that we're trusting a rookie with something as sensitive as this. Of course, we had no choice. But still, you're lucky. I would have killed for this kind of opportunity when I was starting out."

The bitchiness underlying Smith's attitude stung Miranda, but the younger CIA operative reminded herself that this woman was the best of the best. The mere whisper of her name in the espionage world evoked stories of daring exploits and black ops phenomena. And for reasons that were about to be revealed, this superspy was seated at Miranda's kitchen table.

With that reminder in place, she used a respectful tone as she asked her guest, "What kind of opportunity is it, exactly? I mean, red hair and security cameras? There must be more to it than that."

Smith nodded. "Less than five hours ago, a high-ranking government official was framed for murder. If the story reaches the public, that man's reputation will be ruined for life, as will the reputation of the president. We're going to prevent that from happening."

Miranda leaned forward, impressed with the plan, and finally understanding the interest in the security cameras. "We're going to provide him with an alibi? Make it look like he was here with me when the murder occurred?"

Smith glanced over her shoulder at the pair of male operatives who had been quietly pacing Miranda's living room floor. "She's quick, just like I predicted."

"And built," the blonder of the two men added. "Ortega's gonna love her."

"Ortega?" Miranda shook her head, certain that she had misunderstood. "You don't mean Ray Ortega, do you? I mean, I know you and he used to work together—"

"And now he's the director of the Strategic Profiling and Identification Network," Smith confirmed. "More importantly, he's the president's choice for the next director of the FBI—a position with *much* more influence. Ortega's going to kick ass in that job, and there are those who want to keep that from ever taking place."

"So they framed him for murder? My God." Miranda sat back in her chair, trying to absorb the information while marveling at her good luck in landing this high-level assignment. First, Jane Smith ringing her doorbell in the middle of the night. Now Ray Ortega—another legend. This one, an out-and-out hero. And if half of what she'd heard about him was true, a genius at reading people. Not to mention at killing them.

"Earlier this evening, Ortega arrived at a Southern California beach house for a meeting with one of the president's advisors. He found the advisor dead on the floor under circumstances that were clearly arranged to incriminate Ortega himself. His first impulse was to call the police, but he knew it would create a scandal. He could clear his name eventually, of course. But it would ruin his chances of becoming the Bureau's director. He wants that job—not for the glory, but because he wants to clean up this country. The scum that framed him fear him for that very reason. So…" Smith took a deep breath, then explained, "Ortega did the smart thing. The right thing. He called me."

"For an alibi."

"A temporary one. Until he can prove he was framed. Luckily I was in L.A. with most of my team, so we immediately started cleaning up the crime scene. Restaging it so that it looks like a simple break-in gone wrong. Once it was under control, I headed back here.

"Meanwhile, Ortega was smuggled out of town to a private landing strip where we had a plane waiting for him. He flew to Dallas and changed planes, using a fake identity to take a commercial flight home. It took precious extra time, but was necessary. Flight records will have to be doctored, of course. There are a million details," Smith added, as though speaking to herself rather than Miranda.

Then she patted the younger agent's hand. "When Ortega's plane touches down, you'll be there. You'll ride back here with him and enter the building, pretending to be returning home from three dates. The cameras will record every move, then my team will splice the footage into existing tapes."

"Three dates?"

Smith grinned. "One would seem too convenient. So you and Ortega are going to reenact a series of them. It's all in the script we'll provide for you. You'll study it on your way to the airport. Be convincing. A great man's reputation is riding on it."

Ray Ortega. He *was* a great man. And a noble one, if half the stories were true. The thought of someone ruining him, negating all the sacrifices he had made for his country, not to mention all the great deeds he was still destined to accomplish, angered Miranda, and she insisted quietly, "I won't let you down."

Smith surprised her with an actual smile. "Your file is impressive for a rookie. I'll use you again soon if I'm satisfied with your performance."

"You mean, if Ortega's satisfied," the blond man interrupted with a lascivious chuckle.

When Miranda shot him a disgusted glare, Smith chided her. "If you're going to succeed in this business, you'll need to develop a thicker skin. *And* a sense of humor."

Not waiting for a response, the older agent stood up and walked into the bedroom. Miranda trailed after her, watching as she began pulling clothes out of the closet. "First date, this. With jeans. Sexy, but not overwhelming." She shoved a white eyelet shirt that was styled like a bustier into Miranda's hands. "Second date…let's see." She rejected a series of items, settling finally on a medium-length black skirt and a black leather jacket. "With boots. And some sort of camisole or tube top."

Miranda nodded.

"And for the big night, this is perfect." She pulled out a short, sassy dress made of shimmering dark green fabric. "Green eyes, green dress, right? With sandals. No stockings. No bra. A signal dress."

"Signal? Oh…" Miranda struggled not to flush. "Gotcha."

"Remember, you're doing it for your country," the fair-haired man said from the doorway.

"Shut up," Miranda advised him, adding to Smith, "I guess you're right. I've got no sense of humor where this pig is concerned."

Smith nodded, then turned toward the blond man. "Enough with the needling, Mark. Do something useful. Check to see if Ortega's plane is on time."

"I just called. It's ten minutes ahead of schedule."

Smith nodded again, then told Miranda, "Get dressed. Mark will drive you to the airport. You'll study the script on the way there. You and Ortega can spend the ride back getting acquainted. And by getting acquainted," she added dryly, "I mean, having sex in the limo."

"What?" Miranda grimaced. "Is that another joke?"

Ignoring Mark's laughter, Smith explained. "I want the camera to record two people who have been dating for a week and are just about ready to explode from repressed lust. Professional agents will be watching this tape to verify Ortega's alibi, and I want them to either be too embarrassed to study it intently, or so caught up in the erotic elements, they won't notice tiny imperfections in our work. Which means you and Ortega have to put on a convincing show."

Miranda's thoughts flashed back to her father, who had reacted with disdain when she had first announced her plans to join the CIA. "You're too pretty," he had informed her bluntly. "They'll use you like a whore."

Stung, she had reminded him about the awards that covered the walls of her childhood bedroom. Marksmanship and archery—the girl with the perfect aim. But he had just shaken his head, muttering, "You'll see," and she had vowed never to discuss it with him again, a vow she kept until the day he died, six months later.

"Is this a problem?" Jane Smith asked her now, her tone every bit as disdainful as Roger Cutler's had been. "Do I need to find someone else?"

"No, it's fine." Miranda took a deep breath, knowing it was useless—and unwise—to argue with Smith. Better to wait until she met Ortega. Surely he'd understand that they could be convincing for the camera without such extreme tactics. And if he agreed with Smith, well…

"I'll do whatever it takes to help Director Ortega," she announced finally.

The older agent flashed a triumphant smile. "Smart girl. This could make your career, you know. So get dressed. We'll clear out of here.

"And remember. When you walk through your front door and into the hall, the show starts. Don't look up at the camera, but be aware of it. You're a single girl—one who hasn't gotten laid in a while. You're headed for O'Leary's hoping to find the guy of your dreams. Keep the act up until you clear the front walkway. Then go around to the Baker Street side. Mark will be waiting for you with the file. Study it on the ride. Once you hook up with Ortega, follow his lead. He's a pro."

"So am I," Miranda assured her quietly. "Don't worry about Ortega. He'll be in good hands."

During the half-hour ride to the airport, Miranda ignored the suggestive jokes and lame double entendres of her escort, concentrating instead on the script and discovering that this was really a fairly simple assignment. All she had to do was act naturally while keeping in mind the location of the four video cameras—one on the front steps of the apartment building, one in the lobby, the elevator camera, and the one positioned over the exterior of the elevator doors at the end of the hall leading to her apartment.

For the first "date," she and Ortega were apparently just going to talk, and while the security system wouldn't actually record their words, the script reminded them to get into their roles and stay in them. The date would end in the hallway, with Ortega kissing her respectfully.

The second date was also fairly mild. More talking for the cameras, but in an intimate fashion, with occasional nuzzling. A lingering kiss at the door, an invitation into the apartment, from which Ortega would be taped leaving after only a few minutes with a look of frustration on his face, as though he had been sure he was about to score.

Clever, she had to admit. *Sounds like a real second date.*

The third date was scripted as an inferno, complete with make-out sessions in the lobby, elevator and hall. Ortega would again be invited in, and this time he'd stay until early morning, when the cameras would catch him leaving, a satisfied expression on his face.

Most of the footage would be spliced into existing tapes, but this last bit—Ortega's final exit—would be caught in real time, which meant he would actually spend the rest of the night with her.

It was already close to 4:00 a.m., and it would take at least an hour to get back to her place and film the three dates. They had to be finished long before 7:00 a.m., when the residents of her apartment building were first expected to venture into the hallways. Had it been a weekday morning, the timetable would have been almost impossible to plan, but this was Friday night—or more accurately, Saturday morning—and so they had a little more leeway.

"Time for your hot date," Mark announced, slowing his black SUV to a stop on a dark stretch of road near the airport. "Ortega's limo should be showing up any minute."

She nodded. "I'm just going to leave this script with you if that's okay."

"Sure." His gray eyes twinkled. "Enjoy yourself. I know Ortega will."

"Did I mention you're a pig?" she grumbled.

"I'll call you when this is all over. We'll have a drink and laugh about it. No hard feelings."

"I'd love to get together when we're both off duty," she said with a purr. "It'll give me a chance to beat the crap out of you." Jumping from the vehicle, she slammed the door, then rested her thumb and little finger against her cheek in imitation of a phone, mouthing the words "Call me."

Her driver scowled, revved the engine and sped away, just as a limousine rolled into view. It pulled up until the right rear passenger door was within inches of where she stood. Then the door opened, and she had to remind herself to take a deep breath before peeking inside. "Director Ortega?"

"Agent Cutler?" A handsome, dark-haired man gave her a reassuring smile. "Get in. We've got a lot to do, and not much time to do it."

She slid in next to him, still forcing herself to breathe normally, but it wasn't easy. For one thing, he was better looking than she had imagined he'd be. High cheekbones; wavy blue-black hair; an infectious smile. And his eyes were amazing—dark brown with flecks of bronze. She was sure he was well-built, but for the moment, she couldn't get past his arresting face to check out the rest of him.

Of course, she'd find out about the body soon enough....

"Jane really outdid herself," he told her simply. "You've got just the right look. I assume she told you about my history with sexy redheads?"

Miranda flushed. "If there had been more time, I would have done something to bring out more red highlights—"

"It's perfect the way it is. Auburn, right?"

She nodded.

Ortega touched her arm. "This is an unconventional assignment, especially for a rookie. It's okay to be a little nervous."

"I'm just excited," she countered, then she flushed again, fearing he'd misinterpret her enthusiasm.

"Great. So? I assume you've read the script? How would you like to proceed?"

Miranda gave her shoulders a small shrug. "Jane Smith seemed to think we should…well…fool around a little—"

"Jane Smith is a freaking robot about this kind of thing," he interrupted, his jaw muscles visibly clenching. "I apologize for her."

Miranda closed her eyes and was able to breathe normally for the first time since she'd entered the vehicle. "That's okay."

"Do you need a drink?"

"No. Not at all." She gave him a grateful smile. "It really is an honor to assist you, sir."

"How much did she tell you about my predicament?"

"You've been framed for murder. It's outrageous," she added staunchly. "No one would believe you're a killer—"

"I *am* a killer," he corrected her. "But not a murderer. So? What do you say we get acquainted? The old-fashioned way. By talking," he added, his warm smile returning.

He had read Miranda's file—in fact, he seemed to have memorized it—and asked thoughtful questions about her life on the ranch both before and after the accident that put her father in a wheelchair. He remarked on her awards, complimented her performance during training and smoothly integrated some suggestions regarding their upcoming dates, mostly having to do with her comfort level as he repeatedly reminded her that as his date, she always had the right to say "no" to any move he made. If at any time his pace made her uncomfortable, she had only to say one word to make him back off.

Just like a real date....

"According to your file, they've got you in some sort of language immersion program. What's that about?"

"It's something new they're trying," she explained. "Exposing me to twelve different languages at one time. Not so much to learn any of them, obviously, but to be able to recognize them, and identify key words, patterns, that sort of thing."

"Have they said why?"

"No, but I'm dying to find out. Some assignment in an international hub, I'm guessing. Or—" she paused to smile "—maybe they just want to see what it does to my thought patterns."

He nodded in agreement. "Has it affected your dreaming?"

"Not yet. But I'm supposed to keep a dream journal. Do you have a theory?"

"No. But it's fascinating. You'll have to tell me how it all works out."

His mood was so calm, especially given his circumstances, the effect was almost eerie, and so relaxing that Miranda had to shake herself back to attention when the limousine drew to a halt on a side street two blocks from her apartment.

"We'll walk from here," Ortega explained, his tone suddenly brisk. "Remember, even though there's no audio, we'll stay in character—words as well as actions. You never know when someone might be a lip-reader."

"I understand."

The driver opened the door, and Miranda slid out of the vehicle, followed by Ortega. For the first time, she realized how tall he was, and definitely well-built in his black polo shirt and tan slacks. He was staring down at her, the bronze flecks in his eyes sparkling despite the dim lighting, and she barely noticed the limousine pull away.

"Ready?"

She nodded, moistening her lips.

He hesitated, then said quietly, "There's something you should know, Miranda. I won't be acting tonight. I'm extremely attracted to you."

"It's the hair," she said, trying for a light tone.

"You'd be gorgeous even if you shaved it all off." He cupped her chin in his rough hand. "Remember what I said. If I go too far, too fast, resist. I'll slow it right down."

"Okay. Thanks. And vice versa," she added without thinking.

Ortega stared for a second, then chuckled warmly, and for the first time that night she felt as though she had surprised him. Maybe even impressed him.

It was a good feeling, and as she let him take her hand and escort her down the street, she reminded herself that she was more than a pliable rookie. She was a trained officer of the Central Intelligence Agency, with a lot more to offer than just auburn hair and video cameras.

She quickly learned that Ortega was a master at pretending. In fact, he turned their assignment into her best first date ever! He wanted to know everything—her favorite movie, favorite food, favorite book. He teased, bringing a smile to her lips again and again. And through it all, he was respectful and attentive.

And relaxed. She marveled at this above all. He had been framed for murder less than six hours earlier, yet here he was, bantering with her as if they were completely carefree. The alibi would succeed, she realized, not because of hot-and-heavy scenes, but because of this man's attitude.

And the cameras had ample opportunity to memorialize that attitude, as Miranda and her date paused to chat on the doorstep, then again in the lobby. When the elevator arrived, she expected more of the same, and was surprised—and pleased—when he stepped up his attention just a bit, backing her into the corner and telling her in a husky voice how attractive she was.

Then he lowered his mouth to hers for an unscripted kiss so gentle, yet also so thorough, that she actually heard a small moan of delight emanate from her throat.

Ortega buried his face in her hair and murmured, "Nice touch," sending a shudder of arousal right through her.

Conscious that her cheeks were flaming red, she darted through the elevator doors the instant they opened, then turned and motioned for him to join her as an afterthought. His eyes twinkled as he followed her to her door, and when she began fumbling for her keys, he reached for her again, his expression supremely confident.

But Miranda was ready, bracing her arms against his chest and pushing gently, her eyebrow arched in warning. And true to his word, he immediately backed off, a frustrated grin on his face.

"Let's save something for next time, shall we?" she told him.

"Wednesday? I'll pick you up at seven."

"It's a date."

Unlocking the door, she swung it open, then watched

as he ambled back to the elevator. When he turned to give her one last, impish smile, she felt another surge of arousal, and had to dart into the apartment and slam the door shut.

Oh my God....

She leaned against the wall, enjoying the sensation for a moment, then reminded herself they were on the clock. The script allowed a scant two minutes for her to change clothes, sweep her long, loose hair into a braid and redo her makeup, exchanging the gray eyeshadow for a vibrant rust with lip gloss to match.

Forcing herself to concentrate, she completed the transformation, then entered the hallway, doing her best impression of a female headed for a very, *very* promising second date. In the elevator she adjusted her bra and checked her makeup for the benefit of the camera, then she strode through the lobby and out onto the street. She knew Ortega would be waiting around the corner.

And she knew he'd be smiling that relaxed, confident smile that belied his dilemma. As she approached him, she again marveled that he could be so calm. And so handsome. He, too, had changed outfits in the limousine and was wearing jeans with a black turtleneck.

"Miss me?" he asked when she reached him.

"I just don't get how you can stay so calm, Ortega."

He took her arm and escorted her back toward her place. "I actually have an old relaxation technique— something I used to use a lot, then I slacked off. This seemed like a good time to resurrect it."

"It's amazing."

"When all this is behind us, maybe I can teach it to you."

"Thanks. I'd like that," she murmured, surprised that he was again suggesting they'd see each other after the assignment was over. Did he see a future for them? Based on a couple of phony dates?

Phony dates that so far were admittedly better than the real thing....

"You'll find it useful," he assured her. "Especially if you keep working with Jane. Which I don't recommend, by the way."

"Why not? She's the best, right?"

"Hardly." He slipped his arm around her waist and pulled her close as they approached the front steps. "Ready? Showtime."

Their second date was a lot like the first, with a heady kiss in the elevator that Miranda decided to enjoy to the hilt. To her delight, Ortega took the same approach, and by the time he hustled her out into the hall, there was an urgency that told the cameras this couple couldn't wait to get inside the apartment. There would be no rebuffing him at the door this trip, and when she started fumbling for the keys, he commandeered them and had the door open before she could even pretend to react.

The script called for him to stay for five minutes, then leave without ceremony, looking frustrated. She had no idea what they'd actually do for those five minutes, although she knew what she wanted them to do....

But Ortega was all business the moment the door closed. "I'll check in with Jane. You start changing for date number three. I'll let myself out in a couple of minutes."

"Okay." She edged toward the bedroom, disappointed but reminding herself that this was a good sign. He was treating her like a professional. It was time she started returning the favor.

And she was glad to have the extra time to prepare for the big date—the one where they would be manhandling each other. Ortega was obviously attracted to her—either that or he really was the world's best actor. But still, she wanted to drive him wild this time.

For the good of the mission, of course.

So she brushed her hair until it shone, then twisted it and fastened it behind her head with a rhinestone-studded butterfly clip. Now Ortega could nuzzle her without impediment, and if he wanted to be ultra-dramatic, he could pull the clip away and let her hair cascade down her back.

She was dousing herself with perfume when she heard the door open and close—or rather, slam, as the frustrated suitor left in a huff.

Laughing out loud, Miranda took a last glimpse in the mirror, then grabbed a black purse with a shoulder strap as her final accessory. She was almost giddy, and while she knew part of it was the prospect of making out with Ortega, she was mostly feeling proud. This assignment—a huge one—had gone perfectly. Ortega's reputation would be safe and his appointment would go through without a glitch. Jane Smith would be so impressed, she'd invite Miranda to join her team permanently—

Except Ortega warned you against that, she reminded herself as she headed for the door. *You'll have to make him explain that when this is all over. Meanwhile, as he says, it's showtime!*

"How're you holding up?" Ortega asked when she joined him on the side street.

His concerned tone surprised her, and for the first time, she wondered if she was really doing as well with this assignment as she thought she was. Then she decided he was just being a gentleman, so she smiled and assured him, "Piece of cake."

He was wearing a strong, musky aftershave this time, and his hair was slightly damp, as though he'd been grooming it right up to the last moment.

Very convincing, she decided with admiration. *He definitely seems like a guy intent on scoring tonight.*

Intent on scoring, and also *used* to scoring. She had no doubt about that. He was more or less the sexiest man she had ever been this close to, and she figured he knew it. After all, he had worked undercover for years. Certainly in all that time he had seduced a female or two—for his country—and had probably found it surprisingly easy.

Speaking of easy, she warned herself, *try not to be a total slut in the elevator. The script calls for you to enjoy him, not maul him.*

Biting back a laugh, she let him rest his hand low on her back—so low it really wasn't her back at all—as he propelled her toward her building. They flew through the doorway, clearly headed straight to bed. When the elevator didn't come right away, Ortega began kissing her with greed and lust and several other of the very best sins.

As soon as the doors opened, he pushed her into the back corner and before the doors closed fully, he was devouring her, sliding his mouth down from her neck to her breasts, then lower and lower, until he was pushing her dress up to reveal her lace panties. Shocked, Miranda tried to think. Should she protest? Did he expect her to stop him? Was this part of the charade?

Then his teeth were tugging at the wisp of black silk, and she laced her fingers in his wavy hair. The script called for "mindless enjoyment," and this was the very definition of the phrase.

"Ortega..." Her moan was slow and husky.

He seemed to take it as a complaint, and stood up quickly. Then he cupped her chin in his hand and murmured, "You're just so goddammed sexy."

The elevator opened and he whisked her down the hall, taking the keys and working the lock with one hand while holding her close with the other. Then he pushed the door open, half carried her inside, and closed it.

And then it was over.

Miranda leaned against the wall for a second, just to catch her breath. Then she straightened and gave him a smile she hoped was steady. "That went well, don't you think?"

He stared at her, his expression unreadable. Then he murmured, "Yeah. You did well. Nice job."

"Thanks." She bit her lip, wondering if they were just going to stare at one another until dawn. "Would you like a drink? Or coffee? Anything like that?"

He glanced at his watch. "We've got about an hour. At some point, coffee will be good. But for the moment, you're off duty. Do whatever you want. Sleep. Shower. Watch TV. I'll check in with Jane, then just...well, I'll find something to do."

Miranda stepped up to him, concerned. His confidence, his calm, seemed to have abandoned him, and she wondered if he knew something she didn't. Maybe they hadn't done as good a job as she thought. She was a rookie, after all. There were subtleties she might miss that an experienced operative would note.

"What's wrong?" she asked finally.

"Nothing. Everything's great. I just have something I want to say."

She flushed. "You don't have to thank me, Ortega. It's my job—and my privilege—to help a patriot like you."

"You don't understand." He rested his hands on her shoulders. "Promise me you won't take this the wrong way?"

She winced but nodded. "I promise."

Ortega cleared his throat, but his voice was still husky when he told her, "I thought this part of my life was over. This feeling. This amazing, out-of-control, mind-numbing buzz. My God, Miranda, I swear I thought I was past this. But tonight, with you—"

He held up one hand to stop her from interrupting. "Don't take it the wrong way. I'm just thanking you. For making me feel this way. So foolishly optimistic. So completely inspired. I thought this part of me was dead. But tonight…with you…it's the most unbelievable thing I've ever felt."

She stared up at him, speechless for what seemed like forever. Then she whispered, "Thank God, Ortega. I thought it was just me."

His dark eyes widened, then a grin spread slowly over his face.

And then to her shocked delight, he scooped her up in his arms—like some sort of brawny epic hero!—and carried her into the bedroom.

Settling down at a table in the middle of a bustling coffeehouse on the edge of campus, Miranda opened her laptop and pretended to study the screen, while actually listening intently to the conversations of nearby students. She was dressed the part of a graduate student herself in her green-and-white University of Hawaii T-shirt, faded jeans and flat leather sandals.

This was a new phase of her language immersion program. Her assignment? Tracking the discussions she overheard, whether she understood them or not. This particular café was the perfect spot since it catered to international students.

After a weekend of recovering from the Ortega alibi assignment, she had been glad to find distraction in this new adventure. As expected, she hadn't heard from Jane Smith or Ortega at all, but she had read the newspapers, so she knew that at this point at least Ortega was not considered a suspect in the killing of the president's advisor. In fact, his agency, SPIN, was leading the investigation. And from all reports, Jane Smith had succeeded in making it appear to be a simple break-in gone wrong.

But Miranda knew better, and she took great pleasure in imagining Ortega and Smith working behind the scenes to catch the bastards who had tried to frame him. The world might never know what really happened, but justice would be done. And with any luck, Ortega would share the top secret details with her on their fourth date.

She was pretty sure there *would* be a fourth date. He had as much as told her so. It would make the alibi even more believable, for one thing, if they kept seeing each other. And as added incentive, there was the simple matter of the bonfire in her bedroom during that last hour together.

Yes, she was sure she'd hear from him. And maybe from Jane Smith, too, inviting her to join the team permanently. She'd jump at that chance, Ortega's warning notwithstanding.

But for now, she needed to do a good job on this new

assignment. So far, after two days of posing as a student in the coffee house, she had been able to identify most of the languages she overheard, but couldn't distinguish any words beyond simple greetings and pleasantries.

Unimpressive, she decided with a sigh. *Two weeks of training, and nothing to show for it.*

Leaning back in her chair, she closed her eyes and sifted her fingers through her hair as though lost in thought, concentrating on the two young men seated across from her.

She couldn't discern their nationality or language but it was clear they were arguing. Not that their voices were raised. It was more subtle than that—inflection, cadence, the use of very short words.

Maybe this is part of the deal, she told herself, leaning forward and making a note of the observation on her laptop. *Maybe that's what they're teaching you—to pick up on those sorts of things.*

"Miranda Cutler?"

She turned, surprised to hear her name, then surprised again by the sight of a man in a conservative gray suit, so out of place in this venue. Even before he flashed his badge, she knew he was FBI, and her pulse began to race.

This was it. They were going to ask about Ortega. Or better still, they weren't here about the alibi at all, but had been directed to bring her to Ortega on some pretext. Maybe he even wanted her help on the investigation!

"Yes, I'm Miranda Cutler." She pretended to be confused, not wanting to blow her cover completely. "Is something wrong?"

"Why don't we step outside?" he suggested.

She hesitated, then shrugged, closed her laptop and

packed it into the knapsack she had slung on the back of her chair.

"Can't you tell me what this is about?" she asked as she stood and stared into the man's blue eyes, challenging him, but only slightly.

"Outside," he repeated.

He was good at his job, she decided, making a note to practice being so completely nondescript and robotic.

She followed him without further protest, and as soon as they were outside, she murmured teasingly, "You didn't exactly fit in, you know."

"This way." He strode to a black sedan parked in a no-parking zone and opened the front passenger door. "Get in."

It was impossible to engage the gray-suited man in conversation, so Miranda finally stopped trying. Either she was going to be questioned about the alibi or she was being taken to Smith or Ortega. And luckily, she was prepared for either occurrence, so she just leaned back in her seat and forced herself to relax.

She had guessed they were headed for FBI headquarters in D.C., and was relieved when they went to Langley, Virginia, instead. This was Jane Smith territory, although she couldn't imagine why the CIA hadn't sent one of their own to pick her up. Apparently the two agencies were working together, but she was still surprised when the guards waved them through without bothering to glance at the IDs they both produced. Not only that, they allowed the FBI agent to proceed without any additional escort as he led Miranda to a small conference room dominated by a forty-two-inch plasma TV.

They were immediately joined by two men, one of

whom identified himself as Bob Runyon, CIA. The other was FBI, and he and Miranda's gray-suited escort faded into the background, leaving Runyon in charge.

"What's this about?" she demanded for the umpteenth time.

"Sit down," Runyon advised. When she had complied, he pushed a button on a remote control and a video began to play.

Miranda stared at the screen, confused. It was the alibi video, specifically Date Three, just as she and Ortega were dragging one another into the elevator.

Of all parts of that stupid tape to play, they have to pick this one? she complained to herself as she watched Ortega trail his mouth down her body, then up between her thighs. It was mortifying, but she had prepared herself for this moment, so she was able to watch without cringing.

Runyon hit the Pause button at the most humiliating moment possible, then gestured toward the image on the screen. "Care to comment?"

Indignation replaced embarrassment, and Miranda gave him a haughty glare. "How dare you invade my privacy like this. Turn that off. Immediately!"

"Can you identify the man kissing you?"

"Of course I can! It's Ray Ortega, director of SPIN. I've been dating him for a while. Not that it's any of your business." She gulped a breath of air, then insisted, "I demand to know what this is about."

"Drop the act, Cutler. We know all about it. Ortega confessed last night."

Miranda drew back, suspecting a trap. "Confessed to what? Having sex in an elevator? I'll admit it's not our most admirable moment, but since when is it a crime? We were off duty—"

"I said, drop it." Runyon eyed her with a mixture of annoyance and sympathy. "We know he killed Payton. We know you and Smith cooked up this alibi for him. Like I said, he confessed. Take a look." He slid a piece of paper across the table, but when Miranda reached for it, he anchored it to the table with his palm. "Look. Don't touch."

It was a signed declaration, and the signature was purportedly Ortega's. Before Miranda could read more than a few sentences of the text, Runyon pulled the paper back and shoved it into a file.

But a few sentences had been more than enough for Miranda to learn the truth, and it sent a chill through her. Falsifying evidence, killing in self-defense, kidnapping—Ortega had confessed to all of these!

"The good news is, Ortega cleared you of anything but gullibility," Runyon was saying. "He says you were just a dupe. And even if that's not true, you've been pardoned—"

"What?"

"President Standish pardoned you. Pardoned Ortega, too. Jane Smith isn't so lucky. She'll do time for this once she gets out of the hospital. And at least two of her guys are dead. So consider yourself lucky."

Miranda stared in dismay. "I don't understand."

"Yeah, I can see that." The CIA officer's voice lost its edge. "It took me a while to understand it, too. Apparently Ortega killed Payton in self-defense, then Smith cooked up an alibi for him, using you—in more ways than one. Unfortunately, Smith went too far. She kidnapped an FBI agent and a SPIN employee who had figured out what was going on, and she would've killed them both if they hadn't been smart enough to get away. Ortega wasn't part of that. Once he figured out what Smith was really up to, he went after her and her crew and apprehended the ones he didn't shoot. A real bloodbath."

Runyon laughed darkly before adding, "President Standish decided Ortega redeemed himself at the last minute and pardoned him. Unbelievable if you ask me, but no one asked. The good news is, you got pardoned, too. Otherwise you'd be part of the conspiracy and the charges would apply to you too."

"I don't *need* a pardon," Miranda insisted, angry and just a little desperate. "I didn't do anything wrong! I want to make a statement. To clear myself—"

"Not necessary. Ortega cleared you—"

"By calling me a *dupe*? You think that *clears* me?"

"Settle down." Runyon held up a hand to silence her. Then he said with quiet authority, "The only reason for this meeting is to close the loop. Unless you want to press charges against Ortega, in which case, your career is over."

"I don't want to press charges. But I want to make a statement. For the file. Like he did."

"There *is* no file. This never happened." He arched an eyebrow in warning. "This will be classified. Top secret. Only a handful of people will ever know about it. And like I said, it won't affect your career. Unless you let it," he added, his meaning clear.

Miranda's heart sank. Her career—she had worked so hard for it. Now Jane Smith and Ortega had ruined it. Ruined *her*. She had no doubt about that.

Her gaze was drawn to the despicable image on the plasma screen and her gut tightened with disgust. He had seemed so attracted to her. So smitten. But it had all been an act. A way to doubly ensure her loyalty.

She *was* a dupe…

"Cutler?" Runyon switched off the monitor. "Are you okay?"

She glanced at him, amazed by the question. Then she asked, "You said two of Smith's agents were dead. Was one named Mark?"

He nodded. "Friend of yours?"

"No. Just the opposite." She bit her lip. "What about the FBI agent and the SPIN employee? Were they hurt?"

"Yeah, both sustained injuries. One or both are still in the hospital I think." He smiled. "The spinner saved the day according to the report. Some sort of genius or something. Too bad you'll never meet her. You owe her, big-time."

Miranda studied her hands, wondering if he knew how stupid he sounded.

"Any other questions? We need to wrap this up."

"I'd like to read the file."

"Sorry. The less you know the better for you." He cleared his throat. "Do you need counseling? We can arrange it."

"No."

"Good answer." He gave her a reassuring smile. "You're cleared for duty. Just like it never happened. Tomorrow morning you're going to request time off. As a reason, you'll say you never really came to grips with your dad's death and you need to go home for a few weeks, to grieve. Delayed reaction or whatever. It will be approved, no questions asked."

He walked to the door and opened it, then gestured for Miranda to join him. When she had done so, he led her into the hall and closed the door behind them. "It's over, Miranda. Try not to let it get to you. Go home. Hang out with family and friends. Get past this—that's an order—and then come back. Your career will be waiting for you. And Miranda?"

"Yes?" she asked, barely listening to his words.

"When you get back into town, maybe we could have a drink some night after work. Just for fun."

She blinked, sure she hadn't heard him correctly. Then she looked into his eyes and saw interest so stark—so degrading—that she knew he was replaying the images from the alibi tape. That scene in the elevator—

Her stomach knotted violently and she shoved past him, sprinting for the ladies room at the far end of the hall. Bursting into a stall, she fell to her knees in front of a gleaming white toilet.

Just in time to vomit her guts out.

Chapter 2

One year later

"I know you're excited about this, Goldie, but don't get your hopes up. We don't really know much about this girl."

Kristie Hennessy enjoyed the tingle that always shot through her when SPIN Director Will McGregor called her Goldie. Or maybe she was just tingling because he was physically present after a full month of being three thousand miles away, fine-tuning the West Coast office in preparation for transitioning the agency from a stand-alone entity to a division of the FBI.

In the early months of establishing SPIN-West she had been there, too, working side by side with him. *Sleeping* side by side with him. But lately, she had been pulled away from him with increasing frequency and duration, thanks to her duties at the East Coast headquarters, where she provided creative support for FBI agents in the field by supplying them with undercover identities and profiles of suspects.

"It's a foolproof plan," she assured him. "We know all we need to know about Miranda Cutler by watching that videotape. Or at least, *almost* all we need to know."

McGregor groaned. "You're not really going to ask that poor kid if she and Ortega had sex that night, are you?"

"It's the last piece of the puzzle," Kristie insisted. "Oh, look!" She pointed at the young woman approaching the reception desk outside of McGregor's glass-walled office.

With the blinds open, one could see everything happening in the think tank that had made SPIN famous. Of course, had the blinds been closed, Kristie could have kissed McGregor's square jaw, just for luck.

Not that she had his attention anymore. He was openly staring at Miranda Cutler, and Kristie could hardly blame him. The CIA operative was strikingly lovely, despite her stern expression and the hard set to her shoulders. All of that was more than offset by her mane of long auburn hair that was streaked with red and gold highlights. She was wearing black slacks, black boots and a long-sleeved black knit top with a mock turtleneck. No jewelry, no purse. In fact, her only accessories were the gleaming gun holstered at her waist and the badge affixed to the holster. And that hair.

"Put your eyes back in your head, Will," Kristie advised with a teasing smile.

"Right." He flushed. "She just looks so…well, never mind. Let's get this over with."

"It's going to work. Trust me."

He grimaced, then moved to the door and opened it, calling out, "Agent Cutler? Come on in."

As Miranda entered the office, a tentative smile finally appeared on her lips. "Director McGregor, I presume?"

"Thanks for coming." He shook her hand, then motioned to Kristie. "This is Kristie Hennessy, one of our spinners."

Kristie offered her hand to the visitor. "I'm so glad to finally meet you, Miranda. Sit down, won't you? We've got a lot to talk about."

Miranda followed them to the conference table in the corner of the room, but seemed hesitant to take a seat. Then she insisted with unexpected passion, "I've wanted to meet you—to thank you—for so long. I never thought I'd get the chance. I mean, you're the ones, right? They never told me your names. Only that a spinner and an FBI agent apprehended Jane Smith before any innocent lives were lost."

She grabbed Kristie's hand again and pumped it. "You're the spinner, right? And you!" she added in McGregor's direction. "You were with the Bureau before you took this position. You're the agent that apprehended Smith and her team. Right?" Her green eyes sparkled with tears. "Thank you so much for stopping that monster before she succeeded."

The rush of gratitude had a tinge of desperation to it that startled Kristie, and she quickly reassured their guest. "You don't need to thank us, Miranda. But believe me, we've always wanted to meet you, too. Sit down, okay?"

Miranda nodded and took a seat next to McGregor, across from Kristie.

McGregor gave her a reassuring smile. "You're probably wondering why we asked you here today. Like Kristie—Ms. Hennessy—said, we're pleased at this chance to meet you in person. But we also have a favor to ask."

"Anything," Miranda told him. "Just name it."

"It's not a favor," Kristie corrected, sending McGregor a warning glance. "It's an assignment."

"Even better. Name it."

McGregor laughed. "Don't you want to know the details first? It's strictly voluntary. And a little odd."

"Sight unseen it's better than anything I've been doing lately," Miranda replied. "And like I said, I'd do anything for you two."

Kristie sighed, knowing from Miranda's file that indeed her recent assignments had been dismal ones, mostly consisting of dates with politicians or minor criminals. Nothing tawdry—at least, not exactly—but certainly nothing interesting. And definitely nothing that used the marksmanship talents that had earned her entry to the CIA in the first place.

To put it bluntly, Miranda Cutler had been typecast over the last year as a *femme fatale,* and while she was indeed pretty, Kristie had no doubt it was the sexy videotape with Ray Ortega that had short-circuited the young operative's career.

Miranda looked from Kristie to McGregor, as though trying to fathom their hesitation. "It's fine. Really. Ask me anything."

"Okay." Kristie took a deep breath. "How much do you know about Ray Ortega?"

"What?"

"I mean, about where he's been and what he's been doing these last eleven months."

"I have no idea. And I don't care."

Kristie winced, but persisted. "Did you know he left public service—"

"*Left* it? As if he had a choice? He's lucky he isn't in

prison! I'll never understand why President Standish pardoned him."

"Because he saved my sister's life, for one thing," McGregor told her, his voice soft.

"Oh. I didn't know that." Miranda arched an eyebrow. "I'm guessing it's his fault she was in danger in the first place though, right?" When McGregor nodded, her green eyes flashed. "Why are we talking about him? Has he done something else?"

Kristie reached across the table and grasped Miranda's hand. "Ray went into seclusion after—well, after the pardon. He wanted to cleanse himself spiritually. To restore balance to his life. He was riddled with guilt, Miranda. It's so unfair. He's a good man. A great man, really. You know that in your heart, don't you?"

Miranda stared at her for a moment, then spun toward McGregor and demanded, "What's going on?"

"I don't blame you for being confused. What you don't know is that Ortega and Kristie are close friends. He hired her. Trained her to be a spinner. She owes him a lot. Loves him like a brother."

Miranda gave a cool smile. "I guess that makes sense. But it doesn't explain why you asked me here."

"It's simple," Kristie told her. "Ray doesn't want to have anything to do with me—with any of us—anymore. But we need his help. There's a global conspiracy brewing—a dangerous paramilitary cartel—and he's the only person in the world who can thwart it."

"I doubt that," Miranda drawled.

"No, really. He once saved the life of a major player in this conspiracy. A man named Jonathan Kell. We think Ray can get Kell to confide in him."

Kristie had expected Miranda to scoff again, but the

redhead surprised her by smiling with delight. "*That's* what you want? Great! I won't let you down. I'll get Kell to talk. Believe me, I've had practice. And I'm embarrassed to say, I'm pretty good at it. Just tell me what you need to know, and I'll make him spill it."

Ignoring McGregor's chuckle, Kristie insisted, "No, Miranda. You're missing the point. We don't want you to talk to Kell. We want you to talk to Ray." Before the CIA operative could protest, Kristie forged ahead. "I've tried, but he shuts me out. He won't talk to Will—Director McGregor—either. But he feels terrible about what he did to you. How he lied to you. Plus—"

"Kristie, don't," McGregor cautioned.

But the spinner knew she was right. "He fell for you that night, Miranda. I think you can get to him where all the rest of us have failed."

"Fell for me?" Miranda repeated, as though she couldn't trust her own hearing. "You're kidding, right?" Her voice grew strident. "Ray Ortega used me. Lied to me. Made a fool out of me. Humiliated me. Ruined my career. *That's* what happened that night, Ms. Hennessy. You think he feels guilty for it? Good! I hope you're right about that. But don't kid yourself. I was just a dupe, like he said in his stupid statement. I was naïve—"

"You were young and beautiful, with flowing red hair, a perfect face and a great body. And a warm, beautiful smile. Just the kind of female that gets to him. He said it to me himself, when we were investigating the murder together in L.A. He said he met a girl who made him remember what it's like to fall in love—"

"He was lying! To save himself. My God, you're worse than I was. I understand he's your friend, Ms. Hennessy—"

"Call me Kristie. And listen to me, Miranda. I've seen the video. I know what happened between the two of you."

"I beg your pardon?"

"Drop it, Goldie," McGregor muttered.

But it was too late. Miranda Cutler was on her feet, clearly upset by the reference to the alibi tape. "You want to know what happened between us that night? He *screwed* me. Literally *and* figuratively. *That's* what you saw on the video."

"Miranda—"

"When the cameras stopped rolling, Ortega was just getting started. He seduced me, just like he and Jane Smith planned. But don't kid yourself. It had nothing to do with genuine feeling. It was all part of a scheme. Then he planted the idea in *your* head, too. Which makes *you* a dupe, too. Welcome to the club."

Before Kristie and McGregor could even begin to respond, Miranda added unhappily, "I'm sorry. I know you think he's your friend. And I'm sure he cares about you in his own way. But I'm sure he used you, too. Just like he used me. I thought he was this heroic, noble, patriotic guy. He played that part so well."

Settling back down, she murmured, "He had just *killed* a man, but he flirted and teased as though we were really on our first date. *That's* the Ray Ortega *I* know."

"We owe you an apology, Miranda," McGregor told her with quiet insistence. "We didn't know how—well, how fresh all this was to you. Or how deep your feelings ran. Obviously, we don't expect you to contact Ortega."

"I'll contact Kell instead," she interrupted, her passion morphing into confidence before their eyes. "Trust me, I'll get the information you need. Just tell me where to find him. If he's heterosexual, he'll talk to me."

"I'm sure he would," McGregor agreed with a chuckle. "But it's not that simple. Kell's a little unbalanced. Probably harmless, but he's not your normal, run-of-the-mill mark."

"Harmless nuts are my specialty," the redhead assured him, her eyes sparkling.

McGregor's eyes were twinkling, too, and Kristie felt a twinge of jealousy. Then she laughed at herself, deciding that this was a good sign. Miranda's year as a seductress had made her so irresistible, even Will McGregor wasn't completely immune.

Which meant Ray Ortega would be even *more* certain to capitulate!

"I don't think the powers-that-be would be willing to let you handle that part of the assignment on your own," McGregor was explaining to Miranda. "Talking to Ortega is one thing. Approaching Kell is another."

"Aren't *you* running the op?"

"Just the domestic portion."

Miranda's face fell. "So even if I get Ortega to cooperate, I won't be part of the larger effort?"

"If you get Ray to come back here with you, *he'll* be in charge of the op, and I'm sure he'll want you on his team," Kristie told her eagerly. "It works for everyone. See?"

"And even if you can't convince him, we'll put in a good word for you," McGregor added.

Miranda bit her lip, visibly torn by the proposition.

"You can do it, Miranda," Kristie whispered. "You can reach him. I'm sure of it."

Miranda gave her a curious stare. "You're so sure he's a good guy. But if he really is, if he really cares about his country—about SPIN, about you—why is he refusing to help you break up a dangerous paramilitary cartel?"

"It's complicated. He doesn't trust himself anymore. He's sure his instincts are out of whack, so he's gone into voluntary exile."

"And he insists he's already given us all there is to know about Kell," McGregor added. "He was thoroughly debriefed after the mission where he saved Kell's life. That was almost ten years ago. When we contacted Ortega about this—asking for his help—he assured us Kell would be suspicious if he showed up at his place. He said we're better off using the intel from the debrief and just sending someone else in."

"I agree with him. You should send someone else. And that someone should be me."

"Your assignment, if you're willing to take it, is to lure Ray back here," Kristie corrected her.

"Lure?"

The spinner grimaced. "Okay, bad choice of words. Just talk to him. Convince him to come back. Then the four of us will plot a strategy for infiltrating the Brigade."

"Pardon?"

"That's what they call themselves. The Brigade."

"Catchy."

Kristie was relieved to see Miranda could be intrigued, and she decided to make the assignment even more irresistible. "There are five members. We know the identities of four of them, one of whom is Jonathan Kell. But the leader—who calls himself the Brigadier—is a mystery to us. In fact, even the other Brigade members don't know who the Brigadier really is."

"Amazing."

"We're hoping Kell can provide some clue to the

Brigadier's identity without even realizing it. That's the most important piece of information we need at the moment, although we'd also like to get a clearer picture of the Brigade's agenda. So far, they don't seem to have broken any laws. But they're raising a fortune, and training paramilitary personnel. It's all very ominous."

When Miranda glanced at the file in the middle of the table, Kristie slid it over to her, assuring her mischievously, "It gets better and better. Trust me. You'll love this assignment."

"You don't have to decide right now," McGregor added. "Take some time to study the file. Everything we know about Kell is in there. And a lot of information about Ortega, too—about his relationship with Kell, and about his current whereabouts and activities. See how you feel after you've read it."

Miranda locked gazes with him. "And if I help, you'll use your influence to get me on the team that goes after the Brigade? Even if Ortega refuses to come back with me?"

McGregor nodded. Then he seemed to read something in her eyes and murmured, "You trust us, don't you?"

She sighed. "If you keep your word, I'll be eternally grateful. And if you don't, well…" She shrugged her shoulders as if to say it wouldn't be the first time she was duped, and probably not the last.

McGregor turned sideways in his chair and grasped the young agent's hands in his own, forcing her to look at him. "You can trust us, Miranda."

Her cheeks flushed to a gorgeous crimson. "Thanks."

A new jolt of jealousy, much stronger than the last, surged through Kristie and she drawled, "Do you two need a room?"

Visibly startled, Miranda pulled her hands free and jumped to her feet. "Sorry! I'll—I'll take the assignment."

Kristie stood, too, mortified. "I'm so sorry, Miranda. McGregor and I—"

"Forget it." Miranda snatched the file off the table, then insisted, "I'll study this today. Tomorrow I'll make contact. You've got my cell phone number. I'll keep you informed of my progress."

She strode to the door and opened it, and for a moment Kristie thought she was going to leave without saying another word. Then she turned and assured them, her voice ringing with pride, "I can do this. I *will* do this. Thanks again. For everything."

As soon as Miranda had darted into the reception area and disappeared from view, McGregor turned to Kristie and arched a disapproving eyebrow.

"Okay, okay. Stop yelling at me." The spinner covered her face with her hands. "I can't believe I said what I said. Poor Miranda. She must think I'm such a jerk."

To her relief, McGregor started laughing. "I've never seen your jealous side. It was flattering. Horrifying, but flattering."

"Very funny." Kristie gave him a wry smile. "I kept thinking how pretty she was—how Ray wouldn't be able to resist her. Then I suddenly remembered that you kinda like redheads yourself."

"Just because I like *you* in your red wig doesn't mean I like redheads," he corrected. "I fell in love with a wacky blond spinner who has no idea how good-looking she is. There's no one else for me." Resting his hands on her shoulders, he suggested, "Why don't we cut out of here early? We can go back to your place and you can find some way to apologize for making a scene."

"You're not going to make me wear the red wig, are you?"

He laughed again and shook his head.

"Well, then, let's go. I'm just shocked you're willing to leave work early for a change."

"Actually…" He cleared his throat. "If we want to spend some time together, we don't have a choice. My flight to L.A. leaves at ten."

"But you just got here!" Kristie scowled. "This is getting old, Will. We never spend any time together."

"You could come with me. Run your ops from L.A. for a few days."

She was tempted, but reminded herself that if Miranda succeeded in luring—or rather, convincing—Ray to come back, he'd want to work from SPIN headquarters. "Miranda might call…."

"She'll call," McGregor agreed. "With bad news, I predict. Better brace yourself. If he turns her down, you're going to have to let go of him. Maybe for good. Or at least until he's ready to make the first move. Can you do that? Let go of that friendship?"

She sighed. "It's not just for me that I want him back. It's for SPIN, too."

"I didn't think David and I were doing such a bad job running the place," McGregor replied coolly, pulling his hands away.

Uh-oh…

"That's *not* what I meant, Will. You were Ray's choice, and you've been terrific. Sheesh, now we're *both* jealous with no reason." She stepped as close to him as she dared, given the open blinds. "You don't have to compete with him. He's my friend, but you're my everything."

"I'm not worried about competing with Ortega. Mostly because I'd win," McGregor assured her. "He's a dropout. A head case. He almost got us killed, remember? He ruined Miranda Cutler's career. Maybe even her life. Believe me," he added with a growl, "I'm not worried about measuring up."

"Wow." She moistened her lips, confused by the condemnation behind McGregor's words. "Why didn't you say something before we sent Miranda to bring him back?"

"We need his help with Kell. And he's your friend. I know you want to see him again. That's fine with me. I'm not jealous," he added firmly. "Let's just drop it. We've got seven hours before my flight leaves. We can spend it talking about Ortega, or we can spend it having make-up sex. Your choice."

"Close the blinds and I'll make up with you right here, right now," she challenged playfully. Then with a glance through the glass wall to make sure no one was looking, she brushed her lips across McGregor's.

"Speaking of make-up sex," she added mischievously. "Can you imagine the sparks that will fly when Ray sees Miranda again?"

"Unless it was all an act. A way to cement her loyalty, and to put *you* off track." McGregor gave a rueful smile. "I guess we'll find out. Meanwhile, we've got our own sparks to worry about. Right?" He tilted his head toward the door, suggesting, "Let's go."

"Okay." She followed him out of the office, trying to look forward to their unscheduled interlude, but for the first time, a warning bell was going off in her head.

He's a dropout. A head case. He almost got us killed, remember? He ruined Miranda Cutler's career. Maybe even her life.

McGregor's assessment had been harsh, but also true. That was *exactly* what had happened the last time Miranda got mixed up with Ray Ortega.

And now, because of Kristie, she was about to get mixed up with him again.

The more Miranda read about Jonathan Kell and the Brigade, the more excited she became over this new assignment. The file told an amazing story of a young research scientist working for a drug company in South America, investigating the efficacy and potential of various remedies used by the natives of the rain forests. Then a drug lord who styled himself as a revolutionary had kidnapped the scientist, demanding a ransom from the employer and also seeking information from young Kell about his experiments. The drug company refused to pay, leaving Kell to die in a filthy cage in Benito Carerra's jungle hideaway. But not before Carerra tortured Kell mercilessly.

Into this drama had come Ray Ortega, an operative unaware of Kell's plight, sent by the CIA to assassinate Carerra. Ortega seduced Carerra's wife to learn the location of the husband's secret headquarters. Unfortunately, a CIA mole tipped off Carerra, who was ready for Ortega and threw him into a cell with Kell. For two weeks, the men were alternately tortured, starved and neglected. According to Ortega's debrief transcript, Kell had confided that he had been searching for a cure for phobias because Kell himself was riddled with them. Those irrational fears, coupled with the rational ones associated with kidnapping and torture, made the ordeal even worse for Kell. Ortega did his best to help the man stay strong. Stay alive.

And Kell helped Ortega, too, teaching him some relaxation techniques he had developed to help with the phobias. Ortega insisted neither of them would have survived the torture without those skills.

Finally Ortega managed to overpower a guard and confiscate a pistol and crossbow. The two detainees had just reached the vehicle that would take them to safety when a furious Benito Carerra had confronted them, guns blazing. Still cool, even after his ordeal, Ortega had calmly drawn the crossbow, sending an arrow that caught Carerra through the neck, pinning his body to a tree. At the sight of their leader's ghastly fate, the other guards had fled, and Ortega had rushed Kell to a hospital for treatment.

Kell had pledged undying gratitude to Ortega. But he knew his country hadn't sent the operative after Carerra on his account, and he cursed the United States for not intervening sooner. As for the drug company? Kell sued it, claiming that it had abandoned him, despite the existence of an insurance policy that would have paid his ransom, because the executives had hoped he'd be killed and the company could appropriate Kell's valuable research. A court agreed, and Kell was awarded millions, which he used to buy a fortress in the Swiss Alps, where he declared he was no longer an American, and would now conduct and fund his own experiments. Thereafter, he reportedly lived like a virtual hermit, terrified of the world yet also defiant.

And easy prey for the Brigadier, or so the file speculated. The working assumption was that the anonymous leader had promised each of the Brigade members some enticement—be it revenge, security, wealth, or raw power—in exchange for their loyalty and services. Kell could offer his brilliant research; the other three had talents and resources of a military, financial or technological nature.

But even those four men were not trusted with the actual identity of the Brigadier, although SPIN and the CIA hoped Kell might have knowledge Kristie and the CIA analysts could use to deduce that identity.

Miranda shivered with excitement. For the second time in her career, she had an assignment that thrilled her. Inspired her. Made her feel as though she could make a meaningful contribution to her country.

Of course, the last time she had felt that way, it had been a fraud. And she had been a dupe. She couldn't help remembering that as she stared at the map in the file that gave directions to Ortega's retreat in the Sierra Nevada mountains.

But this time, the only potential dupe was Kristie Hennessy. Miranda was going into it with her eyes wide open and her expectations at zero.

And it was always possible Kristie was right. She was, after, all a spinner—a psychologist trained to evaluate others. To predict how they would react, and to plot successful scenarios accordingly. It was because of Kristie that the Ortega alibi mess hadn't led to loss of innocent lives. She was clearly deserving of the trust and respect the SPIN director had placed in her, their apparent love affair notwithstanding.

And even if Kristie's judgment was clouded this time because of her friendship with Ortega, the worst that would happen was he'd refuse to cooperate. Miranda almost hoped he would! She trusted Will McGregor's word that he'd recommend her for participation in the CIA's anti-Brigade op either way, and that was all she really wanted out of this—a chance to redeem herself. To prove her value to the company.

If one more encounter with Ortega could get her that, then all she could say was, *Bring it on.*

Chapter 3

Ortega had chosen a perfect location for his self-imposed exile. A twisty mountain road provided the only access to the parcel, which was surrounded by jagged outcroppings and steep terrain that would discourage even the most adventurous hikers. According to the file, Ortega had installed some sort of monitoring system to alert him when a vehicle approached, which Miranda guessed didn't happen very often, and never by mistake. It was simply too inhospitable a drive for anyone to undertake without a very, very good reason.

By the time she was within a thousand yards of the place, she knew *he* knew she was coming. He would be prepared. And luckily, so was she, mostly because of the eight-month stint she had served on the Farm—the CIA's training facility that doubled as an ongoing societal experiment. During Miranda's stay, she had been inserted into a hostile society with disorienting customs. Surrounded by people she couldn't trust, in an atmosphere of duplicity and challenge, she had honed the skills needed to thrive in such an environment.

She had done well. Now she was headed for another such experience, and she had no doubt she'd survive again. The prospect of seeing Ortega, while distasteful, was overshadowed by the excitement she felt over the anti-Brigade operation. She knew that if she focused on the goal, and didn't get distracted by the alibi disaster and its accompanying humiliation, she'd do fine. And if he tried to manipulate her in any way, well, he'd be surprised. Because thanks to him, she had had a full year of developing her own manipulative skills!

Not that she really thought he'd try anything. A close reading of the file suggested he really did want to be alone, which meant that the worst he'd do would be order her off his property, as he'd done to every other person who had tried to visit him.

If that happened, Miranda could go back to SPIN and report that she had done her best. She had no doubt that McGregor would keep his word. And thanks to a late night phone call she had gotten from Kristie Hennessy, she knew the spinner would accept the truth and move on, too. In fact, Kristie had almost tried to talk Miranda out of going to Ortega after all, belatedly noting what all the rest of them had been trying to tell her: that she "might have" miscalculated, and "maybe Ray won't be as receptive to this visit" as she had hoped.

As the cabin came into view, Miranda was able to confirm the spinner's prediction firsthand. Ortega was standing in the gravel driveway, his hands on his hips, his expression murderous. And despite all of her preparation, she felt a twinge of intimidation, not only from his stance, but from the fact that he looked bigger than she remembered. Bigger and more dangerous.

He was wearing a black cotton outfit resembling a martial arts uniform, but tied at the waist with a simple length of rope. His skin was darker than it had been a year earlier, and his wavy black hair was shaggier than before. Everything about him confirmed the fact that he had radically altered his lifestyle and his relationship with the world.

Stopping her rented Subaru Outback while still twenty feet from him, she took a deep breath, then exhaled slowly. "Okay, Miranda," she told herself firmly. "Like he used to say, it's showtime. Just remember why you're here and you'll do fine."

Pushing the car door open, she second-guessed her attire and quickly grabbed a black hooded sweatshirt along with her knapsack, then pulled the sweatshirt over her bare arms as she exited the vehicle. It was a hot day, and the white sleeveless top she was wearing with her jeans was appropriate and not overly sexy, but still, she didn't want there to be any hint that she was trying to appear attractive. It was bad enough her hair was highlighted to bring out *more* red. She must have been crazy to let her hairdresser talk her into that when she went in for a simple trim!

Standing straight, she pulled off her sunglasses and returned Ortega's stare without saying a word.

Then to her surprise, a broad grin spread across his face. "Miranda?" Striding forward, he added warmly, "You're the last person I expected to see out here. Or anywhere for that matter."

"Hey, Ortega," she murmured, intimidated again, this time because she thought he might be about to do something monumentally offensive, like hug her.

But he stopped a few feet away, insisting quietly, "This is a surprise. But I'm glad you're here."

"It's not a social call. SPIN sent me."

He hesitated, then nodded. "I should have known. I actually thought you were Kristie herself when I saw that the driver was a female. I can't believe she's using you to get to me."

"Yeah, what kind of a monster would use a person for their own selfish purposes?" Miranda drawled.

He winced, then laughed it off. "I'm just glad for the chance to apologize to you in person. I've never forgiven myself for the way I hurt you."

"The hurt lasted about five minutes. It's the burn that had staying power," she assured him, adding with a confident smile, "If you really want to make it up to me, go pack a bag. There's a flight leaving at 2:30. We can make it if we hurry."

"Where are we going?"

"SPIN headquarters."

Now he did step closer, so that she could almost feel the heat of the sun stored in his bronzed flesh. "Why would I want to go there?"

She forced herself not to step back, even though his nearness intimidated her. He had been in good shape the last time they met, but now he seemed even leaner, more muscled, and definitely more physically powerful. "They want you to talk to Jonathan Kell," she explained carefully. "To see if he knows anything that can help Kristie figure out the Brigadier's identity."

Ortega shook his head, visibly frustrated. "She could

crack that case right now if she wanted to. She's got plenty of information, and she's a whiz. She's just using it as a ploy to get me back in the game."

"Come to SPIN with me and tell her that to her face."

"I've already told her…." He shook his head again, then gestured toward his cabin. "Come on. We can argue inside. Want something to drink?"

"No. I'm fine, thanks."

"You're not afraid to come inside with me, are you?"

She laughed dryly. "Actually, I'm dying to see the place. The story is you're trying to get in touch with nature, but I count five antennae and a satellite dish. Kinda high-tech for a nature boy, don't you think?" Without waiting for him to respond she walked past him and up to the front door, which was already wide open.

He caught up to her in a few strides. "For the record, I came here to get in touch with myself, not Mother Nature. But you're right, I've got a lot going on, equipment-wise. I wanted to keep my options open in terms of getting information from the rest of the world. And I have a couple of security systems. Old habits run deep."

Stepping through the open doorway, she scanned the living room, noting the profusion of monitors and computers, as well as shelves lined with books, videotapes and DVDs. An overstuffed recliner in front of a rustic fireplace occupied one corner of the room. The only other furniture, aside from the desks, was a small wooden table and four chairs between the living room and a kitchen. A ladder led to a loft, which she assumed was Ortega's bedroom.

"Come and sit." He crossed to the table and held out a chair for her. "I'll tell you what you need to know."

"About Kell?"

"No. About Kristie. And about that mess with Jane Smith. I owe you an explanation as well as an apology."

Miranda almost growled from frustration. "I don't *care* about any of that, Ortega. I just want your help uncovering the Brigadier's identity. You think you owe me something? Great. Come back to SPIN with me and we'll call it even."

"That part of my life was a nightmare. I've left it behind forever."

"Yeah? Well I'm still *living* that nightmare, thanks to you." She caught her temper, not wanting him to see how fresh the pain still was.

But it was too late.

"I'm sorry, Miranda. How bad has it been?" When she just shook her head, he asked, "What about the language immersion project? Didn't that work out? It sounded so promising."

"They yanked me off that two seconds after you signed your confession. The only immersion I've had for the last year has been with men. I might as well be running my own escort service."

The bronze flecks in Ortega's eyes lit up with emotion. "Those bastards. They promised me you wouldn't pay for my mistake. Then they dared pimp you out?"

"Don't worry. They never actually let me have sex with the subjects for fear I'll fall in love with all of them." She paused to allow the sarcasm in her tone to fully penetrate. "I just flirt with potential assets in bars. Set 'em up for blackmail. Nothing demanding, ergo nothing that I could screw up."

"I'm sorry," he repeated.

She held his gaze in her own. "That's why I need this,

Ortega. My first real chance to redeem myself. I'm not asking you to do it for me. Do it for your country. But in the process, it would really help me out. And like I said, we'd be square."

Ortega exhaled slowly, then settled into a chair, motioning again for her to do the same. "There's a lot you don't know."

"Fine. Fill me in on the way to the airport."

He chuckled. "My country doesn't need me to break the Brigade. Kristie just wants me to come back to civilization because she's worried about me. She and I have a history."

"I know. She told me what good friends you were. Are."

"Did she tell you I once told her I loved her?"

Miranda grimaced, then sat down across from him. "No. That's a new one."

"She didn't take it seriously. She had this idea that I was just infatuated with her alter ego, Melissa Daniels."

"Pardon?"

His eyes twinkled. "Like I said, there's a lot you don't know. When I first met Kristie, she was dressed up in a red wig. That's why I thought you were her— or rather, Melissa Daniels—when your car pulled up today."

"Why would a spinner need an alter ego? She doesn't go into the field, does she?"

"Melissa goes wherever she wants," he explained with a laugh. "Anyway, it was Kristie who figured out I had a thing for pretty redheads. She told Jane Smith about it and that's how you got recruited when I needed an alibi. Jane and I figured the president might ask Kris to help with the investigation, and when she saw what you looked like, she'd be convinced the relationship was legitimate."

"Wow." Miranda bit her lip, then said, "She's got something going with Director McGregor now. Did you know that?"

"Yeah. I think it's great. And I think she was right. I never really was in love with her, although I had a heck of a crush on Melissa." He leaned forward. "She's a great friend. A loyal one. She's worried about me, so she's using this Brigade situation to bring me back. But I won't go. I can't. I'm doing something important out here. Something I need for my own sanity."

"You can't take a little break to visit a friend?" Miranda asked, trying for a light tone.

Ortega leaned back in his chair as though tired of having to explain himself. Then he told her, "I don't expect you to understand. You went through rigorous training, but I went through a completely different program. The kind that teaches a person to suppress his normal reactions. His normal, decent, human reactions. I was an assassin. I did it for my country, and I know it was the right thing to do. But the coldness of it, along with the power, turned out to be something I couldn't handle."

Impressed that he was blaming himself rather than the program or his country, she nodded for him to continue.

"The first time I screwed up was when I was sent to assassinate a CIA mole. The one who sold me out to Benito Carerra. Do you know about that?" When she nodded again, he said, "The mole retired out of the blue. In South America. That's how the agency figured out it was him. They knew he was hanging out with a bunch of drug thugs, so they sent me to take care of it. My assignment was to systematically shoot them all, and I did."

Miranda bit her lip. "You were just doing your job. Any of us would have done the same."

"Except I enjoyed it a little too much. I felt like a god-dammed superman. Then sirens began to wail, and an ambulance screeched up to the door. This little nurse got out and ran inside the building, and she was staring at the bodies, and then at me. Like I was a monster. And she was right."

He stared at the table for a moment, then added, "Out of the blue, we heard someone groaning. One man was still alive. And that little nurse ran to where he was and began trying to save his life. And the contrast...the contrast between her and me..." He glanced up, his eyes clouded. "I took a leave of absence, bought this place, and hung out here for about a year. I exercised my body and my mind. Tried to cleanse the demons away. It worked, or so I thought. And while I was here, I got an idea for a new agency where profilers could work behind the scenes, assisting undercover agents in the field. It would be positive work. Saving lives, not killing them. I went to President Standish and he bought the idea."

"SPIN."

"Yeah, SPIN. It was supposed to be my redemption. But as the agency earned more prestige, I got more power. And it all began to happen again. I fought it, but when Standish told me he was going to appoint me as Director of the FBI, I lost all perspective. Getting that position was all that mattered to me. I told myself it was because of the good I could do, but it was just the power."

She mentally cringed. "I don't need to hear this, Ortega."

"I think you do." His eyes blazed. "That night in

L.A., when the president's advisor told me he was going to recommend against my appointment, we had a huge argument. He took a swing at me, I fought back, and he hit his head. It was self-defense, Miranda, but I still knew it would kill my chances for the appointment. So I called Jane. It was the worst mistake of my life, mostly because of the way it hurt you and Kristie. And McGregor's sister."

"Ortega?"

"Yes?"

"I don't care." She stared straight into his eyes. "I don't care if it was self-defense. I don't care if you're sorry. None of that matters to me. I just want you to go back to SPIN with me and help us ID the Brigadier so I can get my career back on track."

And the amazing part was, she was telling the truth! After all these months of hating this guy, she had finally put him into perspective. She was ready to move on, and if he helped her with that, she would also be able to put *him* firmly in the past, forever, where he belonged.

As though to mark the moment, a clock began to strike twelve, its tone deep and resonant, and Miranda turned toward it, charmed.

Without warning, Ortega jumped up and grabbed her by the wrist. "Come with me."

Startled, Miranda used his sideways motion against him by grabbing his forearm with her other hand and sending him flying back into his chair. As he crashed, and the clock continued to chime, she reached under her sweatshirt and drew her pistol from the back waistband of her jeans in one fluid motion. Pointing it at him, she insisted calmly, "Contrary to popular belief, I don't like being manhandled."

He rubbed the back of his head, then flashed a rueful grin. "Nice move. If I promise not to grab you again, can I get up?"

She nodded and watched as he sprung to his feet. It occurred to her he might have just pretended to let her throw him, just so she'd get it out of her system. Either way, it had felt pretty good.

"I was just trying to show you something," he explained.

"I'm pretty sure I'm not interested."

"It has to do with Jonathan Kell," he told her, his tone mischievous. "Put your gun down and come with me. You'll like it. I promise."

As Ortega took her out the back door and into a clearing, he explained that he always exercised at noon, as well as at dawn and dusk. It was the heart of his cleansing ritual, a vital component of which was the relaxation technique Kell had taught him during their captivity.

Now he was offering to teach it to Miranda as he had promised during their alibi operation. She wasn't sure she trusted his motives, but she wasn't about to pass up this opportunity to learn more about Jonathan Kell, especially because she had a feeling she wasn't going to be able to convince Ortega to come back with her.

But at least she could bring Kristie this glimpse into Kell's mind. Maybe that, combined with the rest of the information, would help the spinner plot a successful strategy.

The huge clearing behind the cabin was empty except for a stump and axe near the house, a bench with a hinged lid and, at the far end of the space, an archery target. In the distance but out of sight, Miranda could hear a stream gurgling. The pine-scented air was so fresh and clean, she could see why Ortega found strength here, with or without his relaxation technique.

"Okay, Ortega. Let's see the miracle routine."

"You're skeptical?"

She shrugged her shoulders.

"Let's try something." He took down a bow and a quiver filled with arrows that had been hung on the side of the cabin. "You're a good shot according to your files. I want you to shoot two arrows. See how you do. Then after the exercises, shoot two more. You'll be surprised how much better you do."

Amused by the challenge, Miranda accepted the equipment. Looping the quiver over her shoulder, she turned her full attention to the bow, testing it, learning its temperament. It had a great feel—not too tight, but ultraresponsive. And there was hardly a breeze to disturb the trajectory, further adding to her confidence.

When she was done getting acquainted with the bow, she pulled an arrow from the quiver, then smiled to see that it was tipped with a hand-hewn obsidian arrowhead. "Where did you get the tip?"

"I made it."

It seemed unbelievable, and she reminded herself that Ortega was a professional liar. "Really? How long did it take you?"

"It took eight months—and a pile of shards and failures—just to make the first one. Now it goes pretty quickly."

"All part of the therapy I presume?"

"Yeah," he said with a laugh. "All part of the therapy."

"Interesting." She took a deep breath, then turned toward the target, threaded the arrow on the string, arched the bow expertly, and released. The arrow flew straight, hitting the target cleanly, about half an inch from the center.

"Nice," Ortega murmured.

She gave him a confident smile, pulled a second arrow from the quiver, and after recalibrating to account for her error, she shot again, this time hitting the target dead center.

"So?" she asked smoothly. "You're saying I'll do better than *that* after you teach me your technique?"

"Smart-ass. You're pretty damned good." He took back the equipment, returned it to its hooks, then eyed her outfit. "Do you have any looser clothes in the car? I'd lend you a gi, but you'd swim in it."

"I'm fine like this."

"I agree. But you won't have the full range of motion."

She took off her sweatshirt and laid it on a nearby bench. "I'll muddle through. Let's see what you've got."

"Okay." He opened the bench and took out a metronome, wound it, then set the speed so that the ticking resembled a slow heartbeat. "I haven't had to use this in years, but it'll help you keep count. Take this seriously though, okay? You'll be glad you did."

Without waiting for a reply, he turned to face east, bowed slightly, and took in a long, slow breath. Then he exhaled and told Miranda, "From the stomach. Shoulders loose, eyes front. As evenly as you can. Try to match the metronome, but don't worry about it. Don't worry about a thing. Just breathe and follow my movements. Clear your mind of anything else."

"Got it."

She could see from his grimace that he didn't think

she was giving due respect to his ritual, but she didn't care. While she appreciated the obvious physical advantage to any form of exercise, she didn't put much stock in the supposed psychological ones. No meditation for her, or finding her chi, or any of that nonsense. If she wanted to tone her mind, she'd read a book.

"Inhale for eight beats. Exhale for eight beats. Repeat that pattern two more times. For the fourth full breath, inhale for sixteen beats—"

"Sixteen?"

"Right. Three sets of eight, one of sixteen. Then start again."

She wanted to object—to remind him she wasn't a pearl diver or mermaid, and couldn't possibly inhale for sixteen beats of that stupid metronome—but he was already beginning to move and breathe, so she joined him reluctantly. It was tough to match even the eight-count beat, especially when paired with the movements. They were typical of any good martial arts form, but done so slowly and meticulously, impatience soon flared in her arm muscles as she tried to follow him. Meanwhile, she had to gulp for air every time she tried to make it through a sixteen-count breath. She probably would have just quit, but Ortega was handling it so effortlessly, her pride wouldn't allow her to give up, so she persevered.

In the distance, a bird was chattering like crazy, and even though she tried to ignore it, her brain was cataloguing the sound, trying to identify the type. Not a crow. A hawk maybe?

Concentrate, Miranda. He said make your mind a blank. Forget about the stupid bird!

Her muscles were aching as they reached a part of the routine where he barely seemed to be moving at all.

Their right arms were outstretched fully to the side, their left arms straight out in front of them at chest level. Their left legs were lifted off the ground, bent at the knees, with their right legs offering the only support. Then Ortega rocked forward, so that all of his weight was on the ball of his foot, and she decided he was right about one thing. These exercises were good for balance!

Would you clear your freaking mind for just one stupid minute! she chastised herself. Then she closed her eyes and listened to the metronome, ignoring Ortega completely. She continued to move, as slowly as possible, but switched to the form from her tae kwon do class. It was a little easier now, and now the eight-count breathing felt almost normal. In fact, in a strange way it felt better than normal.

She wasn't quite sure when the ache left her arms, or the sounds left her ears, or her mind started to relax. She only knew that when it all came together, it was perfection. A moment outside of time, outside of space, outside of herself, yet intimate, at the very core of her being.

Then she lost it, and almost lost her balance in the process. Gulping for air, she opened her eyes and realized that Ortega was standing right in front of her, his face inches from hers, staring at her with open curiosity.

She knew her cheeks were reddening as she backed away from him. Then she admitted, "That was interesting."

"I wasn't sure you'd get there the first time."

"I almost didn't. Then I closed my eyes, and it all came together."

"Closing your eyes is key," he confirmed.

"Then why didn't you tell me to do it?"

"I knew you'd figure it out on your own. That's part of what makes it key," he added with a wink.

"Whatever," she drawled, intent on returning to their former nonrelationship. "Did Kell really teach it to you?"

"He taught me the breathing part. I added the movement. For me, that definitely enhances it. The more you practice, the sooner you'll find the right combination that works for you. Learn to recognize the sensations—the flow—so you can get there without consciously trying. Then it'll last as long as you want."

Miranda bit her lip, wondering if he knew he was beginning to sound like every sex manual she had ever consulted.

"The trick is, don't rush it," he continued, his voice low and reassuring. "Sure, you want to get there, but the idea is to let it happen naturally. Relax. Enjoy the movement. The breathing. When it's time for it, it'll come. And it'll definitely be worth waiting for."

"Good to know," she said, cutting him off before her cheeks got any hotter. "Now what about the Brigade? Are you going to help us or not?"

His chuckle acknowledged the abrupt change in mood. "I told you, SPIN can do it on their own. This is just Kristie's scheme, and I'm not falling for it. You shouldn't, either." His smile warmed. "She's a good friend and I care about her. But she needs to respect my wishes."

Miranda wasn't sure if it was her imagination or not, but Ortega's attitude actually did seem more centered. More balanced. Had the breathing routine really mellowed him that easily?

In any case, there was no doubt that *she* was feeling unusually calm. All of the anger and hurt that usually accompanied any thought of him had dissipated, and she was able to respect what he was trying to say. Trying to do. Yes he was flawed—more flawed than most, or at least, his flaws were more dangerous—but he was trying to minimize the danger, both to himself and to others.

"Maybe it would help if you gave Kristie a timeline for when you'll be ready to talk to her again," she suggested carefully. "She misses you, Ortega. She says you taught her everything she knows. You're practically a hero to her."

"Kristie doesn't just want to talk. She wants to drag me back into the intelligence racket. But that environment is poison for me. I'll never go back to it."

"Which means there really isn't any way I can convince you to come back with me and head up the anti-Brigade team?" Miranda squared her shoulders. "Can I ask a different favor then?"

"Sure. Anything."

"Can you at least talk to me about the time you spent with Kell?"

"I was thoroughly debriefed. Haven't you seen the file?"

"I read every word, but I still have questions."

Ortega seemed about to refuse, then he said, "I'll get us a couple of bottles of water. Then you can ask me whatever you want. Then we'll eat. Then we'll go through the routine again."

She tilted her head to the side, trying to fathom why he wanted her to stay for such a long time. Guilt? Loneliness?

More manipulation? No, that didn't seem to be it.

Settling on loneliness as the most likely culprit, she murmured, "Do you really stay here alone all the time? You never go into Reno or one of the smaller towns?"

"I go down the hill about once a month. To stock up

mostly. And to remind myself there are other people in the world. I'm trying to get centered, but not *self*-centered, so socializing with strangers fits right in. And I haven't completely cut myself off from friends and family. We keep in touch by e-mail. The problem with Kristie is, she doesn't just want to keep in touch. She wants me to return to my old life."

Miranda smiled. "She thinks you're lonely. If she knew you were socializing, especially with women, she might be less obsessed with rescuing you." She grimaced then asked, "That's what you meant by socializing, right? Women?"

"Yeah," he confirmed with a laugh. "That's what I meant. But you're the first woman I've had here at the cabin. And the only woman I'd want here."

Miranda eyed him coolly. "Did you say something about a bottle of water?"

"Yeah," he said, dropping the flirtation without protest. "One bottle of water, coming right up."

They sat under a pine tree, sipping water and munching on apple slices, while Ortega told her the story of his adventure in South America with Carerra and Kell. In some respects it tracked the information in the file almost word for word, but occasionally, she got a glimpse into the ordeal that no file could ever effectively convey.

"The most important thing to remember about Jonathan Kell is that life dealt him a bizarre hand. A brilliant scientist who wouldn't hurt a fly and only wanted to do good. Yet so plagued with fear—fear of virtually everything—that it paralyzed him socially and professionally. That allowed the drug company to take enormous advantage of him. To use his brilliance, but when Kell needed them to pay the ransom, they just cut him loose. His greatest fear—abandonment—was confirmed that day. Abandoned by his employer and associates. And also abandoned by his country."

"His country saved his life. You were CIA and you came through for him."

"Kell knew I was there on a completely different mission. He was grateful to me personally, but not to the U.S. It infuriated him on my behalf that they didn't send someone to rescue me. I tried to explain to him that they couldn't do that, since my op didn't exist officially. I also told him they figured if I was still alive, I'd find a way to escape on my own."

"Small comfort when they're torturing you daily."

"I was trained for that. Kell wasn't."

"That's one of my questions," she admitted. "I get why they couldn't break you. But why didn't Kell—a civilian with phobias—just answer their questions?"

"He did. They thought he was holding out on them, but he wasn't. He tried to tell them about his research, but they were interested in something else that his company was rumored to be developing. Believe me, if he'd known about it, he would have given them every detail. But he says the rumors were just that. Rumors. Or maybe it was another company doing it. There were dozens of little research groups in the rain forest in those days, looking for million-dollar cures."

"Poor guy."

"They'd bring him back to the cage convulsing with fear. It was chilling. They used electrodes on him, and whips, but it didn't take them long to realize all they had to do was come near him and his brain exploded with images ten times worse than anything they could imagine doing to him."

"Do you remember what the other project was? The one in the rumors?"

Ortega nodded. "They called it Night Arrow. Something that made arrows fly straighter, according to Carerra's men. Not a product *you'd* ever need," he added admiringly.

She smiled. "Not much call for that in modern warfare anyway, is there?"

"Right. Unless they could apply it to bullets or torpedoes or whatever. It always sounded like a pipe dream to me. And to Kell. Benito Carerra claimed there were legends of warriors who anointed their arrows with certain magical potions that made them superior or invincible, but aside from the numerous poisons available down there, most potions were just religious concoctions designed to give confidence to the warrior and create fear in the enemy."

"So they kept torturing the poor guy."

"It was brutal. Carerra was such an asshole. I mean, torturing me was one thing. I came after him. But anyone could see Kell was harmless."

"You didn't just come after him, you used his wife to do it."

"So *he* was the victim?" Ortega laughed. "I guess that makes sense from your point of view. You probably wanted to torture me yourself after what I did to you."

"Which was basically the same thing you did to Mrs. Carerra. What was her name? Angelina?"

"It was hardly the same," Ortega protested.

"Really? You slept with her to advance an objective. Sound familiar? Anyway," she said with a sigh, "back to Kell. Everyone assumes he's useful to the Brigade because of his phobia research. Do you agree?"

Ortega nodded. "Our military has spent decades—and millions—trying to find ways to inhibit fear in a soldier. To promote fight-over-flight as a response. They've had success, but the results are always short-lived and the side-effects fairly extreme. Kell probably found something safer or more effective."

"And he would rather sell it to the Brigade because he hates the United States?"

Ortega nodded again. "He's a fairly gentle guy, but if they convinced him they found a way to take down the U.S. and big business—his two enemies—that would definitely motivate him. He used to rant about that kind of thing when we were imprisoned together. Revenge fantasies masquerading as political theory. Poor guy," he added sadly. Then he asked Miranda, "Any other questions?"

"Just one." She gave him an apologetic smile. "You're the founder of SPIN. The original spinner who taught Kristie everything she knows."

"What's your point?"

"You said she has enough information already to figure out who the Brigadier is. So? Doesn't that mean *you* could do it, too? Do you have any theories? Any leads you can give us?"

"I never said she had enough information to figure it out," he corrected her. "Just enough to plan an op to infiltrate the group. Not through Kell—he's too suspicious and way too bitter to trust anyone—"

"Anyone but you."

"Kell's grateful, but not stupid. He knows I was with the CIA. If I showed up at his place wanting to have a beer and talk about old times, he'd know I was investigating the Brigade." He arched an eyebrow. "As I was saying, Kristie can develop a strategy. She has all the information I have, plus she knows which top-notch agents with the right expertise are available, what their skills are, and who the other three Brigade members are. All she has to do is sit in her cubicle and work her magic."

"I agree."

He stared. "You do?"

"Yes. You'd be a huge help to her, but she can do it alone. And you're right. Kell's not stupid. The whole idea of your contacting him was a bad one, which means Kristie really *was* just using it as a way of luring you back." She scrambled to her feet. "Thanks, Ortega. I'll show myself out."

"Wait! You promised to have a meal with me."

"I did not."

He gave her a disarming smile. "We'll spear a couple of fresh trout in my stream and cook them over an open fire. Then we'll do the breathing routine again." Standing, he stepped close to her and murmured, "You'll like it, Miranda. And I think I can get you there faster this time, now that we're in synch."

This time, there was no mistaking the sexual undercurrent to his words. And strangely enough, she was responding. She really wanted to get there faster this time!

He was manipulating her again. Only this time, she could handle it, thanks in part to the calm, centered feeling his relaxation routine had given her. In fact, she might just be able to do a little reverse manipulation.

So she suggested sweetly, "You catch the fish. I'll

practice the routine alone. I'll feel less self-conscious that way. Then we'll have that meal. And *then,* I've really got to go. I want to fly out at a decent hour."

As always, Ortega backed off quickly. "Good plan. I'll just change and get my spear."

She watched him go into the cabin, returning in just a few moments in cut-off jeans and a muscle shirt. As she had suspected, his body was one gorgeous muscle after another, lean and tanned and irresistible.

Just look away, she counseled herself, amused that sex was lurking so stubbornly at the edges of her mind. She definitely needed to do the breathing routine again if she had any hope of maintaining balance with Ortega looking so good.

She turned her attention to the metronome, winding it gently, then setting it on the bench, while her host lifted his spear off its hook on the side of the cabin and disappeared into the trees toward the sound of the stream, calling over his shoulder, "Don't think. Just breathe."

"Okay," she called back, but her mind wasn't on the metronome. It was on the cabin. This was her chance to take a look around without Ortega knowing about it. She didn't know what she hoped to find, but she knew Ortega was a man of many secrets. Many lives. Many lies.

What would it hurt to just double-check that equipment, to make sure it was just a security system, Internet access and satellite television, as he had implied, and not some sort of espionage game being run under the pretense of retreating from the world?

She scooped up the empty water bottles from the bench to use as an excuse if he came back and found

her in the house. Then she slipped through the back
door and into the living room to examine the high-tech
equipment.

Chapter 4

She was almost disappointed to find that Ortega had apparently been telling her the truth. His computer and video equipment, while ultrasophisticated, was not anything a wealthy or connected civilian couldn't get their hands on. Did that mean her host was just what he claimed to be: a good guy with a tendency to go wrong, but not really bad deep inside?

Miranda wasn't quite ready to conclude that yet, so she took a moment to glance at his books, tapes and DVDs, just in case a suspicious theme presented itself. She found instead a very eclectic and engrossing collection—just the sort of items one might expect to find on a spinner's shelves.

She was just about to admit defeat when she saw an empty tape container in front of the VCR.

Let's see what you're watching these days, she told

her host as she picked up the box and read the provocative label: Surveillance Video.

For a guy who's been out of the game for a year, you've got some strange viewing habits, Ortega.

After a quick peek out the back window to ensure he was still busy, she checked to see that the tape was in the player. Then she turned on the TV and pressed the Play button. A grainy black-and-white image appeared, and for an instant, Miranda was simply confused by the low-tech quality of the recording.

Then realization shot through her and she stared in disbelief at the image of herself and Ortega, chatting and flirting—or more accurately, drooling over one another—while waiting for the elevator in the lobby of her apartment building.

Oh, God...

She punched the Stop button, her stomach knotting with disgust and self-loathing every bit as fresh and intense as when she had first viewed the video on a forty-two-inch screen at Langley. It took every ounce of willpower not to rip the tape from the machine and tear it to shreds. Instead, she carefully replaced the carton, then pressed the palms of her hands against her eyes and forced herself to grasp the truth.

Ray Ortega wasn't some sexy spiritual guru living in harmony with nature. Nor was he a top-secret mastermind running sophisticated black ops from a mountain retreat.

He was a pervert—a loser!—sitting alone in the middle of nowhere watching videos of Miranda to get his rocks off.

Somewhere in the distance, a metronome was sending her a rhythmic signal from outside the door, and while she couldn't quite make herself breathe normally, it did help her pull herself together. Locating a pen and paper, she wrote:

Hey, Ortega, I decided to just get going. I've got all the info on you and Kell I need. I'll pass it along to Kristie, and I'll try to make her understand why you need to stay out of the intelligence game permanently. Thanks for teaching me the breathing routine, I'm sure it will come in handy, assuming they ever give me a decent assignment. I doubt we'll ever meet again, so goodbye.

Then she grabbed her pistol from where she had left it on his kitchen table, shoved it into her knapsack, and hurried to the rented SUV. In seconds she was speeding down the mountain, still a little shaken up, but only because she had allowed herself to get upset over seeing the video again.

Or more accurately, over knowing Ortega watched it whenever he needed a cheap thrill. And since it was in the player, she could only assume he had watched it very recently. No wonder he had been so pleased to see her!

Well, Miranda, she told herself grimly, *you wanted closure, didn't you? I think you just got it.*

When her plane touched down at 10:00 p.m., Miranda dialed the telephone number marked "SPIN—nighttime" in the Brigade file. Kristie Hennessy answered on the first ring, identifying herself as S-3. When she found out her caller was Miranda, she acted as though they were long-lost sisters. Then she gave her the address of her apartment and promised to have hot chocolate and cookies awaiting her.

Miranda was actually in need of something stronger, but still, she was amazed and pleased at the reception. She had been thinking about this mission—studying the file for the entire plane ride—and she needed to discuss it with someone. Anyone. But most particularly with a spinner. So she took a cab straight to Kristie's apartment without bothering to go home first.

The spinner answered the door on the first knock, as though she had been lurking on the other side for hours.

"Miranda! Thank God." Grabbing her guest by the arm, she pulled her into the living room. "I was beginning to think you got lost."

"Thanks for inviting me over at this late hour—"

"Are you serious? I've been dying of curiosity ever since you called. Tell me everything. No, wait! Do you want something to eat first?"

"I'm fine."

"Perfect. Come and sit. Tell me everything."

Miranda took a seat on the couch, while the spinner sat on the coffee table directly in front of her, her blue eyes alive with anticipation.

"It's not good news, you know," she warned Kristie.

"Was he horrid? Will—I mean, Director McGregor—thinks he's a head case. He didn't do anything crazy, did he?"

"No, of course not." Miranda bit her lip to keep from laughing. "I thought he was your best friend."

"He is. I adore him. But that doesn't mean *you* have to." Kristie eyed her hopefully. "Do you?"

"Are you nuts? He *is* a head case. But the visit wasn't a total waste." She leaned forward, eager to share the plan she had developed on the plane. "Did you know I'm claustrophobic? I mean, is that in my psych profile?"

The spinner grimaced. "You lost me."

"You've seen my psych profile, right? I'm a little claustrophobic. Which means I have something in common with Jonathan Kell. A link to him."

"Miranda?" Kristie cocked her head to the side, her expression sincerely confused. "What happened with Ray?"

"He's fine. I promise. Don't worry about him anymore."

"I want details."

"Okay." Miranda shrugged. "During the day he communes with nature. At night, he watches X-rated footage of yours truly. He's happy as a perverted clam."

Kristie's blue eyes had widened. "X-rated footage?"

"The alibi video," Miranda explained with a laugh. "He labeled it 'surveillance tape,' but a better title would have been 'Nude Dupes on the Loose.'" She gave Kristie a sympathetic smile. "He's a head case, just like your boss said. But the good news is, he and I talked a lot about Kell. And I had time to study the file on the plane. I'm convinced you and I can crack this case— come up with the Brigadier's identity—between the two of us."

"Pardon?"

Miranda laughed again. "I've got my confidence back. Courtesy of Ray Ortega. Finding out that he's got demons—*lots* of them—made it easier for me to let myself off the hook. All we have to do now is make the CIA see that I'm not a screwup. For that, I need your help."

When Kristie just stared at her, she added gently, "He's not coming back. Maybe not ever. But definitely not soon. He honestly doesn't trust himself to make wise choices. I actually respect that part of him, by the way. I'm not so sure about the porno videotape stuff, but even there, I'm willing to cut him some slack."

Kristie cocked her head to the side. "You don't hate him anymore?"

"I don't feel anything, actually. He's a part of my past. *Finally.* Now all I have to do is impress my superiors, and life is good." She smiled to ease the blow of the next statement. "I need your help with that. You're a spinner, I'm an operative. Get me in to see Kell, okay? I'll take it from there."

Kristie opened her mouth as if to speak, then closed it and took a look around the room, presumably for allies. Then she murmured, "What do you mean? Get you in to see Kell? Alone? That's not possible. We promised to try to get you on the team—"

"On the team, I'll be relegated to a supporting role. That won't get me out of escort duty. I need something spectacular. Something SPIN-worthy." Before Kristie could protest, she explained, "I'm claustrophobic—that's right up Kell's dysfunctional alley. I'm a former lover of Ray Ortega, Kell's idol. And I've got a freakish amount of sex appeal for a person who's never had a decent relationship. That works for *all* guys. How much raw material do you need?"

Arching an eyebrow, she added firmly, "Spin me something daring. Something wild. I promise I can handle it."

Two hours later, Kristie was pacing the floor, while Miranda half dozed on the couch, muttering again and again, "You're overthinking it. Just get me into Switzerland. I'll do the rest."

The spinner's bloodshot eyes flashed. "I don't care what Ray told you, I don't have enough information!"

"Then forget Kell. Target one of the other Brigade members. That's what Ortega was suggesting, you know. He said Kell is way too suspicious to fall for something like this."

Kristie shook her head. "It has to be Kell. I feel that in my bones. And I love the claustrophobia angle, but I need more. I need Ray."

A phone rang at that moment, and Miranda drawled, "Maybe that's him."

The spinner frowned. "Who would call this late? It's not my operative phone, and Will's too polite to call after midnight unless it's an emergency."

Miranda glanced at the identification screen. "It's a 213 area code."

"Oops!" Kristie sprang for the phone and punched the speaker button. "Will? Hi."

"Hey, beautiful. Did I wake you?"

"Even if you did, I'd never complain," she assured him. "Is everything okay?"

"That depends on what you're wearing," the director's sexy voice told her.

As Miranda bit back a smile, Kristie insisted, "This isn't a good time, Will. I've got something boiling on the stove."

"At midnight? Just as well, since this is partly a business call. Have you heard from Miranda Cutler?"

Kristie winced. "Why do you ask?"

There was a long silence, then McGregor—*Director* McGregor—said, "Because I'm in charge. And because I'm concerned about her. And because Ortega called me a few minutes ago, asking if she's okay."

"Well…" Kristie gave Miranda an apologetic shrug.

"In that case, good news. She's right here. Miranda, say hello."

"Hi, Director McGregor."

The silence was much longer this time. Then he muttered, "What's going on?"

"Everything's fine," Kristie insisted. "Miranda's plane got in late, so I told her to come here. That's okay, right?"

"Of course. How did it go, Miranda?"

"Ortega and I had a very cordial exchange."

"He said you disappeared without saying goodbye. He thought it was going well, then suddenly, you were gone. So he asked me to follow up."

"I left him a note," she replied coolly. "It was clear he wasn't going to help us. He did his best to brief me about Kell. That's why I came to see Kristie. But I didn't see any reason to hang around. I can't believe he called you," she added ruefully.

"He feels like crap about the way he and Jane Smith used you. He was worried he blew it again. I promised to check on you, and now I have."

"Right." Miranda smiled in relief while motioning to Kristie to pick up the receiver. "I'll give you two some privacy now—"

"Wait, Miranda." McGregor's tone had become businesslike. "I'm supposed to keep your superiors informed. I'm going to honor our agreement and ask that you be assigned to the anti-Brigade team, but that won't happen for a few days at least. Should I tell them you'll report for duty tomorrow morning, pending new developments with the team?"

"Miranda's exhausted, Will," Kristie interrupted. "Can't you tell her supervisor I need her for a few more days? To debrief her properly once she's rested?"

"She visited Ortega for less than four hours and you need days to debrief her?" McGregor protested, but his tone was teasing. "What's going on, Goldie?"

Miranda waved her hand for Kristie to keep silent. "Director McGregor? Ortega told me the same basic story that's in the file, but the nuances are intriguing. I want to be sure I communicate them to Kristie while they're fresh in my mind."

"Fine. Check in with your interim supervisor—"

"My what?"

"Sorry, I thought you knew. Your regular team leader didn't know anything about Ortega and the alibi situation, so when we asked to borrow you, the agency reassigned you temporarily. To a guy named Bob Runyon. He apparently knows the whole story."

Miranda winced. "He's the one who broke the news to me after Jane Smith was apprehended. I'll check in with him and let him know what's going on."

"Excellent." McGregor's tone softened. "It sounds like you did a great job, Miranda. I'll be sure the powers-that-be hear about it. And when it's time to put the team together, I'll use my best efforts to get you on it."

"Thanks. Good night, sir. I'll just get that boiling pot off the stove while you two say goodbye."

Kristie picked up the receiver. "McGregor?" She listened for a few moments, then murmured, "Me, too. 'Night."

Miranda gave her a teasing smile after the call had been disconnected. "Lucky you."

"I know. That's why… Well, never mind." Her tone became brisk. "What's the story with Bob Runyon? Your reaction wasn't positive."

"He's a pig, but I think that will work to our advantage." She paused to join in Kristie's laughter, then added, "I'll go see him tomorrow and convince him to give me a couple of weeks off. Plenty of time to make round trips to South America and to Switzerland."

The spinner rubbed her bloodshot eyes. "You really think there's something in the drug company files we can use?"

"It stands to reason. Look how much you know about me from reading my psych profile and the rest of my personnel file. I'm hoping they have a really thick one on a nut like Kell, along with detailed files on his experiments. I know Ortega included a lot of that in his debrief, but—"

"But the more detail, the better? I agree. You'd make a good spinner, Miranda."

"Puh-leeze. I'd go crazy sitting in front of phones and computers all day. That's why we're the perfect team for this." She hesitated, then asked carefully, "I don't want to get you into trouble with Director McGregor. I'm assuming that won't happen, given how valuable you are to him, and given…well, you know."

"He'll have a fit, but if we succeed, he'll get over it. You just have to promise—and I mean, *promise*—to follow the plan exactly. You're going to South America for a simple break-in, right? And then, if we decide to send you to Kell, it will be short and sweet. Information gathering, not heroics. I won't go any further with this unless I have your word on that."

"You've got it."

"And one more condition." The spinner's expression grew grim. "When all this is over, you're going to get some counseling."

"Huh? Where did *that* come from?" Miranda shook

her head. "I keep forgetting you're a shrink. But trust me, that visit to Ortega's today was pure therapy for me. And I honestly think I'll benefit from the relaxation technique he taught me. I've definitely put those demons to rest, once and for all."

"I wasn't talking about you and Ray."

Miranda scowled, reminded once again that the spinner had seen her psych profile. She was about to assure her that she had completely recovered from her father's moody dominance, but even Miranda knew that wasn't true. So she stuck her hand forward for a shake instead. "Okay, S-3. You've got yourself a deal."

"Mr. Runyon? Sir? They told me to come right in. I hope I'm not disturbing you."

"Come in, Miranda."

Miranda struggled not to laugh as Bob Runyon motioned for her to take a seat, taking visible care not to let his gaze drop from her face to her body, even for an instant.

Still, she imagined he had already noticed her high, high heels and short, short skirt, both of which were as extreme as she had dared wear to headquarters, along with a gauzy black blouse that was sheer enough to afford a glimpse of her lacy bra. This was one of her favorite vamp outfits, and considering the fact that the CIA had taught her to dress this way, it seemed only fair to demonstrate to them, up close and personal, how proficient she had become.

"Director McGregor suggested I report to you, sir."

"Give me a minute…" He leafed through a pile of folders until he found the one he wanted. "Obviously McGregor told you I'm functioning as your interim. I hope that's not a problem for you."

"Absolutely not, sir. I was actually glad to hear it."

He looked up from the file. "Somehow I doubt that."

"Because of the way I acted the last time I saw you?" Miranda sighed. "I was hoping you wouldn't hold that against me."

"Against *you?*" He cleared his throat. "I thought it was *my* behavior that was the problem. Not that I did anything wrong," he added quickly. "But I should have been more sensitive. I apologize."

Miranda leaned forward, and this time, he apparently couldn't resist an eyeful of cleavage.

Then she told him simply, "I was so embarrassed about the things I let Ortega do to me. And so mortified that you had seen them, and probably thought I was either naive or a slut—"

"No, no! Nothing like that. I have nothing but the greatest respect for you, Miranda."

"But that tape. The way he kissed me. The places he kissed me. And the way I obviously enjoyed it." She bit her lip. "When you asked me to have a drink with you, I thought to myself, what if we ride in an elevator?"

"Oh, God! I wasn't suggesting anything like that."

Miranda smiled. "I've had a lot of time to think about that. And the truth is, that's what normal healthy adults *do* in elevators when they're dating. Right? It was a mistake with Ortega, but with you—" She stared at her hands, pretending to be embarrassed. "I mean, not that you're interested anymore. But still, it's nothing to be ashamed of. I'm really sorry I reacted the way I did."

"Right." He cleared his throat, and she knew he was having trouble following the conversation. That was a very good sign.

"It's the company's fault for asking a good-looking single guy to debrief me," she added lightly. "They should have used a woman. Then we wouldn't have gotten our signals crossed. I wouldn't blame you if you didn't want to date *any* redheads anymore, much less date me. My loss, right? For scaring you away?"

"No. I mean—" He flushed, then suggested carefully, "Whenever you're ready, I'm definitely still interested."

"Really?" She gave him a shy smile. "Maybe when I get back from vacation, we can have that drink and talk."

He seemed to want to respond, but no words came out of his mouth, so she prompted, "Did you want to hear about my visit to Ortega's hideaway?"

He nodded, his eyes glazed.

"I thought it would be awkward, but we were both very professional. I mean…" She bit her lip. "It was obvious he hadn't been alone with a woman in a while, so that got a little awkward. For him though, not for *me*. I was all business."

"How long were you there?"

"About three hours. We spent most of the time in his cabin, because it was so warm outside. I was wearing a halter top and shorts, but I was still roasting. He gave me some very valuable intel that I've been sharing with one of the spinners."

"Your assignment was to bring *him* back to SPIN, not just intel."

"I tried everything I could think of. Everything except going all the way. Director McGregor made it clear I wasn't expected to go that far."

"No one wanted you to do anything like that," Runyon assured her. "I'm sorry if I implied otherwise."

"You've got to stop apologizing to me for doing your

job," she told him with a sigh. "You know, I have to say, the contrast between you and Ortega is really unbelievable. There he was, thinking only about himself. And here you are, worried about me. It means a lot, Mr. Runyon." She hesitated, then murmured, "Bob."

"You're a valuable member of my team," he assured her.

"Your *interim* team. But I'd love to make it permanent. Maybe we can discuss that when I get back."

"From vacation? You mentioned that earlier. I didn't realize you were scheduled for one."

"It's a new request. Is it a problem? I just feel like I've finally put my past behind me. And I'd like to do what you suggested last year. Visit my dad's grave. Talk to my old friends. Then come back here all eager and fresh. Ready to make new memories. Maybe even in elevators," she said, blushing on cue.

Runyon licked his lips. "How long do you plan on being gone? McGregor recommended you for the anti-Brigade team and—" He laughed sheepishly. "Well, I had my doubts about that. But now that we've spoken, I definitely want you with us."

"And *I* definitely want to *be* with you," she told him breathlessly. "But the spinner says it will be two weeks before the op is planned and ready. Perfect timing, right? When I get back, I'll be at your disposal."

"I'll process the paperwork right away, transferring you to me. And Miranda?" He stood and walked around the desk, then waited for her to stand before telling her softly, "I really do apologize for that video business. I shouldn't have played it in front of you. I realize that now."

"Do you know what I think, Bob?" she replied, gazing up at him with widened eyes. "Someday, when

we're both ready, we should watch that tape again. Together. Just so you can remind me, once and for all, that
I didn't do anything wrong in that elevator. I just did it
with the wrong guy."

Miranda was still laughing at herself when her plane
took off later that morning. She usually didn't indulge
in such over-the-top seductions, but Runyon had been
the masculine equivalent of a bitch in heat, and she
hadn't been able to resist making his heart pound even
faster. He'd live. And meanwhile, she could chalk it up
to broadening her range of vamp skills, although she
prayed that she wouldn't need them so often in the future if she and the spinner succeeded.

She took it as a good omen that Kristie had already
accomplished a lot. Miranda was traveling in first class
under the alias Jennifer Aguilar. Her only carry-on lug-
gage was her purse and a DVD player in a padded case
with six romantic comedies on disks nestled in plastic
sleeves.

Stowed in the bowels of the jet were the tools of Miranda's trade, spinner style. Her favorite was an ornate
barrette that was actually a tiny digital camera. There
were also eyeglasses that would help her see in the dark
during the break-in, along with a miniflashlight that
produced a powerful beam.

Last but not least, she was equipped with tranquil-
izer darts and a high-tech shooting "straw" made of
silicon. Kristie had learned that the drug company's
security system consisted of a six-foot-high iron
fence, a padlocked gate, and four semivicious Dobermans. No security cameras, no voice prints, no reti-
nal scans…

In other words, a piece of cake.

Miranda wanted to lean back in her leather seat and enjoy the luxury—after all, she hadn't been pampered since the time she had pneumonia just weeks before her father's accident—but she found herself studying the files again. So much was riding on this. Her career. Her self-esteem. Her true emotional break from the Ortega fiasco.

And Kristie Hennessy's reputation.

Miranda was fairly sure McGregor would forgive Kristie any screwup—one only had to see them together to know that. But the spinner had built something for herself, using instinct, intelligence and guts, and Miranda wasn't about to ruin it. She'd never knowingly do that to a dedicated professional.

And certainly never to a friend.

She checked into her five-star hotel, discovering quickly that it catered to ultrawealthy Americans who wanted a jungle experience without the heat, humidity and bugs. In fact, as nearly as Miranda could tell, they just wanted lush foliage and tropical drinks, and she might have joined them in the decadent Rain Forest Bar, but she wanted to get a few hours of sleep before the break-in.

She also needed to locate the vehicle Kristie had arranged for her. The desk clerk had already given her the keys in a sealed envelope marked "Señorita Aguilar." Once she checked out her accommodations—a sumptuous suite with a fully stocked bar and a huge bed draped with designer mosquito netting—Miranda went for a stroll in the parking lot, occasionally pushing the alarm button on the key chain until finally a set of headlights on a shiny black Mercedes convertible flashed in response.

Miranda knew without checking that there was a loaded pistol and a C-4 kit under the front seat. The trunk almost certainly contained a set of chain cutters and a lightweight black cotton outfit, complete with tennis shoes, in Miranda's size. Reassured that the op was set, she returned to her suite and enjoyed a room service order of Canopy Kabobs and Tropical Fruit Salad, washed down by Safari Seltzer. After slipping out of her clothes, she set the alarm on the nightstand to wake her at midnight—with "Sounds of the Jungle Night," no less. But she didn't climb into bed just yet.

Instead, she rummaged in her suitcase until she found the metronome she had purchased on the way to the airport that morning. Then for the first time since she left Ortega's place, she practiced Jonathan Kell's breathing technique as she moved through her tae kwon do form.

Eight counts in, eight counts out, three times. Slow and steady. Then one impossibly slow set. She had to gulp for air a few times before the rhythm established itself, then her motions and her breathing attained a fluidity that moved her easily toward the goal of complete balance. A new sensation—the feeling that her lungs had infinite capacity, that she could inhale forever—began to seduce her. Then the metronome reminded her to exhale, and that, too, was amazing, as the air flowed up through her, an inexhaustible source, replenished even as it left her.

Now the three slow breaths seemed too hurried, and her body yearned for the fourth one. When it came to her again, she floated—serene and in perfect harmony. And because she didn't struggle to maintain it, she stayed there, still breathing, but no longer making a conscious effort. She didn't know how long it lasted, but when it ended, she felt no loss, no regret. She felt only peace.

My God, Ortega, no wonder you do this....

She moved through the form one last time, just to re-introduce her body to reality. Then she glanced at the clock and realized sheepishly that the entire experience had lasted less than thirty minutes. It had seemed like at least an hour!

She felt so refreshed, it seemed silly to think about sleeping. Yet she also knew she would fall asleep in seconds, thanks to the absence of worry or stress. And she needed to be at her best for the break-in, so she entered the cocoon of netting, slipped between satin sheets, tucked her blowgun under the fluffy pillow and nestled down for a nap.

Awakened by the recorded sounds of birds cawing and waterfalls crashing, Miranda switched off the alarm, then dressed in a sexy black-and-white striped sundress and low-heeled sandals. Then she twisted her hair into a long, loose braid, grabbed a black canvas shoulder bag containing the straw, darts and a flashlight, and headed down three flights of stairs to the ground floor.

The lobby was deserted, although from the sound of things, the bar was hopping. Outside, a doorman was busy attending to a group disembarking from a stretch limousine, so Miranda was able to scoot into the parking lot without attracting attention. Once at the Mercedes, she drove quickly to an unlit area, where she changed into the black outfit and sneakers before following the rest of the route she had memorized on the plane.

It took less than forty minutes to reach the building

that served as both laboratory and warehouse for Bio-GeniSystems, Inc, the company that had refused to pay Kell's ransom ten years earlier. As Kristie had fore-warned, the place was surrounded by a high chain-link fence topped with barbed wire. There was a main gate in the front, with a wider one for deliveries in the back. Both were padlocked.

It seemed completely deserted, but the intel had been accurate thus far, so Miranda assumed the Dobermans would be there soon to greet her. Closing the car door as quietly as possible, she tucked the pistol in her waistband and loaded the dart gun, hoping that it would suffice. It was designed to hold two projectiles in its cylinder, which meant she would need to reload once. On the other hand, it would be silent and nonlethal, which was just how she wanted it.

Popping the trunk, she retrieved the chain cutters, which she then used to slice easily through the padlock cables on the back gate. Immediately the dogs began to bark from somewhere in the dark recesses of the lot, so she threw the tool back into the trunk, then pushed the gate open and braced herself, the high-tech straw in her lips and her special glasses ready to detect heat from the animals' bodies as soon as they came into view.

It was almost surreal, seeing them as blurs of pulsating yellow and red before they took actual shape before her eyes. As soon as the first two dogs bounded into range, she fired, dropping them.

A third animal leapt toward her, his fangs bared, and for a split second she considered using the pistol, but by then her fingers had managed to get the third and fourth darts in place, so she blew one into the monster's neck just as his body reached her. The impact of his huge, unconscious form almost knocked her off her feet, and to keep her balance she dropped to one knee, pushing the carcass aside, alert for the last dog's arrival.

To her amusement, this fellow seemed to be rethinking his options. He ran up to within a few feet of her, then whined as if to say, "Don't shoot me."

Miranda extended her hand and he moved to her cautiously, then licked her fingers. "That's a good boy," she told him softly. "Don't worry. This won't hurt a bit. You'll sleep for a few minutes and you probably won't remember a thing. Okay?" Jumping to her feet, she took a few steps backward, smiled into his trusting brown eyes, and shot him with a dart.

Turning her attention to the back door of the facility, she saw that it was secured by an excellent dead bolt. Unfortunately for BioGeniSystems, there was a window within inches of the entrance, and no alarm system, so Miranda simply shattered the glass, then reached inside and unlocked the door.

"I trained for eight months for this?" Miranda asked with a laugh, then she turned on the slim flashlight hooked to her waistband and surveyed a half-empty storeroom. On the far wall were two doors, one marked "Lab," the other, "Office."

Praying that she would find a wealth of information on Jonathan Kell, she headed into the office and was pleased to find a tall set of file cabinets along one wall. Another door led to a small outer office, which in turn had a door to the front parking lot. The blinds in the outer office were closed tight.

Locating the file drawer labeled "K", she transferred the flashlight to her teeth and began searching until she found a four-inch thick folder with Jonathan Kell's name emblazoned across the front.

Personnel records. Background checks. Disciplinary reports. Counseling notes. It was more than Miranda could have wanted. She quickly photographed what she needed, then returned the file to its spot.

There had been nothing about Kell's actual experiments or research, so she searched through the remaining cabinets for more records, then put the barrette back in her hair for safekeeping and moved into the laboratory. Expecting it to be spotless and high-tech, she grimaced when she found long metal tables littered with tubes, vials and equipment in complete disarray. Kristie had mentioned that BioGeniSystems had gone downhill in recent years, mostly due to inferior staff, but also because of the simple glut of similar companies operating in the area with little or no success. There were even rumors that the company had begun working with drug lords in the area, developing methods of refining and purifying illegal substances—a far cry from their original purpose of healing.

There were three regular file cabinets in the lab, along with a fourth one made of stainless steel that was styled more like a safe, complete with a combination lock. Checking the unsecured drawers first, she found five slim bundles of records labeled Jonathan Kell, and quickly photographed them.

Then she stared at the locked cabinet, intrigued but also fairly certain that it contained nothing of use to her. Kell hadn't worked here for ten years, after all. The safe probably contained current secrets, not old ones. Or maybe it housed the payroll.

Still, she had to open it. After all, Kristie's scenario

called for BioGeniSystems to assume that this break-in was the result of industrial, rather than governmental, spying. And no self-respecting industrial spy would pass up the chance to see what a competitor considered so valuable it had to be locked up!

Balancing the flashlight on a table with its beam directed at the safe, Miranda dug in her shoulder bag for the C-4 that Kristie's contact had planted in the car. Kneeling, she briefly examined the lock as well as the cabinet's structure. Then she rigged the explosive directly under the main hinge and stepped back just as it detonated cleanly.

Setting the door aside, she knelt again and examined the handful of files in the interior. They were all labeled "HeetSeek." The only other contents were a set of six blue test tubes hanging in a chrome rack. Flipping through the papers, she bit her lip, not quite understanding what she was reading. Then she saw two words that sent her mind flashing back to her recent conversation with Ortega.

What was Kell rumored to be working on?
Something called Night Arrow.

"It really did exist," she murmured, stunned by the revelation. "But Kell didn't know about it. So these bastards didn't just betray him by refusing to pay the ransom. They kept secrets from him and he was tortured because of them!"

Knowing that the dogs would wake up shortly, she decided to just stuff these files into her bag rather than taking the time to photograph them. It would fit with her cover, she decided, and she didn't trust herself to know what to copy and what to ignore. She also wanted to take one of the beautiful blue tubes, but was a little concerned about the danger if the HeetSeek liquid proved to be volatile. The last thing she wanted to do was blow up that beautiful Mercedes and get thrown in a prison for industrial espionage. The CIA would disown her more quickly than BioGeniSystems had dumped Kell!

She decided to take a small amount in a more secure receptacle, so she took one of the tubes from the chrome rack and moved to a messy workstation. Locating an empty vial made of clear glass, she propped it up in a beaker. Then she uncorked the test tube, careful not to allow any fumes to reach her nostrils as she transferred some of its contents—a clear, thick liquid—into the slender vial. Then she tightly capped both receptacles. Relieved that she had survived thus far, she tucked the sample into her pants pocket, praying that none of the substance would leak and make contact with her skin. As soon as she got back to the car she would transfer the vial to the trunk, just in case it indeed proved dangerous.

As she carried the half-empty test tube back to the safe, she was so completely intent on HeetSeek and its implications, she momentarily forgot her actual mission. And the dogs. And the fact that unidentified substances were not the only source of danger for a CIA agent on an unsanctioned op in a foreign country.

Then a rough voice brutally reminded her of that danger, shouting orders at her in Spanish as overhead lamps began to blaze, flooding the room with light so bright it stabbed at her eyeballs. Completely disoriented, she spun toward the voice, and as she did so, the test tube of HeetSeek slipped from her grasp, crashing to the floor at her feet.

She jumped back, certain that the room would now

be rocked by an explosion, and when nothing happened, she almost laughed with relief.

Then she raised her hands above her head, looked directly into the angry eyes of the armed men in the doorway, and said with a cheerful smile, "I guess I'm busted. And so is my loot."

Chapter 5

There were four men, three of whom were wearing uniforms and were armed with pistols. The fourth man hung back a bit, clearly more intimidated by the situation than his captive was. He was dressed in casual, golf-style clothes and from his rumpled hair and bleary eyes, Miranda guessed he had been pulled out of bed unexpectedly.

But why?

According to SPIN's intel, BioGeniSystems didn't use armed guards either directly or as part of a contract with a security company. Even assuming they did, she wondered how they had discovered the break-in so quickly. Was it possible she had triggered a silent alarm at some point? It didn't seem likely, given the otherwise poor security.

After instructing her to keep her hands raised, one of the guards stepped forward and frisked her, then turned to show her Glock to his companions, oblivious to the fact that he had failed to detect the vial in her pocket.

The man in the golf clothes spoke for the first time. "Who do you work for? What else have you touched besides the—the contents of the safe?"

Miranda licked her lips, intrigued. He didn't want to mention the term "HeetSeek." Apparently it was so confidential—so valuable—that he didn't even trust his own men to know about it.

"What else was worth touching?" Miranda asked with a wry smile. "My employers offered me a fortune if I could snag the Night Arrow formula for them. Imagine what they would have given me for an actual sample! Too bad it broke."

"Night Arrow?" a female voice asked in obvious disbelief, and a lovely, well-dressed woman pushed her way through the group of guards. Ignoring Miranda, she said to the unarmed man, "You told us that was just a myth!"

"It is. It is." He shrank from her angry gaze. "We ran experiments on it, just to be sure it didn't work. And it doesn't. I swear it, Señora Carerra."

"Carerra?" Miranda looked more closely at the woman, impressed. "Are you Angelina? The widow of Benito Carerra?"

The woman's brown eyes narrowed. "Who are you to dare ask my name?"

Miranda smiled. "You and I have something in common. We were both screwed by Ray Ortega."

Angelina opened her mouth as if to speak, then she closed it and just studied Miranda for a few moments.

Then she surprised everyone by murmuring to her guards, "Leave us for a minute. I'd like to speak with Miss… Miss?"

"I'm Jennifer Aguilar. I was hired by Cornucopia Pharmaceuticals to steal the Night Arrow formula."

"Cornucopia," the unarmed man muttered. "Those bastards."

Angelina glared at him. "Apparently they knew the truth, that you have been working on this all along. Step outside with my men, doctor. And hope that Miss Aguilar here puts me in a better mood, or you will wish you hadn't lied to us."

When he and the others had left, the dark-haired woman instructed Miranda simply, "Talk to me."

Miranda shrugged. "I heard all about it. From Ortega himself. It was one of the missions that made him famous, you know. Seducing you and then using the information to kill your husband. I went through something similar, but in my case, it was my career that he killed, not my husband."

"Go on."

She sighed. "Do you think I dreamed of *this?* Industrial espionage? I had my sights set higher. But Ortega ruined that."

"You wanted to work for the CIA?"

"Exactly. I made it into their training program. Then Ortega used me for one of his ops. Made a complete fool out of me and enjoyed himself—sexually—in the process. I was tossed out on my ear after he was done with me." She didn't have to feign the passion in her voice as she added, "I wanted that career. I *earned* it. I could have made a difference. But that—that bastard ruined everything for me. And the same thing happened to you. Right?"

Angelina hesitated, then asked carefully, "Aren't you forgetting something? It's true, Ortega used me. But he also believed that by killing Benito, he was rescuing me from a very cruel man."

"And what if he had failed in his mission? Did he ever once think about what would have happened to you if he *hadn't* been able to kill your husband?"

Angelina arched an eyebrow. "I see you truly hate him. As do I. It was arrogant of him to assume I wanted to be rescued. Who was he to decide such a thing? To use me the way he did?"

"I'm sorry," Miranda told her softly. "I know how it feels to be duped by him. And then abandoned to pick up the pieces of a shattered life."

"I survived, and now I am stronger because of it. You will be, too." Angelina walked to the safe and examined the rack of vials. "You took only one? The one that broke?"

"Yes. That and the files. They're in my bag."

"Leave them. Take nothing but your keys, and then go quickly. I will see that you are not prosecuted."

Miranda stared. "Really?"

"We are sisters, are we not? Come." She took Miranda by the arm and led her into the warehouse area where the men were waiting. "Miss Aguilar is leaving now. I want each of you to forget this ever happened. Is that clear?"

When the doctor protested that they should turn Miranda over to the authorities as a burglar, Angelina reminded him, "Are you ready for that kind of publicity? Do you want the world to know about Night Arrow?"

"No," he admitted.

"Then we will let her go. And she will tell no one what she found. Is that not true, Miss Aguilar?"

"I'll tell them there was no sign of Night Arrow anywhere," Miranda assured her, adding softly, "If I had known you were associated with BioGeniSystems, I never would have taken this assignment. But still, I'm glad we had a chance to meet. Sisters, just like you said."

Angelina beamed. "I am pleased, too. Now go home. Find another way to earn a living. And be strong, Jennifer."

"I will." She took one final look at this woman who had been through so much, been trampled so often, yet somehow had evolved into the most confident, least victimlike female Miranda had ever met.

Living proof that there really is life after Ortega, Miranda told herself, impressed.

And inspired.

Flashing Angelina a grateful smile, she backed a safe distance away from the group, then turned and sprinted for the door.

"I still can't believe she let you go."

"I know." Miranda helped herself to a third slice of pizza from the box on Kristie's coffee table, then settled back in one of the spinner's overstuffed easy chairs. "To her, I was a kindred spirit, thank God."

"It was a brilliant move, telling her about you and Ray. It could have backfired, but instead, it was your ticket out of there."

"Of course, she also didn't want the world hearing about Night Arrow. So she might have let me go anyway."

"*After* checking out your story. Verifying your background. And maybe letting her guards teach you a lesson. You definitely caught a break. Of all the people to walk into BioGeniSystems in the middle of the night…"

"It's like you said. They must be doing some illicit testing in their lab at night. For the Carerra drug cartel.

She runs it now, right? And even ten years ago, her husband had heard rumors about Night Arrow. That's why he was torturing Kell in the first place." Miranda sighed. "You're right. I was lucky it was her. Not just because she let me go, but because it taught me something."

"Let me guess," Kristie protested with a groan. "Life after Ortega? Are we going to go through *that* again?"

Miranda laughed. "It's more than that. Really. I like seeing a victim turn into such a confident person, period. You know about my father, right? He *never* recovered—emotionally—from his accident. But Angelina Carerra went through something just as horrible. Plus, she started out as such a…well, for lack of a better word, such a doormat, right? According to Ortega, she was scared to death of Benito, and extremely submissive and easily manipulated. But the woman I met last night was bursting with confidence. Exuding strength. And that's what she said to me: 'Be strong, Jennifer.' It was very inspiring."

"It's unusual for a person to change that much," Kristie mused. "Maybe she never really was as weak as people thought. Maybe she acted that way because Benito wanted a submissive woman, so she played the part in those days. After he died, she was able to be herself."

"No. If she'd been that strong ten years ago, she never would have married him. According to Ortega, Benito Carerra wasn't just an abusive husband. He was a full-out megalomaniac, viciously dominating everyone—his soldiers, his family, even the politicians that protected him."

Kristie arched an eyebrow. "Ray freed her from all that? And she isn't at all grateful?"

"Why should she be? He didn't do it out of concern

for her. It was just another mission to him. But to her, it must have been terrifying." Miranda sighed. "I give her credit for not being bitter. She has definitely moved on. That's what I want to do. So?" She eyed the spinner hopefully. "How long do you think it will take for you to finish the Kell scenario?"

"You're such a slave driver," the spinner said, laughing. "Give me a couple of days, okay? I have to study these files on the sly, you know, so I won't get much done at the office. Why don't you come over again tomorrow night and I'll share whatever I've learned up till then."

"What about the sample of HeetSeek? Are you going to get it analyzed?"

Kristie nodded. "But not until you're back from Switzerland. I don't want McGregor to hear about it before then." She picked up the vial from the table. "I wish you could remember more of what those files said."

"They referred to it mostly as Night Arrow. And they did tons of trajectory tests, most of which failed. But not *all* of them. If only I'd photographed those pages, too."

"It's lucky you didn't. The only reason they didn't search you for a camera was because you had actual files stuffed in your bag." The spinner's blue eyes sparkled. "You really think the natives in that region used it on their arrows to give them heat-seeking properties?"

"That's the myth. A myth that's been circulating for years, so maybe our government knows all about it already. Right? It's probably been tested to death with no success."

"Hard to say."

Miranda smiled, sensing that the spinner didn't want this to be a myth at all. And who could blame her? It was such an amazing concept—arrows flying through the darkness, guided by the heat emanating from their intended victim's body!

"I guess I'll go home." She stood and stretched. "McGregor will probably be calling you soon. I don't want to be here for the 'what are you wearing?' part of the show."

"I still can't believe I let you overhear that on the speakerphone. How mortifying."

"It's romantic," Miranda countered, adding cautiously, "You two are great together. Once you really let go of Ortega, who knows what might happen. Right?"

Kristie frowned. "You make it sound like I'm interested in Ray romantically. I'm not and I never was." She hesitated, then admitted, "But you're right. It bugs Will a little. Or maybe a lot. Not romantically, but professionally."

"That's understandable."

"Pardon?"

"Where would Ortega fit in if he came back? Not the FBI, that's for sure. No way could President Standish appoint a killer, even if the killing was self-defense. So? Would he come back to SPIN? Is there room enough for him and McGregor?"

"Probably not," Kristie admitted. "But there are other agencies. Other jobs than director. He's an amazing strategist."

"And his last official act was to plot himself an exit strategy," Miranda reminded her. "Maybe you should respect that. He wants to be alone. Except of course for his monthly trips into Reno for sex, and his quality time with the X-rated videotape."

"You make him sound like such a pervert," Kristie complained. "That tape is actually very romantic, you know."

"Puh-leeze."

"Have you ever really watched it?"

"No, thank God."

"Hold on." The spinner walked over to a bookcase. "It's here somewhere."

"You're kidding. Am I the only person in America who doesn't own a copy?" She grimaced as Kristie pulled a tape from a box and stuck it into her VCR. "This is nuts."

"Just watch."

Miranda scowled, but sat on the couch, waiting for the show. It began with a poorly lit shot of herself and Ortega entering the apartment building. He held the door for her and she smiled up at him, her expression radiant. They laughed and chatted and teased, all the while gazing into one another's eyes as though the rest of the world simply didn't exist for them.

His demeanor was so respectful. So protective. So devoted. Even when he finally kissed her for the first time in the elevator, he seemed more smitten than aroused.

And through it all, Miranda stared, bewildered by the performances—her own as well as Ortega's. It really *was* romantic. In fact, it was mesmerizing. Even the one blatantly erotic moment when he knelt in front of her in the elevator had an innocence to it. A sense of discovery, and generosity, and hope.

"He really orchestrated this perfectly, didn't he? Can you believe what a dupe I was? But you're right," Miranda admitted with a sigh. "It's really not X-rated at all. That's a relief, at least."

"Poor Ray," Kristie said sadly. "It kills me to think of him spending the rest of his life alone."

"It's his choice. Plus…" Miranda gave a teasing smile. "Don't you want to get married and have little

McSpinners someday? That might not happen with Ortega around."

"Go home," Kristie advised dryly. "And take your X-rated videotape with you."

Miranda spent the next day studying background on Kell and the other three known Brigade members: a financier named Alexander Gresley, an expert in secure communications named Victor Chen and a mercenary known only as Tork, who was reportedly a gigantic brute.

In her free time, she also browsed the internet for Information about Switzerland, Amazon myths and heat-seeking technology. But she resisted the impulse to research the various psychological therapies available to transform helpless victims into formidable, confident people. While she told herself her interest stemmed from her amazing encounter with Angelina Carerra, she knew that it—like many things in her life—was ultimately about her father, the quintessential victim.

She took breaks from her study to perform Ortega's version of Kell's breathing technique at dawn, noon, and dusk, knowing that her teacher was doing the same in the clearing outside his mountain cabin. Even though he wasn't actually performing the moves at the same time as she, given the time difference, it was fascinating to pretend that he was. Now that she knew he wasn't really a pervert watching pornographic tapes of her in the wilderness, she was able to appreciate his dilemma, and to feel gratitude toward him for sharing his technique with her. She reveled in the balance she had already learned to achieve, and dreamed of the day when she would truly master the technique.

Of course, Ortega had mastered it, yet when he

needed it most, it had let him down. So she warned herself not to overestimate it. Or him.

Definitely not him.

"No, no, no, no, no." Miranda shook her head frantically that evening when Kristie Hennessy unveiled her final scenario for uncovering the Brigadier's identity. Despite the fact that they had agreed to target Jonathan Kell, using Ortega as their link, Kristie had decided at the last minute that it was better to go after Alexander Gresley, the London financier. The spinner explained that she had taken to heart Ortega's comment that Kell would be too suspicious if Ortega contacted him, and had decided they shouldn't use the Ortega connection at all.

"We're supposed to be using *your* instincts, not Ortega's," Miranda complained. "He had his chance to be involved with this and he turned you down. Now he's controlling our every move like some sort of Dead Hand? I don't think so. You said it yourself—Kell's the key. What's changed?"

"Getting to Kell through Ray was the key. That's a little different."

"We *are* going through him. Right? We're saying I've got claustrophobia. Somewhere along the line I met Ortega, and he told me about Kell's experiments with phobia. Now I've come to Switzerland for a firsthand lesson."

"It's not credible. Traveling all that way because of a little claustrophobia? Kell will be suspicious."

"Not if you *make* it credible. Put your spin on it. Isn't that why they call you a spinner?" Miranda laughed in frustration. "Don't let Ortega psyche you out, Kris."

"Do you want to plan a successful scenario? Or do you just want to prove Ray wrong?" When Miranda didn't answer right away, Kristie reminded her, "You agreed to let me call the shots. I have to feel good about it—in my bones—or I won't send you out there alone."

Miranda hesitated, then nodded. "Okay. Tell me about Alexander Gresley. What makes him such a good mark?"

"He likes women," Kristie explained, adding with a wince, "Sorry."

Miranda shrugged. "That's okay. It's what I do, for now at least. He's in London, right? And he's some sort of financial wizard?"

"Right. He spends his free time at a club there, gambling, carousing, and whatever. So that's where we'll send you. It's called Club Fortuna."

"I like the sound of that. Anything in particular about the guy I should know?"

"He's very well-connected, politically and socially. We only found out last week about his membership in the Brigade. He operates on the edge of the law, but never quite gets caught doing anything blatantly illegal. He's never been married. No kids. Benevolent to his employees. Lucrative for his associates. Brutal to his enemies. We think he had a competitor killed once, but again, no proof. Still, you've got to be very, very careful. Don't let anything distract you from the primary objective," she added, arching an eyebrow for emphasis.

Miranda groaned, knowing that the spinner was referring to her lapse in South America, when she had become so enamored of the tubes of Night Arrow, she had forgotten to keep an eye out for guards. "I'm never going to live that down, am I? In my defense, those test tubes were a gorgeous shade of blue."

Kristie laughed. "Well, Gresley's got enough money to offer you sapphires, so keep it together."

"Okay." Miranda cleared her throat. "If for some reason I fail with Gresley, then I'll move on to Kell. Agreed?"

"No. Absolutely not. I told you, he'll be too suspicious if you just happen to be a old friend of Ray's stopping by for a lesson." The spinner hesitated, then admitted, "I almost had a workable idea this afternoon but it fell apart."

Miranda leaned forward eagerly. "Come on. I'm dying of curiosity."

"Okay." Kristie picked up the vial of HeetSeek. "Kell was tortured over this, just like you said last night. If he heard it actually existed, he'd want more information. At first I thought about posing you as a scientist, but it would take weeks, and we don't have that kind of time. Then I thought we'd re-use Jennifer Aguilar."

"Of course! I could tell him I broke into Bio-GeniSystems as an industrial spy and found the Night Arrow formula. I'd say the files mentioned his ordeal. I did some research and found out he was ultra-rich, so I decided to offer the formula to him instead of the company that was paying me peanuts to steal it."

Kristie nodded. "Something like that. But the scientific community is a small one, and I'm sure Kell keeps informed about it. He might have contacts at Cornucopia, for example. Or he might have used some industrial spies himself from time to time. Who knows?"

"Still, it's a better angle than just vamping Gresley."

"It would be if Kell were rational. But he's got all those phobias, so he doesn't mix with strangers. And ever since his experience with Benito Carerra, he's paranoid as well as phobic. He might be willing to pay Jennifer a fortune for Night Arrow, but he wouldn't want to socialize with her without getting a lot of information about her background first. It's too risky."

"So? If I'm not Jennifer Aguilar, who am I?"

Kristie handed her a thick manila packet. "Miranda Duncan. An aspiring actress. I wanted to make you a model, because Gresley has a thing for them, but you're not really tall enough. No offense," she added quickly.

Miranda laughed. "Don't worry. My days as a professional escort have been bad for my career, but great for my self-esteem. If I can get Gresley alone, I can get him to talk. And I kind of like the actress angle."

"I actually tied the escort jobs into it a little. That's how Miranda Duncan pays the rent while she's waiting for her big break. You'll tell Gresley you came to the casino to meet a client, but he never showed up. Tell him you really needed the money."

"That's good. *You're* good." Miranda sifted through the contents of the package, which included a passport, plane tickets, hotel reservations and a detailed bio, as well as information about the phony escort company— Prudently Yours—that employed Miranda Duncan. "Looks like you thought of everything."

"Your flight leaves early in the morning. Do you have everything you need in terms of clothing? You're welcome to borrow stuff from Melissa's side of my closet. She has a couple of amazing dresses, and tons of size-seven shoes. Would those fit you?"

"I'm a seven and a half. What size do *you* wear?" Before Kristie could respond, she added wryly, "*Please* say it's a seven, or this Melissa girl is going to really start freaking me out."

Kristie gave a mischievous smile. "Luckily, she and I are the same size."

"Well, thanks for the offer, but I have plenty of shoes—*and* dresses—thanks to the CIA. There's one outfit in particular. A sleeveless copper lamé with a plunging neckline. Hangs like a dream. I have a rinse to put on my hair so that my highlights turn the same shade of copper. The effect is pretty cool."

"Ooo, sounds gorgeous. Is it a short dress?"

"Knee length, but with slits up to the eyeballs. Melissa can borrow it anytime she wants."

"McGregor would love it," Kristie admitted. "Maybe I'll take you up on that for his birthday."

Miranda watched as her new friend bit her lip, clearly conflicted by talk of McGregor. Smiling sympathetically, she told the spinner, "Should we clue him in? Now that we have a solid plan that isn't at all dangerous, he might go along with it."

"No way. He'd say it's outside of SPIN's jurisdiction. Which of course it is, technically."

"I'm CIA," Miranda reminded her. "It's well within *my* jurisdiction. Just a little outside my authority."

"Just a little," Kristie drawled. "The trip to South America, not to mention the break-in, could already get us both fired."

"Unless we get the Brigadier's identity," Miranda reminded her. "And we will, so don't worry."

Kristie nodded. "So? We're set?"

"I think so."

"If I've forgotten something, just let me know. In addition to the dedicated phone number for the escort service, you've got my direct SPIN lines, here and at the office. Call day or night. I can get money, papers, information to you within minutes."

"Okay." Miranda repacked the envelope, still disappointed that they were now targeting Gresley instead of Kell. She knew she needed to trust Kristie's instincts, but also knew in her gut that Kell would be so thrilled to get his hands on Night Arrow, he might just set aside his suspicions and meet with Jennifer Aguilar, industrial spy, who would then seduce him into betraying the Brigade.

The vial of HeetSeek was still on the coffee table, so Miranda murmured, "I usually carry cards with me on assignments, with the name of a fake escort service, and a phone number for appointments. That sort of thing. Not really necessary, I suppose, but sometimes they ask. Maybe I'll stop at an all-night copy shop—"

"Not necessary. I can print some up right here," Kristie assured her, jumping up and crossing to her desk. "I should have thought of cards. That's a nice touch."

As soon as the spinner was absorbed with her work, Miranda took a deep breath, then snatched up the vial and slipped it into the pocket of her sweatshirt.

With any luck, the Gresley plan would work. But Miranda wasn't coming home without the identity of the Brigadier—not after all this!—so if Miranda Duncan couldn't get the information out of Englishman, Jennifer Aguilar would have no choice but to get it out of Jonathan Kell.

As Miranda walked past the endless panels of floor-to-ceiling mirrors that lined the entrance hall of Club

Fortuna, multiple images of her metallic dress shimmered wildly, thanks to the huge chandeliers that blazed overhead. She was pleased with the effect, noting in particular how the copper highlights in her hair were accentuated by the sumptuous lighting. She couldn't have asked for a better introduction to Alexander Gresley's world, and only hoped that he was one of the throng of men at the bar who were openly staring at her.

The CIA had taught her to make an entrance, and so she didn't shrink from the attention, nor did she respond to it. She had learned that the best approach was to pretend her admirers didn't exist, at least, not right away. Pausing a few yards from the bar, she scanned the room, paying attention to the lights, the fountains, the music and chatter emanating from the casino in the distance—and then, as if noticing them for the first time, she looked directly at her audience and smiled in delighted surprise, sizing them up with unabashed curiosity just as they had been doing to her.

She licked her lips, her gaze settling on one particularly attractive man, then on another. Then she sighed, consulted the tiny watch face on her diamond wristband, and turned away from the onlookers, back toward the doorway. She wanted everyone to know that she was being kept waiting, and that she wasn't accustomed to such disrespect.

"May I help you, Miss?"

Turning, she smiled into the face of a well-groomed man in his early thirties dressed in a black tuxedo.

"I'm Edward," the man told her, bowing slightly. "Is this your first visit to the Fortuna? I'd be happy to find you a table. Or if you're here to gamble, I can help you get situated. Either way, several of the gentlemen at the bar are insisting on buying you a drink, so allow me to serve you."

"Aren't you sweet?" She looked at her watch again. "I'm meeting an acquaintance, but I guess he's running late. Perhaps you know him? John O'Neill? He's an American banker. I understand he's a member."

"I didn't realize Mr. O'Neill was in London. It will be wonderful to see him again." The waiter inclined his head toward the casino. "Mr. O'Neill usually sits in the alcove with some of the other longtime members. Would you like to wait there? I'm sure it won't be long."

Miranda bit her lip. "Our arrangement was to meet here, in the entrance. But he's already forty minutes late. And this feels so public. So, yes, thank you. The alcove sounds lovely."

You're a genius, she told Kristie as she followed the waiter through the bustling casino. *I don't know how you knew about John O'Neill, but he's definitely my ticket into the sanctum sanctorum of this place.*

Kristie had explained to Miranda that the Fortuna was a club within a club. Anyone off the street with acceptable attire and a big wallet could play there, but most of them never saw the real Fortuna, which was tucked in the back where a second bar and an elite staff saw to the needs of the ultrawealthy members. Knowing that Alexander Gresley spent almost every evening in the exclusive section of the club, the spinner had studied the member list until she found an American bachelor whose appearances at the club were rare and whose schedule tended to be unpredictable. She then confirmed that he hadn't been to London recently and was not expected there in the next few weeks.

Against that backdrop, she had provided Miranda with enough information on O'Neill to allow her to field questions from anyone but the closest of friends. If in fact Miranda had the bad luck to come face-to-face with one of O'Neill's best buddies, she'd have to wing it. But the spinner had assured her such a confrontation was unlikely, and Miranda had already learned that Kristie's scenarios were generally foolproof, so she wasn't worried.

The casino was crowded, but nowhere near capacity, which Miranda attributed to the fact that it was Sunday night. Still, there was a contagious excitement to the atmosphere, as the sounds and smells—bells ringing, cards being shuffled, cigar smoke wafting in tiny clouds, the roulette wheel spinning wildly—assaulted her. She had a real fondness for roulette, not because she ever walked away with winnings, but because the wheel always let her break even, and she appreciated that mixture of luck, risk and dependability.

It was tempting to pause and place a bet, just to see if her luck was with her that evening, but she was anxious to make contact with Alexander Gresley. After that, she could use her love of the game as a fun way to flirt with the target. Plus, it would help explain why she wasn't willing to drink too much, an issue that always came up in these escort situations, where the men felt compelled to try and gain the upper hand by plying her with liquor. And as a paid escort, she was supposed to go along with their every whim, assuming it didn't endanger her.

"Watch your step," the waiter instructed her as they reached a staircase covered with red carpet that led to a mezzanine. Two men flanked the banisters, and while they were dressed in tuxedos with respectful expressions on their faces, their presence was clearly meant to discourage nonmembers from proceeding any farther. Miranda gave each of them a flirtatious smile, and was pleased when their eyes twinkled in return, showing her they knew *exactly* what she was, and how pleased the members would be to meet her.

She climbed the steps slowly, making sure the slits in her skirt flared to reveal as much leg, along with her provocative lace-topped stockings and sexy black garters, as possible. Then she followed the waiter along the inner wall, which was made of frosted panels of glass that allowed the members a sense of the larger casino without lessening their privacy. Finally they reached an ornate set of double doors, again guarded by two well-dressed men.

"This is Miranda Duncan. Mr. John O'Neill's date for the evening," the waiter explained. "Mr. O'Neill instructed her to wait at the bar, but I felt she'd be more comfortable in the alcove."

"We didn't realize Mr. O'Neill was in London," the taller of the two guards murmured.

Miranda smiled. "I don't have many details, other than the fact that he wanted me to meet him here. I flew in from New York just for the opportunity."

The opportunity...

It was a simple code, well understood by those in the escort trade, and by the high-class bouncers who were expected by customers to distinguish between a paid date—to be treated with the utmost respect—and a hooker.

"Do you have a business card?" the man asked, adding with an admiring smile, "I'm sure the other clients will be asking me for it."

"You're sweet." Miranda dipped into her black beaded bag and handed one of Kristie's newly printed creations to each of the guards. "As I said, I work mainly in New York, but for special occasions, arrangements can be made through my office." Arching a playful eyebrow, she insisted, "I could easily be persuaded to spend more time here. It's charming."

The man smiled, then swung the doors wide open. "Let us know if we can be of service, Miss Duncan. Edward will find you a table. I'm sure Mr. O'Neill will be here directly. He's quite punctual as a rule."

She gave a grateful nod, then followed the waiter into the alcove, aware of the stares that greeted her. The room was sparsely populated, again reflecting the reality of the Sunday evening, and while she imagined there were usually quite a few female guests earlier in the weekend, tonight Miranda was the only one in sight. Of the dozen or so men, most were seated alone, in leather wing chairs, reading the newspaper or smoking a cigar. In addition to the wing chairs, there were six tables scattered around the room, each with two straightback chairs, none of which were occupied.

Edward led Miranda to a table near the bar. "What can I get for you, Miss?"

She hesitated, then pulled a credit card out of her purse. "Just seltzer with a squeeze of lime, thanks."

"There's no charge. And if there were, Mr. O'Neill would cover it."

Miranda gave him a wistful smile. "I'm beginning to think I've been stood up, so please don't put anything on Mr. O'Neill's tab. It will complicate things on my end, if you get my meaning."

"Would you like us to try and contact him?"

"I'll do that myself in a bit, thanks." She gestured toward a hall at the far end of the room. "Is the rest room through there?"

The waiter nodded. "Also the members card room and several private meeting rooms."

She smiled again. "Thanks, Edward. I'll be fine for the next few minutes or so. After that, I'll try calling Mr. O'Neill, and if I don't have any luck, I'll probably just leave. If I don't see you again—"

"You'll see me," he assured her. "I intend to check back often. And now if you'll excuse me, I'll arrange for your drink."

She loved the way he bowed before walking away, but decided she probably looked far too content for a working woman who was apparently being stood up. So she frowned toward the door, then looked at her watch again before surveying the men in the room, most of whom had stopped staring at her and had returned to their reading.

There was no Alexander Gresley in sight, which meant she needed to check out the card room. She was about to wander in that direction when one of the members came over to join her.

"You can't possibly be alone," the short, balding man said to her.

"I've been telling myself that for almost an hour," she answered with a wistful smile. "I hope we're right."

"I'm Robert Combes. May I keep you company until your lucky fellow arrives?"

When she nodded, he sat down quickly, as though expecting her to change her mind.

Her drink arrived at that moment, and Combes frowned. "That won't do. We should have champagne, don't you agree?"

When Miranda hesitated, the waiter intervened by suggesting, "I'll see that our finest bottle is brought up, sir, while Miss Duncan makes up her mind."

"Brilliant as always, Edward," Combes assured him.

Edward smiled. "I see you're in good hands, Miss Duncan. Excuse me while I find out if Mr. O'Neill has arrived."

"Thanks, Edward." Miranda watched the waiter disappear from the room, then she gave Combes a smile meant to dazzle him. "I have a confession to make."

"I'd be honored to hear it."

"I have the most sinfully decadent urge. To watch a card game. Would you escort me? Perhaps you'll bring me good luck."

Her new friend practically fell over himself as he sprang to his feet and helped her scoot back her chair. Then he sheepishly offered her his arm and they strolled past the amused members and down the hallway to the cardroom. To Miranda's dismay, there were only three additional men, and again, no Gresley.

The players ignored her, concentrating on their hands. In contrast, Combes began to show more obvious interest, resting his hand on the small of her back as though signaling to the others that he was staking a claim.

Fortunately, Miranda was used to this kind of touching. And for some reason it actually bothered her less than usual.

Because men don't disgust you as much as they used to, she explained to herself. *That's the best part about seeing Ortega again. You've been blaming every man you meet for his transgressions—for daring to take your honor under false pretenses. But guess what? I think you're over it!*

Or at least, almost over it. Once she picked Gresley's brain for information that would help her uncover the Brigadier's identity, she could finally get her career back on track. *Then* life would be good. She might even find a normal guy to take her on a *real* date instead of an assignment for a change!

A burst of laughter emanating from one of the meeting rooms caught her attention, especially when one of the card players got up and ambled over to the half-closed door.

"What's going on?" she asked Combes.

"Nothing," he murmured, clearly embarrassed.

She pursed her lips, wondering if Gresley might not be in the meeting room. She had almost been ready to call it a night, letting Combes see her back to her hotel, then wrangling an invitation to return with him to the Fortuna the following evening. But maybe that wouldn't be necessary after all.

Then she heard one of the men in the meeting room call out to a friend at the card table, "Gresley and his new girlfriend are putting on a show."

Gresley!

Delighted, Miranda tugged at Combes's sleeve. "Did you hear that? A show! Can we see?"

"It's nothing a lady would enjoy, believe me," Combes explained, scowling slightly.

She took a deep breath, wondering what to do now. Given the reference to Gresley's "new girlfriend," it would probably be difficult—if not impossible—for Miranda to get her mark alone long enough to make any progress. But at least she could meet him, and send a signal that she'd like to get to know him better. With any luck, he'd arrange to be there the next night *without* his girlfriend, and she could suggest they go somewhere to talk, hopefully his town house, where she could flirt and interrogate in the style that had been so successful for her in her career.

So she slipped her arms around Combes's neck and murmured, "I'm not feeling like much of a lady at the moment. Indulge me, won't you? Let's see the show."

His gray eyes darkened with unmistakable arousal. "Whatever you wish, my dear. I'll indulge you, and then perhaps, you'll return the favor."

"Great." Another peel of laughter told her Gresley and his girlfriend were becoming more entertaining by the second, and she was determined to find out what was going on. If nothing else, it would help her know what to do when she hooked up with him the next night. So she darted across the room ahead of Combes and sidled through the doorway into the meeting room to find a group of boisterous males, drinks and cigars in hand, watching a man who was seated. In front of the man was a scantily clad young woman, kneeling in a position that left little doubt about the nature of the "show."

Miranda didn't even attempt to stifle her gasp of horror as she stared at the couple. She was only dimly aware of the other onlookers, and when Combes laid a hand on her arm, she shook it off as though he were the lowest form of pest.

She wanted to look away, but her gaze was trapped by the leering expression of the man staring down at his "girlfriend."

Alexander Gresley, forty-one years of age, twice divorced, a billionaire financier with a ruthless reputation and a supposed fondness for women. The picture in the file had perfectly captured his round face, thinning black hair, and a precisely manicured moustache. But nothing in the file could have prepared Miranda for Gresley's depravity.

"Miranda?" Combes whispered.

The sound of her name roused her, and she noticed that the other men in the room were now looking at her rather than the X-rated display. Outraged, she sent a disgusted glare in every direction, and was about to stomp out of the room when Gresley raised his eyes and noticed her for the first time.

She wanted to spit in his direction, but settled for raising her chin in a gesture of dismissal. Then she spun on her heels and stormed back into the card room, ignoring Combes's pleas that she wait for him. Striding down the hall and through the alcove, she burst through the double doors, announcing to the tall guard who had admitted her, "I'm leaving. Please don't give my name or number to any of those lowlifes."

"What happened?" he demanded, trailing her as she sped down the stairs. "Did someone make an improper advance?"

"Improper? I doubt they know the meaning of the word."

He caught her gently by the arm. "Do you want to speak to the manager? If Mr. O'Neill complains, we'll need to know the facts—"

"Just call me a cab. I'll be in the rest room, composing myself. If that fool Combes asks for me, tell him I'm gone."

"Whatever you say, Miss Duncan. I'll have Edward drive you personally. We're terribly sorry—"

"Tell Edward I'll meet him outside." She hurried to the ladies room in the general casino, and after double-checking that she was alone, she dialed Kristie's number.

"This is S-3. Please identify yourself."

"Kristie? It's me. I only have a minute, but I need you to get me a flight out of here. I can be packed and at the airport in two hours."

"You don't sound happy," the spinner told her sympathetically.

"Long story short? We're aborting this part of the op because Gresley is a depraved pig. Believe me, you don't want to know more."

"Oh, no! Miranda, I'm sorry. I mean, we knew he was sort of a pig, right? But depraved? As in kinky?"

"Depraved as in liking an audience when he gets his rocks off. No chance of me getting him alone and then charming the pants off him—the pants come off first! And as much as I want the identity of the Brigadier, I'm not getting it on my knees, if you get my drift."

"Yuck! Where are you?"

"In the bathroom at the Fortuna," Miranda said. "They're bringing a car around for me because I made a scene. I'll take a cab from my hotel to the airport."

"Okay, good. In two hours, you'll be on your way back home, safe and sound."

"No. Not home. Geneva." Miranda heard female voices and muttered, "I've got company. I'll call again from the hotel. Bye."

Leaving the stall, she saw two young women fixing their makeup and giggling in front of a mirror, crowing about their victories, both romantic and gambling. She was tempted to warn them—to insist they run screaming from the building before they fell into Gresley's clutches—then she scolded herself for overreacting.

It was just a shock, that's all. Get a grip. Start thinking about Jonathan Kell. He may be a strange guy, but he can't possibly be as repulsive as Gresley!

Smiling grimly, she splashed some water on her face, but it didn't help. She needed fresh air, so she hurried back into the casino and strode quickly toward the mirrored entryway.

"Miss Duncan!"

Miranda whirled toward the unfamiliar male voice, determined to take the speaker's head off, especially if it was some obsequious manager pretending to be shocked that a group of distinguished English gentlemen had misbehaved. She wasn't really ready to speak to *any* man just yet, with the possible exception of Edward. And even *he* wouldn't be safe unless he had his car keys in his hand and a very submissive expression on his face.

But the face that greeted her was far from submissive. In fact, in its own way, it was chilling.

It was also disgustingly familiar.

It was Alexander Gresley.

Chapter 6

Recovering quickly, Miranda gave her former target a disdainful stare. "You must have a death wish."

Gresley surprised her by chuckling. "Apparently. But I couldn't allow you to leave without apologizing. Believe me, Miss Duncan, that particular event was not intended for eyes as hauntingly beautiful as yours."

"Puh-leese. Is that supposed to make you seem *less* slimy? Because FYI, it's having the opposite effect." She glanced toward the doorway. "My chariot awaits, so buzz off."

He moved to block her retreat. "You don't know who I am, do you?"

"The Prince of Darkness?"

"In some circles, as Dante would say." He flashed a self-impressed grin. "But I can also be generous and contrite. I'm hoping you'll allow me to demonstrate one, if not both, qualities."

Miranda licked her lips, carefully evaluating this development. Gresley possessed information she needed to resuscitate her career. And given his demeanor and interest, she had a feeling he'd behave himself, at least for a day or so, if only to redeem his image before launching any offensive attacks.

On the minus side, she could barely look at him without retching. That wasn't a good sign. She hadn't actually vomited over a man since that incident with Runyon a year earlier, but it was still fairly fresh in her mind.

But that was before you and Ortega made up. And before you started doing the breathing exercises. You're calmer now. More balanced. Take a deep breath, then exploit this creep the way he exploited that poor girl in the meeting room. Call it karma. Call it justice. Or just call it serendipity, 'cause he's standing right there, Miranda, and he's your ticket outta escort duty.

"Don't make me beg," Gresley was saying, his voice soft with lust. "From the moment I first saw you, staring at me, judging me, I knew we were destined to become good friends. We just need to bypass this unfortunate introduction."

Without giving Miranda a chance to respond, he pulled her business card out of his pocket and exhibited it to her as if to remind her he was a potential customer, and presumably a lucrative catch. Then he murmured, "Tell me what you want. I'll give you anything."

"I want respect. And—" she gave a sheepish shrug "—a rain check, if you don't mind."

"Beg pardon?"

She pouted as she rubbed her jaw. "I have the most

excruciating toothache. The only reason I didn't cancel my appointment with Mr. O'Neill was that he's a new client, and I didn't want to make a bad impression."

It was her best routine, cultivated from dozens of lame dates with even lamer informants. While most women used headaches as their primary excuses, Miranda had quickly discovered that men were resourceful enough to work around that particular ailment. But a toothache? That made kissing painful. And as for Gresley's favorite indoor sport? It was almost impossible for a girl with an impacted molar!

She could see from his puzzled expression that he was wondering what use she'd be to him in her condition. To add to his dilemma, she stepped closer and murmured, "I can't keep calling you the Prince of Darkness. Do you have a human name?"

He laughed. "You may call me Alex. And you must allow me to introduce you to the Gresley family remedy for toothaches. I promise, it will work."

"But will it cost me my soul?"

Gresley's pale blue eyes twinkled. "I'm not interested in your soul, Miranda. Just restoring your mouth to health. Do you like Scotch?"

"Is *that* the remedy?" She smiled. "I was practically raised on it."

"I have a twenty-five-year-old vintage Macallan at my town house. And my driver is waiting for us at the door." He paused to look her over, openly admiring the copper dress and its contents. Then he offered her his arm and suggested, "Shall we?"

To Miranda's relief, Gresley was a perfect gentleman during the short limousine ride to his town house. Not that she was concerned for her own safety. The man was in passable shape, but no match for her. She was quite certain she could literally kill him with one arm tied behind her back. The driver would present a more formidable challenge, but there was a tinted privacy panel between him and the passengers, so even he wasn't a threat, at least for the moment.

From her study of Gresley's file, she knew just what questions to ask him to put him at his ease and make him feel self-important. By the time he ushered her into an elegant sitting room on the second floor of his home, they were laughing and chatting like old friends. He seemed harmless and only slightly depraved, but she reminded herself of the scene at the Fortuna, and the way he had treated that other girl, so she didn't let her guard down.

When he finally left her alone, explaining that he wanted to instruct the servants not to disturb them, Miranda scooted over to his desk and began to snoop, but found nothing. Then a nearby briefcase caught her eye. There was no lock on the clasp, so she opened it and found a pad of lined paper covered with handwritten notes and labeled "Manifesto." Thrilled, she dug through her purse, located the barrette-camera, and snapped shots of the notes.

She had barely returned to her seat on the lavender silk sofa when her host reappeared, carrying a tray containing a bottle and two cut-crystal glasses. "You won't find anything this smooth at the Fortuna," he assured her.

Miranda gave him a smile, then took a sip of the Scotch, swishing it in her mouth as though treating her injured tooth. "I think it's infected. This has been going on for almost two weeks. If your remedy doesn't work, I might have to break down and go to the dentist." She shuddered. "I hate those needles. And the drill. The very thought of a dentist terrifies me."

Gresley edged over so that his thigh was pressed against hers. "I have an associate who could help you with that little problem. His research in the area is phenomenal."

Miranda licked her lips. "He does research about people who are afraid of the dentist?"

"All phobias, actually." Gresley nuzzled her neck, then trailed his lips up to her mouth.

"Ow! Oh, sorry." She pulled away, grimacing. "Maybe we should just call it a night. It's late, and my mouth is getting worse instead of better."

Gresley scowled, and seemed about to complain, when a doorbell sounded from the ground floor. "Ah, help has arrived. I took the liberty of sending for someone to assist you. You'll be feeling better in no time at all. Excuse me for just a moment."

Miranda stared after him as he left the room. Was he actually telling her that Jonathan Kell was at the door? Here in London? What fantastic luck! And to think she had almost flown to Geneva that night!

Think, Miranda, think, she pleaded with herself. *You've got to completely change your approach to Kell. You don't need to refer to Ortega, or lure him with the vial of HeetSeek. Gresley is giving you the perfect entrée—a dental phobia! Kell will see you as an instant kindred spirit.*

All she needed now was a way to dump Gresley and pick up Kell. The phobia angle was nice, but she had a feeling the copper dress would be at least as effective a tool, so she crossed her legs, allowing maximum skin to be exposed by the slit.

When the door opened, she licked her lips and prepared to smile, but her coquettish expression faded before it began when she saw that Gresley was accompanied by two men, neither of whom were Jonathan Kell.

The first was the burly driver who had transported them from the Fortuna. The second was a slightly built gray-haired fellow carrying a black leather case.

"Miranda Duncan? May I present Phillip Makepeace, my personal physician. He's here to take care of that toothache."

Miranda stood and backed away, annoyed. "I told you, I don't like needles. Or anyone touching my mouth, dentist *or* doctor. Send him away."

Gresley shot his driver a curt glance. "Take hold of her."

"No!" She held up her hand in warning. "The escort service trained us for this, you know. And they have excellent lawyers, or barristers, or whatever the hell you call them over here. So just back off before you buy yourself a shitload of trouble." Her eyes narrowed. "I can guarantee you, I'm not worth it."

"I'd prefer to be the judge of that," Gresley said with a sneer. "Settle down. You'll get double your standard fee." Turning back toward his driver, he barked. "Do as you're told! *Now.*"

When the physician pulled a syringe from the bag, Miranda pretended to whimper. "No. Please let me go."

Her behavior had the desired effect, making the driver less wary as he rushed her, his huge hands outstretched.

Using the same technique that had worked so well at Ortega's cabin, she grabbed his forearm and used his own momentum to propel him past her, sending him crashing into a curio cabinet that shattered upon impact, raining glass and splinters down on him.

He was dazed, but she knew he wouldn't stay down for long. She could possibly sprint past the other two men and out the door without further engagement, but her adrenaline-charged system wanted Gresley, who was frozen in disbelief. So she strode up to him and smashed her fist into his face. And while she yelled from the pain that shot through her knuckles, she knew from the sound of his jaw shattering that his agony was far worse than hers.

But just to be on the safe side, she also kneed him brutally in the groin, then watched in satisfaction as he crumbled to the floor and curled into a ball.

"Better have a dentist look at that mouth," she advised him with a tart smile. Then she spun on the doctor, who was backing toward the doorway, the needle still in his hand.

"Drop it and run," she warned. *"Now."*

But he was looking at something behind her, and she knew the driver was back on his feet, so she turned to him, arching an eyebrow as she spied the pistol in his bloodied hand.

"Do you guys really want another round of this?" she demanded.

"Give her the injection," the driver said to the doctor, ignoring her completely. "Then care for Gresley."

"Be serious," Miranda protested. "We both know you won't shoot me. Dr. Feel-Good here signed on for some good old fashioned date rape, not a full-blown murder."

The physician nodded. "We should just let her go. If she complains to the authorities, we'll say she tried to rob Gresley. It will be her word against ours, and she's a whore. An American whore."

"Professional escort," she corrected him with a wink.

"And I will indeed walk right out of here. And we'll all pretend this never happened, right? I won't even send you a bill for ruining my favorite dress."

The driver scowled but nodded. "Go on then. Be quick about it."

"Put the gun on the floor and kick it under the sideboard first," she told him.

"You'd like that, wouldn't you? So *you* can get it and shoot *us*."

"The last thing I want is my fingerprints anywhere, let alone on a gun. Which reminds me…" She walked over to the coffee table and upended the tray so that both of the glasses, along with the bottle of expensive Scotch, flew to the ground and shattered. "There. That's better." She sighed and suggested, "Give the gun to the doctor then. I'm pretty sure he won't shoot me."

The driver grimaced, then handed the weapon to the physician. "There. He has it. Now get out of here."

Had the doctor seemed even the least bit comfortable with the gun, Miranda would have cut her losses and left, despite knowing Gresley would send the driver to hunt her down the instant he regained consciousness.

But the poor physician's hand shook visibly as he pleaded with her, "Do as he says. And quickly!"

So she flashed a triumphant smile, and before the driver could reassess the situation, she had grabbed the doctor and wrenched the gun from his hand, then jumped back so that she had both men in her line of fire. "Okay, doc. Inject your buddy here, and be quick about it."

"Pardon?"

"Either you shoot him with the needle or I shoot him with the gun. Your choice." To the driver she added sweetly, "It won't hurt a bit. It'll just make you sleepy and cooperative. Right, doc?" Waving the pistol she added in a deadly serious tone, "Do it."

The physician and driver exchanged glances, then the latter rolled up his sleeve, muttering, "Bitch."

Miranda watched in amusement as his eyelids began to close within seconds of receiving the injection. As he slumped to the floor, she wished him, "Sweet dreams, a-hole." Then she asked the doctor, "Do you have another dose in that bag for yourself?"

He nodded, completely cowed, and sat down on the floor next to his bag. "May I use a clean needle?"

"Be quick about it."

A groan sounded from Gresley's direction and she saw that he was struggling to sit up. "Hey! Get back in your fetal position," she ordered him, and to her delight, he immediately complied.

Meanwhile, the doctor had prepared a second injection and was looking up at her as if awaiting instructions. She nodded, and he immediately plunged the needle into his arm.

"Nighty-night," she said cheerfully as he slumped over in a heap.

"Okay, Gresley," she murmured, double-checking the pistol's chamber to be sure it was loaded. Then she walked over to him and stared down, announcing quietly, "Your turn."

"My God, Miranda, you're freaking me out!"

"I didn't actually shoot him," Miranda assured the spinner. "I just thought about it. You've gotta admit, he deserved it."

"He was unconscious," Kristie reminded her.

"That's how he likes his women. I really wanted to give him a taste of that medicine."

The spinner sighed. "Exactly how much of that Scotch did you drink?"

Miranda laughed. "I'm drunk on something else."

"What?"

"Power. Ortega was right. There's nothing as intoxicating."

"Can I quote you?" Kristie asked dryly. Then she sighed again. "The important thing is, it's over."

"For the moment. But Gresley'll try to track me. Can you lead him on a wild-goose chase?"

"No problem. I'll make a fake Miranda Duncan trail for him to follow. You switch to Jennifer Aguilar's passport. I'll make your reservation under that name. The sooner you bring that new information about the Brigade home, the sooner we can work on it together."

"Nice try, partner," Miranda said, laughing. "But I'm headed for Kell country. I'll send the Gresley intel to you electronically before I check out of here."

"We don't need Kell anymore!" The spinner's tone was now panicked. "You succeeded! That was our deal."

"We don't know what we have yet. Our best strategy is for you to sift through the new intel while I try to get more in Switzerland. Also, you need to get Jennifer's credentials in order. Make her a high-class call girl from Reno, okay?"

"Excuse me?"

Miranda laughed. "It was your idea, remember? You said we needed the connection with Ortega for Kell to trust me. So Jennifer can't be an industrial spy. And I was thinking about Ortega's monthly trips to Reno. I'm guessing he doesn't want complications, so he probably uses professionals. So just give Jennifer the minimum credentials. In case Kell checks. An apartment near the casinos, for example. Credit cards. That sort of thing."

"I'm sure Ray doesn't use prostitutes."

"Hey! Who are you calling a prostitute? I'm a professional girlfriend," Miranda said, teasing. "Anyway, I'd better get going. Gresley probably won't look for me tonight—he'll be too busy rushing to the hospital. But I don't want to take chances."

"I didn't think to send a disguise with you."

"It's cool. I've got my hair in a twist and covered mostly with a scarf. And I'm wearing jeans and a sweatshirt. A far cry from the copper outfit. Plus I've still got the chauffeur's gun, although I'll have to ditch it before I go through security at the airport. After that, Gresley will be expecting me to take a flight to the States, so I'll be safer going to Switzerland. See what I mean?"

"This has gotten completely out of control. There wasn't supposed to be any danger," Kristie reminded her. Then she insisted unhappily, "I'm so, so sorry I didn't catch the fact that Gresley was a freak."

"It's not your fault. He's surrounded by enablers who protect his secret. I just wonder how he's going to explain his busted jaw," she added with pride.

"Like I said, this has gotten out of control."

"Don't worry. It's fine. I'll call you from the airport to get the new itinerary. And Kristie? Thanks. I couldn't do this without you."

"That's the point, Miranda. You *can't* do this without me, and you haven't given me time to plan a new scenario."

"There isn't time for that. So we'll just modify the old one. It'll be fine, I promise."

"I must be out of my mind."

Miranda laughed at the mournful tone, then glanced at her watch and announced, "Gotta go. 'Bye!" before the spinner could make another try at convincing her to come home.

Four hours later, on a flight to Geneva, Miranda's adrenaline-laced high had abandoned her, and she began to second-guess her decision to head for Kell's fortress without a well-thought-out, spinner-approved plan. Did she really expect to waltz into the place and charm a crazy man into revealing the Brigadier's identity to her?

Plus, to be totally honest with herself, she knew she intended to do much more than that. She wanted to find a way to bring the Brigade itself down. To prove once and for all that she was more than a pretty face and a good shot.

The problem was, she was beginning to think she might *not* be more than that. After all, she had made a gigantic mistake in South America, letting Angelina Carerra sneak up on her, thereby losing the HeetSeek documents. Now she had made a second strategic error in London, going to Gresley's place alone even though she had seen firsthand what a depraved fellow he was.

It would be even worse with Kell, she knew. If she made a mistake—any mistake—she wouldn't survive. He was so unstable, so prone to fits of paranoia, he would almost certainly overreact if someone dared invade his sanctuary. From all reports, there were dozens of armed guards and massive security at the fortress. Compared to that, Angelina's guards and Gresley's driver had been child's play.

Which meant Miranda had two choices. She could return to the States and give Kristie a chance to plan a solid scenario for her. While that option might take days, even weeks, it would increase her chances for success, not to mention, for survival.

Or she could proceed with her original instinct and tap into Kell's devotion to Ray Ortega, the man who kept him alive during weeks of torture, and then liberated him by shooting an arrow through his captor's throat. It was a powerful image, and one she intended to invoke often.

Jonathan Kell loved Ortega. And Jonathan Kell had phobias. Enter Jennifer Aguilar, a woman who also loved Ortega, and was loved by him. And by coincidence, she had a nearly debilitating case of claustrophobia. The latter would be easy to feign, given the fact that Miranda really did experience mild discomfort and eventual panic in closed spaces.

As for feigning love for Ortega? That would be easier than she had expected, thanks to the experiences of the past week. She had grown to crave her sessions with the breathing technique, and credited it to a large extent with her success in South America and again in London. Her ability to stay calm, to think under pressure, had mushroomed, and she owed it to Ortega and Kell.

Beyond that, she had meant what she told Kristie hours earlier. She had stood over Gresley's motionless body and had felt a surge of power—of domination and righteousness—like nothing she had ever experienced. Wasn't that what Ortega had tried to explain to her?

I couldn't handle it....

She hadn't understood it then, but she got it now. And while she could feel superior for having resisted it to some extent, she had felt the pull—embraced the possibility, if only for a moment—and she understood that for a black ops assassin, the day could easily come where pulling back was no longer an option.

So what are you saying? she asked herself ruefully. *You're starting to like the guy? The guy who ruined your life?*

No, she didn't "like" him. But she was beginning to understand what had seduced him. And maybe she even understood his decision to banish himself, although it still seemed selfish and cowardly.

But at least he wasn't a heartless monster anymore. That was progress.

And since she had to pretend to be in love with him, it was fortuitous that she had watched them together on the alibi video. The perfect couple, falling in love for the cameras. The perfect guy—charming, seductive, attentive. *That* was the Ortega she needed to focus on now.

He's got zillions of good points, she reminded herself, opening her laptop and creating a document entitled "Ortega," then dividing the page into two columns: Plus and Minus, as she had done countless times in the past when agonizing over a boyfriend.

It's time to explore the kinder, gentler, sexier side of this guy, she told herself. *So you can convince Kell how hooked you are.*

Forcing herself to be honest, she made her first entry in the Plus column: The Best Sex Ever.

Why deny it? It was not only true, but amazingly so.

The second entry, "bronze flecks in his eyes," was equally undeniable, and just the sort of thing a real girlfriend would count. Smiling ruefully, Miranda added "great body," and "sexy smile," followed by, "taught me the breathing exercises" and "taught Kristie to be a great spinner."

Unfortunately, that seemed to be it, so she started on the Minus column, and within seconds, it was disturbingly longer. Worse, Miranda couldn't help but notice that the entries in that column seemed a little more serious.

"Liar," "criminal," "ruined my career," "uses other people, then throws them aside," "refused to help his country when called upon," "turns his back on his friends," "frequents prostitutes…"

Miranda scowled. This wasn't going as well as she had hoped.

Okay, so he refused to help his country this time. But what about all the times he did help it? Put that in the Plus column at least. And didn't he save McGregor's sister? Although, it's kinda canceled out by the fact that he got her into danger in the first place.

She sighed, admitting that Ortega still wasn't boyfriend material. On the other hand, didn't high-priced call girls use slightly different criteria? For them, "best sex ever," "generous," "pays on time," and "not too kinky" had to be the only criteria that mattered, right?

This was definitely going to take a little work. But when all was said and done, he *was* a hunk—and she was a normal female—so getting there might just turn out to be fun.

"You're out of control, Miranda," Kristie Hennessy announced to her empty apartment as she paced the floor, willing the phone to ring. "I should have stopped you. *Call,* dammit! Or I really *will* stop you."

The spinner wasn't accustomed to these feelings. She was always in complete control of her ops. And the

few times she had decided to bend the rules or take outrageous chances, those had been *her* decisions! But
somewhere along the line, Miranda had apparently
mounted a coup.

If the phone conversation right after the Gresley incident had alarmed Kristie, the call from the London airport had been worse, and the last call, from Geneva, had
scared her half to death. Her operative had been so full of
herself—so frightening confident—Kristie had intention-
ally tried to make her feel insecure, even going so far as
to refer to the poor girl's father! But nothing had worked.

Miranda—or rather, Jennifer—was on a roll. Or
maybe a "role," given how completely she had embraced
the part of Ray Ortega's mistress. It would have been
funny if it hadn't been terrifying. After all of Kristie's
efforts to bring the two of them together, based on a show
of heat in the video, Miranda was now going too far in
the opposite direction, insisting that Ortega was a hunk.

A hunk? Kristie literally cringed as she remembered
how giddy her operative had sounded. And while she
had to admit it would probably fool Kell, at least temporarily, she feared what it must be doing to Miranda's
psyche. To her sense of self-worth. The CIA agent despised Ray, yet here she was, convincing herself that he
was God's gift. It was downright scary.

When the phone finally rang, she leapt on it, ready
to threaten the rogue agent into submission. "Miranda?"

"Goldie? Are you okay?"

"Oh!" She sank onto the floor, loving the sound of
McGregor's husky baritone. "Hi, Will. It's so nice to
hear your voice."

"You sound stressed. What's going on?" When she
didn't respond right away, he demanded, "You were ex-

pecting a call from Miranda Cutler? I thought she was on vacation."

Kristie took a deep breath, then admitted, "Miranda and I are getting to be pretty good friends these days. I'm worried about her, Will. She's all alone, with a lot on her plate."

"If she's got you for a friend, she's not alone anymore," he observed quietly. "She's lucky."

"That's true."

"You sound kind of lonely yourself, S-3. Have I been neglecting you?"

"If I said yes, would you come back early?" She bit her lip, then insisted, "I know you need to be there until the end of the week—"

"I'll catch a plane right after work tomorrow night. How's that?"

Kristie closed her eyes, grateful beyond words, and more madly in love than ever. "That sounds good. Thanks, Will."

"My pleasure." He cleared his throat and added, "I've been wanting to talk to you anyway. About Ortega. So this will be good."

Oh, God...

The spinner stared at the receiver, wondering what to say next. But the words came without any conscious effort by her. "I love you, Will McGregor. I love working for you, I love talking to you, I love making love to you. And I need you, because I'm going crazy here by myself."

"Hey!" His tone had become wonderfully protective. "Maybe I should come now."

"No, no. Tomorrow night is great. Perfect. I can't wait. We have so much to talk about, just like you said."

"Okay, sweetheart. Try to get some sleep. You know I love you, right?"

She bit her lip, then murmured, "That's good, because tomorrow night I'm going to dump a humongous problem on you. It's not fair, but it's going to happen."

"Dump away," he told her simply. "That's what I'm here for. Don't you know that by now?"

Chapter 7

The information photographed by Miranda at Gresley's town house turned out to be invaluable. After sending the "manifesto" electronically to Kristie, she also placed a copy on her laptop's hard drive to study, even though she would have to erase it before she went to Jonathan Kell's fortress. The reclusive scientist was just suspicious enough to check her computer, and she wanted him to find some games, some amusing Internet sites concerning fashion and "tips for pleasing a man," and a datebook showing appointments—booked by eager male patrons far in advance—with every third weekend per month reserved for Ray Ortega's exclusive use.

Creating a call girl's fantasy calendar on the airplane ride had been fun and relaxing, but once she arrived at the hotel room Kristie had reserved for her, Miranda's only indulgence was twenty minutes of breathing exercises before settling down with Gresley's Brigade file. Almost immediately, she knew one thing for certain about the Brigadier—he wasn't an American. No American, however disenchanted, could have written so dismissively about the United States.

Miranda had been trained to handle anti-American propaganda. In fact, she had been trained to spew it. But the Brigadier's statements still rankled her. It wasn't so much that he referred to her country as a lumbering, ineffective behemoth that had outlived any possible usefulness. What bothered her, and what told her the guy wasn't an American citizen, was his contention that the U.S. had *never* been anything special. Had America not been protected by two oceans, the Brigadier insisted, it would have never have come into existence, and certainly would have been easily wiped out, "and good riddance for that."

Not that the Brigade was fond of any other country, either. In fact, according to the group's core philosophy, the very concept of a "nation" had outlived its usefulness. Individual nations, especially democracies and republics, were paralyzed by their giant bureaucracies and terrified of their citizenry. They were incapable of responding quickly to threats, and thus were vulnerable to complete destruction.

Destruction by whom? Miranda was fairly certain the Brigade saw itself in that role, although the file didn't quite come out and say it. Instead, it simply theorized that small, strategically placed cadres, similar to terrorist cells but populated by mainstream players—global bankers, scientists and philosophers—and supported by easily deployable mini-armies, could better respond to the realities of the 21st Century world, and thus, would naturally begin to spring up and take over. Eventually, these cadres would interlink to form a network that could protect and dominate the world with their quick responses and streamlined procedures.

Miranda was sure this new intel was burning a hole in Kristie Hennessy's virtual pocket. The spinner would be desperate to turn it over to the CIA immediately, yet if she did so, she'd have to explain its origins. If she did that, the CIA would recall Miranda and fire her, and Kristie's job would also be in jeopardy. Yet to withhold the information probably felt like quasi-treason to the spinner.

Still, Miranda was confident her friend wouldn't betray her trust, at least not for another day or so. Which meant Miranda had to gain Kell's confidence quickly so that he would give her the remaining pieces of the puzzle before the CIA took action to end the operation.

To earn Kell's trust, she planned to convince him they had a lot in common—namely, they both loved and admired Ray Ortega, and they both had debilitating phobias. As for pretending to be Ortega's mistress? Well, how difficult could that be? He was an objectively attractive man, so her feelings would be inherently believable. Better still, she had actually slept with him once, which would help enormously.

And luckily, their night together had been memorable, from the fake foreplay, to the incendiary rush of true heat between them when he had carried her to her bedroom and devoted himself to making an impression. She had refused to dwell on any of that for months thereafter, knowing he had just done it to earn her loyalty if the police decided to question her. But now she had an excuse to think about it, not to mention a reason to finally savor it.

Plus, there was the fact that she hadn't been with anyone since Ortega. That alone made the experience stand
out in her mind. She had been so distrustful of men
thereafter, and so intent on salvaging her derailed career,
she hadn't even considered dating. Ironically, she had
spent a lot of time with men, professionally speaking.
She had flirted with them in bars, perhaps allowing
them to nuzzle or paw her just a bit on the way to her
hotel room, where she would begin to strip for them. But
by the time she was down to lacy lingerie, a bright light
would flash, and she'd know that the CIA camera crew
had gotten the photograph they needed to turn the mark
into an asset.

At that point, her job was usually done. If the man had
been a gentleman, more or less, she would often stay to
go over the terms of the deal with him. Sometimes she
would even apologize. But if the guy had been a slimeball
in any sense, she'd just put her clothes on and leave, knowing that the officer in charge would take it from there.

Compared to those losers—the last and most disgusting being Alexander Gresley—Ortega was actually a
catch! Especially the Ortega she had met at the mountain
cabin, who had radiated physical health, spiritual balance
and raw sex appeal. Now that it served her interests to
admit it, she reminded herself of the erotic overtones to
the breathing lesson he had given her. They had reached
a moment of mutual harmony and shared trust, despite
their past, and that moment could have turned into an afternoon of lovemaking had she allowed it.

Feigning severe claustrophobia would be much
more complicated than pretending to love Ortega. Miranda had tried it once on the airplane—concentrating on the closed-in feel of the cabin, the lack of

outside air and the impossibility of exiting—and her pretend panic had begun to quickly resemble the real thing, so much so that she could only quell it by turning up the air jets on the console above her seat until they were blasting oxygen in her face, allowing her to inhale and exhale deeply and rhythmically until calm returned.

At the inn, there was less opportunity to practice, since it was only three floors high, with no elevator. Also, Kristie had made a point of requesting a room with a balcony, explaining to the front desk that Jennifer Aguilar had severe claustrophobia and needed to know she could get out into the open on a moment's notice. Miranda had continued to make such comments upon her arrival, just in case Kell decided to check up on her.

If he did call the inn, they would probably tell him that the American tourist had spent the afternoon and early evening going for a run, then camping out on the balcony of her room, where she could be seen performing a martial arts routine in slow motion, or simply sipping her seltzer water and gazing at the spectacular view of the Rhone Valley afforded by the inn's location on the side of a slope at the upper edge of the village.

She hoped she cut an intriguing figure, with her form-flattering wardrobe, elaborate makeup and carefully styled hair, all of which seemed designed to capture the attention of men, and did so successfully. But she ignored their advances in favor of spending time alone, and outdoors. Why?

Because she was a call girl on holiday who was already in love with one of her customers, so she had no reason to be looking for male companionship on this particular trip. And Kell would understand that her tiny room—the best the inn had to offer, and lovely in its own way—felt uncomfortably confining to her.

Or at least she hoped he would. Her plan was to spend at least a few hours with him, but her dream was that he'd invite her to stay at his fortress rather than the cramped quarters at the inn. His home was reportedly huge, built from the remnants of an old monastery about an hour outside the village at the top of an unpaved road. The inn-keeper explained that the village residents had no reason to ever use the road, and the tourists—mostly hikers—who came to the area quickly discovered that it was a mistake to approach Kell's gated sanctuary, wisely opting instead to take the cable cars at the other end of the valley that carried them to more hospitable glacial trails.

Awakening with confidence her first full day in Switzerland, Miranda still felt a pang of doubt when the car she hired reached the outskirts of Kell's property. There she was confronted by the infamous gate, manned by two armed guards, one of whom walked toward the vehicle with his rifle aimed directly at the driver.

"Don't worry," she murmured in hesitant French as she opened her door and prepared to charm the guard. "This will just take a moment, and then you can go back to the village. I will call you to come back for me when I'm finished here."

The driver frowned. "You are certain you wish to visit Monsieur Kell? He is a strange man."

"I'll be fine. Thank you." She slipped out of the front seat, slung her oversized purse on her shoulder, and ambled over to the guard, announcing cheerfully, "I'm here to see Jonathan Kell. I would have called for an appointment, but no one in the village had a number I could use. Can you tell him I'm here?"

The armed man's eyes narrowed. "Does he know you?"

"My boyfriend saved his life once, ten years ago. That practically makes us family, don't you think?" She flashed a flirtatious smile. "Just tell him I'm here, sugar."

He shook his head. "I'll tell him, but if you don't have an appointment, he's not going to see you. Even when I tell him how—well, how harmless you seem."

"Harmless?" She laughed. "I've been called many things, but never that. I must be losing my touch."

The guard laughed, too. "Come on. Let's see if you can charm the boss."

Miranda trailed after him, pleased by his reaction. Apparently Kristie had been correct when she predicted that Kell's guards, while well-trained, were undoubtedly bored senseless and eager for entertainment, particularly in the form of a sexy female. Unlike their counterparts, such as soldiers guarding military facilities, or private security for financial institutions, Kell's men knew they were simply defending a delusional man against imaginary dangers. Twelve guards to do the work of one or two, with nothing to do all day but discuss their crazy employer and hope for something—anything—to divert them.

Punching in a code on a panel next to the main gate, the guard escorted her through a smaller entrance for foot traffic, where a second guard stood outside a booth, his rifle also poised and ready, his eyebrow arched. "We aren't expecting anyone."

"She's special, Joe," the first guard assured him. "Her boyfriend saved Kell's life."

"Yeah?" Joe shrugged his shoulders, then explained the gesture to Miranda, saying, "Kell made us send his own cousin away last month, so don't get your hopes up. What's your name?"

"Jennifer Aguilar."

He scribbled it down. "And the boyfriend who saved Kell? What's his name?"

"Ray Ortega."

Joe nodded, then stepped into the booth, reminding the first guard, "Keep an eye on her, Mike. Or the boss will have a fit."

In less than a minute, Joe called out for them to join him.

Miranda followed Mike into the booth, but when he started to close the door behind her, she made a point of asking that he leave it open. She could see from the glance he exchanged with Joe that he was offended by the implication that she didn't trust them, but he complied with her request.

Joe motioned to an intercom affixed to the wall as he announced, "She's here, boss. Go ahead."

"Miss Aguilar?"

"Hi, Mr. Kell. Thanks for agreeing to see me."

"I haven't agreed to anything yet. What's the purpose of this visit? Did Ortega send you?"

"No. He doesn't know I'm here. It's a surprise," she explained, adding, "It's a long story, but I think you'll like it. After all, Ray saved your life, right? I'm sure you'd love to do something special for him. Wouldn't you?"

"You're telling me Ortega didn't send you? And you have no way of proving to me that you're his girlfriend, much less that I should allow you into my home?"

"But—"

"Go back to the village, Miss Aguilar. Don't bother me again unless Ortega calls ahead to vouch for you.

And even then…" His tone grew wistful. "I just don't see any point to this."

"I can prove to you I'm Ray's girlfriend. And I can explain exactly why you need to see me. But I'd rather not give intimate details this way, over a stupid box. Can't we talk face-to-face? Just for five minutes?"

"No. Joe, are you still there?"

"I'm here, boss."

"Disconnect this call using the standard protocol. Understood?"

"Sure, boss. Right away." Joe punched a button on the intercom, and Miranda noted that a green light on the instrument panel went out, replaced by a yellow one.

But not red, which she found curious. Yellow would seem to denote a standby mode. Was that what Kell meant by "standard protocol"? Was it possible he was still listening, either from curiosity or more likely, paranoia?

In any case, she had nothing to lose, so she sank down onto the only chair in the booth and covered her face with her hands. "I must have said something to offend him. Ray will be so angry with me! He and Mr. Kell went through so much together, they're almost like brothers. This was supposed to be a wonderful adventure, and now look what I've done."

"Our boss doesn't meet with strangers. Period. It's nothing personal, miss. You didn't say anything wrong. I promise."

"I should have told him about my claustrophobia. But it's so embarrassing talking about it over a silly intercom. I just assumed he felt so close to Ray that he'd do this for him, no questions asked. I was so stupid, and now I've come all this way for nothing."

Joe exchanged nervous looks with the other guard,

then murmured, "You have claustrophobia? That's why you asked us to leave the door open?"

She nodded. "Isn't it the silliest thing? I've had it all my life. But lately, it seems to be getting worse."

Joe pursed his lips. "Is that why you want to see Mr. Kell?"

"Yes. Ray told me Mr. Kell is a scientist who used to do research into phobias. I was hoping he could help me. I thought he'd do it for Ray. And I also thought he'd be especially sympathetic, since he has phobias himself. Or at least, Ray said he used to. I guess I was naive. Or presumptuous. Or both. I should have realized he'd want some sort of proof that I wasn't a reporter or fortune hunter or something. Right? I mean, he's obviously rich if he can hire professionals like you to guard his home." She rolled her eyes. "I must look like such an idiot."

"Actually, you look great," Joe said with a smile. "Whoever Ray Ortega is, he's a lucky guy. And in my opinion, Mr. Kell should make an exception for you. Just to get a look at you if nothing else."

"What a sweet thing to say." She stood and touched his cheek. "Thanks, sugar. And when you see Mr. Kell, please apologize to him for me. And ask him not to hold this against Ray, okay? It's *my* screwup, not his."

A buzzer sounded, and Joe pushed the intercom button. "Go ahead, sir."

"Miss Aguilar?"

"Mr. Kell? Oh! Thanks for calling back. I owe you an apology—"

"That's not necessary. Joe? Bring her up to the house. I'll send Samson down to help Mike man the gate. And Joe?"

"Yes, sir?"

"Keep an eye on her. If she does anything suspicious, shoot her and throw her body in the woods with the others."

"Sure thing, boss. We'll be right there." He pushed another button, and this time the light turned red. Then he told Miranda with a laugh, "There aren't any bodies in the woods, by the way. Kell's just a little wacko on the subject of strangers."

"Thanks." She touched his cheek again, then turned to the other guard and insisted, "Thank you, too. Mike, is it? I'll be sure to tell Mr. Kell how sweet you've been to me."

"Tell him I was ferocious," Mike suggested wryly. "That's what he pays me to be."

"I was terrified," she assured him. "What girl wouldn't be? Two big strong hunks with guns? I'm sure I'll have wild dreams tonight. About you guys having your way with me."

"Yeah, I'll be dreaming about you, too," Mike admitted.

Joe cleared his throat. "Come on, Miss Aguilar. We'd better get you up there before he changes his mind. Mike? Go ahead and dismiss her car. Once Kell meets her, I have a feeling he's gonna want her to stay."

After the flattering reaction of the guards at the gate, Miranda wasn't prepared for the reception she received as she stepped inside the stone fortress and was immediately thrown up against a wall by a burly man who proceeded to frisk her with obnoxious thoroughness.

"Hey, Carl. Go easy on her," Joe protested. "She's a guest. And she's a nice girl."

Miranda flashed her admirer a grateful smile, then she straightened her sundress and gave Carl a haughty glare. Unmoved, he dumped the contents of her purse onto the floor and rifled through them with his foot.

Miranda bit back a smile, knowing that the mixture of cosmetics, brushes, sunglasses, chewing gum and brightly colored condom packages confirmed her reputation as "harmless." She hadn't even brought the barrette-camera onto the premises, although it was tucked into a pocket of her overnight bag back at the inn. Knowing of Kell's paranoia, she had anticipated the search, and had chosen her accessories, as well as her nonthreatening outfit—a lightweight cotton dress, thin sweater, sandals and lacy lingerie—with care.

Carl reached down to retrieve her wallet, passport and cell phone, stuffing the phone into his pocket, then sifting through her money and identification. "She's clean, boss," he pronounced finally.

"Then why do I feel so dirty?" Miranda murmured.

"He was following *my* instructions," said Jonathan Kell, stepping out of the shadows. He was wearing a surgical mask over part of his face, with a pair of huge blue eyes staring at her over it with hesitant curiosity.

"Mr. Kell? Oh, thank you *so* much for seeing me!" She leapt toward him, intending to wrap her arms around his neck, but Carl grabbed her by the shoulders and shoved her down to the stone floor.

It took every ounce of willpower she possessed not to fight back, but she forced herself to stay on her knees. "Ow! Be careful." She glared up at Carl. "If that leaves a mark, my boyfriend will kick your sorry ass."

"Just keep your distance from now on," he warned her.

"Right back atcha," she retorted, scrambling to her feet, then arching an accusatory eyebrow in Kell's direction.

She could see that the altercation had upset her host, and she realized that he would have been scared to death if she had actually succeeded in embracing him. First of all, he would have thought she was trying to kill him. Beyond that, he had a fear of germs that simply wasn't compatible with casual displays of affection. Add to that his well-known fear of anything or anyone new, and she was probably lucky he hadn't had a full-fledged heart attack right there on the spot.

But he had apparently survived, because he suggested softly, "Why don't we go into the drawing room?" Then he turned to Joe and instructed, "You can go back to the gatehouse. Tell Samson to check the grounds and then let the dogs out."

"This early?"

"We can't be too careful."

Joe shrugged, then gave Miranda a reassuring smile before disappearing through the front door.

She followed Carl and Kell into a huge room with walls made of stone and a beamed ceiling that was at least twenty feet above their heads. The windows, while beautifully crafted of stained glass, were obstructed by bars, adding to the cold effect despite the fire that was blazing in the massive fireplace at the far end of the room. There was a square oak table with four chairs, a black leather sofa and two wooden rocking chairs, all close enough to the fire to keep the chill away. The floors were made of stone, with no carpets or rugs.

"If I promise not to try and hug you again, will you send monkey boy away?" Miranda asked, taking a seat on the sofa. "I don't want to talk about my personal life in front of him."

"Monkey boy?" Kell smiled for the first time, but sobered quickly, then sat in one of the rocking chairs. "I'd like Carl to stay. I don't generally meet with guests alone."

"He stole my phone."

"No one is allowed to bring communication equipment into my home. We'll return it when you're leaving."

"So?" She gave him a teasing smile. "You really are scared of everyone? But *look* at you!" She eyed his short, light brown hair, glowing skin and well-built body. "I was expecting someone pale and thin and quivering, but you're a good-looking guy. Do you work out? Or are you afraid of that, too?"

Kell frowned but didn't respond.

"Don't be offended. Ray told me you have *inner* strength, and that's what really counts. Plus, he says you're a genius, which is one of the reasons I thought you'd be a lot nerdier." She smiled again. "So? What has he told you about *me?*"

"Pardon?"

"Obviously, he hasn't mentioned me by name. But hasn't he told you he has a girlfriend? I mean, we've been seeing each other for almost six months. You guys keep in touch, right?"

"An occasional e-mail," Kell admitted. "But he never mentioned a girlfriend."

"Oh, really?" She folded her arms across her chest and looked into the roaring fire as though upset.

"It's not the sort of thing he and I communicate about," Kell told her quickly. "And now that I think about it, it's been more than six months since I heard from him."

She bit her lip, genuinely touched at his attempt to soothe her hurt feelings.

"I'm sure he would have mentioned you. You're so beautiful. Just his type, right? I mean, you look a little like the pictures I've seen of his ex-wife." Kell blanched. "You knew he was married once, didn't you?"

Miranda smiled. "You know Ray. He'd never lie to someone he cared about. So of course he told me. And given what I do for a living, *his* past is pretty tame, don't you think?"

"What do you do for a living?"

"She's a hooker, boss," Carl interrupted. "Her wallet is filled with men's business cards."

Miranda gave him a furious glare, then turned to Kell and explained. "I'm not a prostitute. I'm a professional girlfriend. There's a big difference."

"A professional girlfriend? How many boyfriends do you have?"

"About a dozen, give or take. But Ray's the only one I'd go to Switzerland for. I'd go around the world for any of them," she added with a wink. "But Switzerland? That's true love."

"Ray is your customer?"

"Client. And only because he wants it that way. He's a lot like you," she reminded him. "Living all alone. Keeping the world at a distance."

"He's nothing like me," Kell corrected her. "I live alone because I'm protecting myself from the world. Ortega thinks he's protecting the world from himself. *His* act is selfless. Mine is selfish."

Miranda licked her lips, intrigued by the simple assessment. Wasn't it true? Ortega believed his inability to handle power made him a threat, so he stayed at his cabin, all alone, rather than make another mistake that could hurt another innocent victim, like McGregor's sister.

Or Miranda.

That goes in the Plus column, she admitted to herself, remembering the chart of Ortega's pros and cons she had made on the airplane. She had deleted it before they landed, but it stayed in her imagination, and given the fact she was pretending to be in love with the guy, it was comforting to know that the list of minuses wasn't so much longer than the pluses as she had first thought.

"Miss Aguilar?"

"You'd better call me Jennifer," she told Kell. "We're practically related, you know. Because we both love Ray. Right?"

Kell stared at her for a moment, then nodded and turned to Carl, instructing him, "When Samson gets back, tell him to go into town and pick up Miss Aguilar's things. She's going to be staying with us for a while."

When a cell phone began to ring in her living room, Kristie thought at first it was Miranda, and she sprang for it, intending to beg, threaten or cajole her friend into coming home. Then she realized it was the new phone she had purchased as a dedicated line for "Miranda Duncan's" employer, and she grimaced.

Get it together, Kristie. You're the proprietress of an escort service. Time to act like it.

Using a soft, throaty voice, she purred into the phone. "Prudently Yours. This is Daniella. How can I help you this evening?"

"I'm attempting to locate one of your girls," a man

with a British accent informed her, speaking carefully, as though every word mattered. "Her name is Miranda Duncan. Any assistance you can offer would be greatly appreciated."

"Are you a client, sir?"

"In a sense, yes."

"May I have your name?" When he hesitated, Kristie asked him with pretended hesitation, "You aren't by any chance Mr. Alexander Gresley, are you?"

"Yes, I am he."

"Oh, Mr. Gresley! Miranda will be *so* glad to hear you've called us. She was worried you'd be upset over her faux pas the other evening. Let me assure you the agency will pay for that bottle of Scotch. Miranda tells us it was quite expensive, and she feels just terrible about spilling it."

"I beg your pardon?"

"Isn't that why you're calling?"

"The Scotch?" He cleared his throat. "What else did she tell you about our encounter?"

"Well, just that it wasn't much of an encounter at all, thanks to her toothache. It was all my fault, Mr. Gresley, so don't blame Miranda. I knew she wasn't feeling well, but Mr. O'Neill was a new client and I didn't want to disappoint him. And he had specifically requested a certain type of companion. Believe me, I've learned my lesson. Just send us the bill—"

"I'm not calling for reimbursement. I'd like to send Miss Duncan some flowers. Can you tell me where she is?"

Kristie sighed into the phone. "We have a policy. And I can't imagine why you'd want to send her anything, considering what poor service we gave you."

"According to my contacts, she flew to New York, and from there, to San Diego, where she went to hospital for her tooth. Is that true?"

"I'm impressed," Kristie told him, trying not to sound too self-satisfied that her fake trail had fooled him. "Your contacts are well-informed. Miranda will be flattered to know you went to so much trouble to find her."

"And?"

"Well…" Kristie hesitated for dramatic effect. "The poor girl did go to the emergency room in San Diego, just like your contacts said. But once the doctors diagnosed the massive infection in her jaw, we had her transferred to a private facility that works with us on surgical matters. Not usually teeth," she added with a giggle. "But still, they know how to take good care of our girls. I can't give out information about them, per our contract, but Miranda will be released by the end of next week. Should I have her call you then?"

"I'd rather surprise her."

I'll bet you would, the spinner rebuked him silently. *Surprise her with a pair of thugs to rough her up, right?*

Aloud, she cooed with delight. "I'm sure she'd love that. After all she's been through, a little extra pampering would be so sweet. I won't breathe a word of it. I'll just call you as soon as I have the release date. She'll probably check into the Hilton for a few extra days of recuperation at our expense. You could show up with flowers and candy—ooo, I'm getting goose bumps just thinking about it."

"As am I," Gresley assured her. "Do I have your word, then? It will be our little secret? If I'm going to cross an ocean to surprise her, I don't want to be disappointed."

"I won't breathe a word. Give me a number where

you can be reached, and I'll call you with her room number as soon as the facility releases her."

She was grinning as she recorded the information. Then she said a heartfelt goodbye—forever—to Alexander Gresley. If he called again in a week, wondering why he hadn't heard from "Daniella," he'd discover that the line had been disconnected, with no forwarding number. And in the meantime, if Miranda's mission proved successful, maybe the Brigade would be on the run, and Gresley would have bigger problems than just exacting revenge from a pugnacious working girl with a mean right hook!

The call had been so much fun—just the sort of thing she loved about her job as a spinner—she almost forgot for a moment about her dilemma. It all seemed so harmless—Gresley chasing Miranda in San Diego, when she was actually a continent away. But a continent away wasn't any safer. In fact, it might be even worse, if the Brigadier ever found out that a CIA agent was trying to infiltrate his organization.

The spinner was just sinking back into gloom when she heard a brisk knocking on the door to her apartment. And suddenly, her only thought—in fact, the only word that existed in the world for her—was McGregor.

Lunging for the door, she yanked it open, prepared to throw herself into her lover's arms and beg his forgiveness for keeping secrets, while thanking him for showing up ahead of schedule.

But it wasn't her lover who stood on the other side of the threshold. It was Ray Ortega. Except not exactly the Ray she had been best friends with for more than a year before his exile.

This Ray was leaner, meaner, bronzer and all-around more intimidating, from his perfect body to his thick, collar length hair. He looked nothing like a bureaucrat, and everything like a warrior, and she stared for a moment before recovering.

Then she threw herself against his iron-walled chest, wrapped her arms around his neck, and cried, "Ray! I knew you'd come back."

"Don't get carried away. I'm not really back. Just looking for Miranda Cutler."

"Does this mean you've changed your mind about helping us ID the Brigadier?" She interrupted herself to pull him into the living room. "Sit down. Visit with me. You look so great."

"So do you," he murmured, adding quickly, "How's McGregor?"

"Perfect."

"Good. So…" He cleared his throat, then asked carefully, "Any idea where I can find Miranda?"

Chapter 8

Ortega took a seat beside Kristie. "The CIA told me Miranda was at her family's ranch, but no one there has seen her."

"You went to her ranch? That's so romantic."

He scowled. "I went there to find out why she took off from the cabin without saying goodbye. I was concerned I might have said something that disturbed her."

"Not exactly." Kristie winced. "It freaked her out that you had a copy of the alibi video handy. She figured you used it for—well, you know. Kicks."

"The tape?" He winced. "I'll explain that to her when I see her. So? Do you know where she is?"

"You mean, Miranda?"

"That's who we're talking about, isn't it?" he said with a growl, then his expression softened. "She won't be too happy to see me, I suppose. But at least this time, I can make sure it ends on a better note."

"Miranda deserves that," Kristie admitted.

"Sounds like you two have become friends. I don't know why that surprises me."

"Because we're so different. But yes, we've become friends. Which makes this a little awkward."

He nodded. "I didn't come here to put you on the spot. I was just concerned when I couldn't find her. And I figured you might be in touch with her. So? Do you know where she is?"

"If I did, I wouldn't feel comfortable telling you," she reminded him.

"She told the CIA she'd be at the ranch. I assume she's just marking time until the Brigade op gets underway."

Kristie nodded.

"What's she going to do if they try to get in touch with her and can't find her?"

Kristie shrugged.

"I get why she wanted to avoid *me*. But giving inaccurate information about her whereabouts to her supervisor is a bad move. I'm surprised you and McGregor went along with that."

"McGregor doesn't know anything about it," Kristie corrected him. "It's my fault. Completely."

"What do you mean, your 'fault'?" Ortega pursed his lips. "You've been holding out on McGregor? And Miranda's been lying to the CIA, even though she's desperate to get her career back on track? Why is this beginning to sound a little nuts?" He closed his eyes, repeating stubbornly, "She's desperate to get her career back on track. Which means, this has nothing to do with avoiding *me*. She's secretly working on the Brigade case, right?"

"I really couldn't say."

"In other words, you're helping her plan some kind of harebrained scenario? Behind McGregor's back? You're doing the same goddammed thing to *him* you used to do to *me?*" He shook his head in disbelief. "Where's she staying? I checked with her apartment manager and he said they hadn't seen much of her lately. Are you saying she's been staying here with you? While you two plot behind everyone's back?"

Kristie stared down at her hands folded in her lap. "Like I said, I really can't say."

The room grew so silent, she was actually afraid to look up at him. She didn't need to anyway, because she had seen that expression countless times before. That vein along the side of his temple, throbbing. The metallic specks in his eyes, glinting. The frustration welling visibly inside him, ready to spill over onto the source of his heartburn. "I'll give her the message, Ray. Can't we talk about something else?"

"Is she in Switzerland?" Before Kristie could even try to respond, he yelled, "Goddammit, she *is* in Switzerland! And she went alone? Is she nuts? *Are you both nuts?*"

He jumped up and strode to the front door, growling over his shoulder. "I hope McGregor cans your ass. And if Miranda's still alive when I get there, she's going to wish she wasn't! God*dam*mit!"

He stormed through the door and slammed it from the other side, leaving Kristie to stare after him, her heart sinking. She had never seen him this angry, and she had seen him angry a *lot*. Surely he'd calm down before he reached the fortress, but what if he didn't? He'd decimate Miranda's scenario. Ruin their chances of ever cracking the Brigade. And definitely get them both fired.

Hurrying to the phone, she dialed Miranda's cell number. Predictably, there was no answer, but it rolled over to message mode, and she waited impatiently for the beep, so that she could warn her friend that Ray Ortega was on his way, ready to storm the fortress, throw her over his shoulder, and carry her out of there....

The beep sounded, but Kristie didn't say a word. She was too preoccupied with the image of a hunky bronze warrior sweeping an auburn-haired female off her feet and carrying her off into the sunset.

It was so perfect.

And if Kristie warned Miranda, it would never happen. Miranda might even be stubborn enough to find his interference offensive if she learned about it ahead of time.

But if she didn't—if it just happened without warning—even an independent, self-sufficient woman like Miranda would have to admit it was romantic, wouldn't she?

Except Miranda hated Ray. And McGregor thought he was a head case. In fact, everyone but Kristie thought the intelligence world was well rid of him. If Kristie was right, then there was no problem. But if she was wrong, if Ray was the man everyone else thought he was—dangerous, selfish, unbalanced, and a liar—then Kristie had to warn Miranda, and she had to do it right away.

Disconnecting the call, she continued to hold the phone in her hand, not quite sure whether or not to put it down. Her loyalties were torn in too many different directions. Ray, her best friend. Miranda, her newest friend. McGregor, her everything. Somehow, if she wasn't careful, she was going to betray all of them at once.

She was so distracted, she didn't notice the sound of a key in the lock of her front door, or the knob being turned. But when the door opened, and McGregor stepped into view, his blue eyes twinkling with anticipation of their reunion, her whole body snapped to attention.

Walking quickly to him, she wrapped her arms around his waist. "Thank God you're here."

"Yeah, I missed you, too." He tilted her face up so that he could look directly into it. "Are you okay?"

She took a deep breath, then blurted out the truth without attempting to hide anything. "Miranda went after Kell alone. Well, not completely alone, because she had me spinning for her. But now Ray found out, and he's furious. He's on his way there. And if he's not careful, he'll blow her cover. Except he's always careful, so of course he won't. But it's going to be a mess. A romantic one, I think. But still, a mess. And somehow, it's all my fault."

McGregor surprised her by disengaging himself from her arms and taking a full step backward. "Miranda's in Switzerland? Without authorization? And you knew about it?"

She nodded.

"You *arranged* it?" He seemed almost dazed, then rallied enough to murmur, "Okay. Let's hear it."

She gave him a quick rundown, trying not to notice how green he turned when she detailed the mission to South America, or how narrow his blue eyes became when she described the altercation with Gresley.

"So?" she asked finally. "Am I fired?"

"If this goes south, I'll definitely have to fire you," he confirmed.

"And if it succeeds?"

"Then I'll probably be stuck with you indefinitely."

Ignoring her groan, McGregor folded his arms across his chest, then leaned back against the kitchen counter. "So? What was it like, seeing your mentor again?"

Uh-oh…

She licked her lips, then admitted, "It was a relief. I thought he'd never leave that mountain again. Not for anything. But he left it for Miranda."

McGregor shrugged. "And?"

"And he looked different. Acted different. He's still my friend, and I still care about him, but he doesn't really fit in anymore. I guess I'm the only one who didn't know that." She stepped closer. "Miranda asked me an interesting question the other day. Whether I would want Ray to be the director of SPIN again if he decided to come back."

"That *is* an interesting question."

"Is it?" She smiled wistfully. "To me, it made no sense. Because I couldn't imagine anyone but you as director now. I wanted Ray back as a friend. As a valuable resource. And because I didn't want him to be lonely. He'll always be the founder of SPIN and I'll always give him credit for that. But you're the perfect director for us." She touched his cheek. "I see now that I must have been sending you mixed signals. Sorry."

He nodded. "The question is, what do we do now?"

"About us?"

"I meant, about Miranda."

"Oh." She grimaced. "With Ray there to help her, she'll be fine. I mean—" she scanned his blue eyes anxiously "—you don't really think he's a head case who can't be trusted to do the right thing, do you?"

"I don't know." McGregor's tone was solemn. "I never knew the guy very well. All I knew was, he gave you a rough time when you worked for him. Then he almost got us all killed. Now he's been off on his own for a year, doing God knows what."

"Purifying himself."

"Give me a break," McGregor drawled. "Guys like that don't just leave the game forever, Goldie. It's in their blood. Either he's fooling himself, or he's fooling us. If that's what's going on—if he's using us for his own clandestine purposes, like last time—"

"He isn't!"

"How can you be so sure?"

"I have to be sure. Because if I'm wrong…" She tried to steady her voice, failed, then explained unhappily, "If I'm wrong, what's going to happen to Miranda?"

"Come on, Jonathan. It's a beautiful day! We're in the Swiss Alps—the prettiest place I've ever been. Let's go outside."

Miranda's host gave her a pained smile. "That's the claustrophobia talking."

She laughed. "You're kidding, right? This isn't exactly a closed-in space. You live in a freaking barn."

"I've been having trouble with allergies lately. And there are security concerns as well. We're safer indoors."

"What a nut." She gave him a smile to assure him she was just teasing. "How many phobias do you have, anyway? I've noticed at least eight since I got here. That's just the tip of the iceberg, right?"

He scowled, but she could see he was secretly enjoying the banter. In fact, she had the distinct impression he hadn't had this much fun in a long, long time, and it was little wonder. His home was so barren, so cold. Yet for all his strangeness, Kell seemed like a decent man at heart. He was simply scared of his own shadow, not to mention, everyone else's.

"You've been here for three hours and you still

haven't told me what I need to know about your condition," he reminded her sternly.

"What's there to say? I've got it, I want to get rid of it. So hypnotize me, or give me an injection, or something. It's been ten years. I'm sure you've come up with some new therapies by now. Those old breathing exercises you taught Ray just don't work for me. I do them, but the results are pathetic."

"Okay." He pursed his lips. "Besides claustrophobia, what are your major phobias?"

"That's the only one."

"Not possible. A phobic person tends to have a cluster of them."

"Or in your case, a whole herd of them."

Kell bit back a smile. "Do you want my help or not?" He studied her intently. "What about bugs? Rodents? The dark? Germs?"

"Everyone's afraid of the dark. And bugs and rats give everyone the creeps."

"But if you're claustrophobic, they're probably triggers for you. That's all I'm saying. They trigger your panic, correct? And then you can't breathe." He opened a tube of antibacterial cream and rubbed some on his hands as though the mere mention of rats and germs had upset him.

Miranda shrugged her shoulders. "I had a rough experience on the plane. If it hadn't been for the overhead oxygen jets, I would have started climbing the walls."

"That's because claustrophobia isn't fear of small places at all. It's fear of running out of air. That's why a small room with a window that opens is fine, while an elevator of the same size is instantly scary."

"Elevators. That's why I'm here, you know. Ray has

a fantasy about sex in elevators, but I can't handle it. We discovered that the night we met. He let it go for a while, then finally started teaching me the stupid breathing exercises."

"Just so he could make love to you in an elevator?"

"No." She smiled. "It's also because he doesn't want me to be afraid. He's so brave—so big and strong and fearless—he just can't stand to think of me being scared. Plus," she added with a wink, "the danger of being discovered turns him on. Sex in elevators, sex in the back of limousines, sex in alleys. I'm okay with the alley, but the other two get me panicked."

"Not your typical relationship," Kell murmured. Then he cleared his throat and asked, "Does it bother him that you have sex with other men?"

"Actually, it's probably a relief for him, as long as they don't hurt me. I can't make any demands for fidelity from him when I'm fooling around with other guys, right?" She sighed. "I don't really understand him. Such a great guy, but living by himself, except for his one weekend a month with me."

"He hasn't told you why he turned his back on society?"

Miranda shook her head. "I've always assumed he was bitter. That's why it surprised me this morning, when you said he was protecting the world, not himself. Why would the world need protection from an insurance investigator?"

"Ask Ortega. It's not my place to say. Although…" Kell arched an eyebrow. "How does he explain the way he met *me?*"

"You were kidnapped and held for ransom because of your science stuff. Ray's company insured your employer, and he went down there to investigate, in case they filed a claim. The bad guy grabbed him, too, and threw you both in some icky, dirty cage. You kept his spirits up with your breathing technique until he managed to kill the bad guy and free you both."

"That's what he says? That *I* kept *his* spirits up?" Kell's eyes clouded. "I wouldn't have lasted a week without him there."

"It's criminal that your company didn't pay your ransom right away. Especially because Ray says your research probably earned them zillions of dollars."

"It *was* criminal. They assumed I'd be killed, and they could keep all the profits. Unfortunately for them, Ortega saved me. Then I sued them for half of their net worth."

"And then you moved here." Miranda tried for an innocent tone. "Why didn't you just come home to the United States?"

"The U.S. betrayed me. Did nothing to help me when I was captured. So I renounced my citizenship."

"And now you're Swiss?"

"I have no country. No such antiquated allegiances. The era of nations is over, Jennifer. That's what I learned in that cage. If your country can't protect you, can't save you, what good is it to you?" He flushed and added quickly, "Sorry. I didn't mean to preach."

"It's okay. It's kind of inspiring, actually. But most of us can't afford to think that way. You're rich. So you can be your own country in a way, right? You have your own guards here to protect you. People like me have to rely on our governments to do that."

"Except, your government is too big and bloated to protect you efficiently. And it's too corrupt to even try."

"That's depressing," she told him with another sigh.

"I agree. But times are changing. Nations are collapsing under their own weight, and another form of protection—a smaller, more efficient one—is forming. We live in an amazing time. Frightening, obviously, but also amazing."

"You think the big countries are breaking up into little ones?"

He shook his head. "It's not about geography anymore. Not with supersonic travel and global communication. The next era of human history will be about mobility, power and response, not geography."

She smiled. "Where did you get these ideas?"

"I told you. They were born in that cage in South America. The corporation that employed me didn't rescue me. My huge, wealthy country didn't, either. It was one man who saved me, where all the power and money in the world had failed."

"You make Ray sound like a hero," she murmured.

"He was. Probably still is. If you knew what I knew, you'd feel privileged to be his girlfriend."

"Then help me have sex with the poor guy in an elevator. It's really all he wants."

Kell burst into laughter. "When you put it that way, how can I refuse?"

"So?" She smiled impishly. "You've found something new, something more effective? I knew it! Once Ray told me what a genius you were, I knew that in ten years, you'd find something better than stupid breathing exercises. Is it hypnosis? That makes more sense than breathing."

Kell laughed again. "I investigated hypnosis for years, but with no success. I finally came full circle and discovered a pharmaceutical solution. Unfortunately," he added more soberly, "it's a new drug, so the long-term side effects are unknown. I can give you a couple of doses—enough for you and Ortega to have some fun together. But for sustained relief, it's still the breathing exercises, I'm afraid.

"On the other hand," he continued, his blue eyes sparkling, "you will be amazed at what the drug can do for you for a few hours. It won't just alleviate your claustrophobia. It will empower you in ways you can't imagine. For a few hours, you'll feel invincible. And in many ways, you'll *be* invincible."

"Wow." Miranda stared into his eyes, thrilled to have confirmed what they all has suspected—Kell's useful-ness to the Brigadier was rooted in a new discovery. One with military applications. And she was going to get her hands on it.

"Can I try it now, Jonathan?"

"I want you to get a good night's sleep first. The drug is very powerful. And I've never tried it on a woman."

"Okay. First thing in the morning then? And tonight, you can tell me bedtime stories about the new form of government you've dreamed up."

"I beg your pardon?"

She winced, realizing she had gone too far and aroused his suspicions. "It's just so fascinating for me, talking to a genius like you. The men I know don't have these kinds of big, bold ideas. The men I know," she added with a mischievous smile, "spend their time dreaming up sex fantasies, not new forms of government."

"Ortega doesn't talk to you about government? Cur-rent events? None of that?"

"Why would he? He's not really into politics."

Kell gave a harsh laugh. "Since when? He's probably the most political guy I've ever met. It's interesting that he claims to love you, but lies to you the way he does. I'm beginning to think he doesn't deserve you."

Miranda licked her lips, then said softly, "He saved your life, Jonathan."

The scientist immediately flushed. "Excellent point. I didn't mean to sound critical of him. I meant it as a compliment to you. You're a very intelligent woman, you know."

"Usually men compliment my hair. Or my body. It's sweet that you actually respect my mind," she said, biting her bottom lip as though confused and flattered. "It means a lot, especially from you."

He stared at her for a moment, then caught her off guard by asking, "Do you think Ortega would mind if I slept with you?"

"Hmmm?"

"I'd pay you, of course. I mean, it's what you do for a living, isn't it?" When she didn't answer right away, he held up his hands and insisted, "Forget I said it. Obviously I've offended you."

"No, sweetie." She grabbed his hands in her own and squeezed them gently. "You asked me if Ray would mind, and I'm pretty sure the answer is 'yes.'"

"Oh. I see."

She nodded. "The other men don't matter to him. But you're like a brother. He says that all the time. And even though I'm a professional, I'm also his girl. He pays me, and puts up with my clients, just to keep things from getting too serious. But in his own way, he loves me. A lot, I think. And he loves you, too. It would seem icky to him. See what I mean?"

Kell's cheeks were scarlet. "Absolutely. I despise myself for suggesting it. You won't tell him, will you?"

"No. I promise I won't. And I'll tell you a secret." She leaned forward and kissed his lips. "I wish we could do it, too. And not just because I'm grateful that you're going to cure me. You're very attractive. Handsome, smart and rich." She smiled impishly. "I love those qualities in a man."

"Never mind," he scolded, but he was clearly relieved that she was flirting with him as though his gaffe had never occurred. Then he insisted, "If you're going to take the power pill tomorrow—"

"The what?"

He flushed again. "That's what I call it. You'll find out why. Anyway, you need to prepare yourself so that the hangover will be less intense. Do you take vitamins?"

She nodded. "For my hair."

Kell chuckled. "They work very well. I'll give you some extra vitamin C to take. Some calcium, too. You'll eat a high protein dinner, then get some sleep. I can give you a sedative—"

"No thanks. I feel so safe here, I'll sleep like a baby, I'm sure."

"I'm glad you feel safe. It's nice having company." He cleared his throat. "Can you stay for a few days?"

"Maybe even longer."

"I'd like that," he admitted. "But I'm afraid you'll need to leave by Friday. I'm expecting guests on the weekend, and they aren't the sort of men you'd want to meet. Believe me."

Miranda's instincts jumped to attention. "Really? Business or social?"

When he hesitated, she suspected it was because his

visitors were political. Did that mean the Brigade was getting together? Probably not the Brigadier himself, since he didn't meet with them in person. But maybe the rest of the group?

Which meant Gresley would be there, assuming he'd had his jaw wired or otherwise repaired by then. Too bad. It would have been such a coup to wrangle an invitation to a Brigade meeting. She'd just have to make the most of the time between now and then.

Kell finally responded, admitting, "I don't know these men well, but I promised them they'd have my undivided attention. For a business deal, like you said."

"That's okay. I love being with you, but I'm also dying to get home and see Ray." She cocked her head to the side. "I guess you're not really afraid of strangers after all. You're fine with me, and you're letting these men visit. Have they stayed here before?"

"All but one. I've never met him in person, and frankly, I'm scared to death of him," Kell told her with a wry smile. "But this business is important to me, so I'll force myself to handle it."

Miranda stared, speechless. Was it possible the Brigadier was attending the weekend meeting? If so, she could learn his identity by surveilling the premises, which would be easy to do with the right equipment and a nice, safe spot along one of the hiking trails. She was sure Kristie could arrange for the equipment, but contacting the spinner was a problem, since Kell's guards had confiscated her cell phone and she was sure they monitored all communications from within the fortress. They had even taken custody of her laptop when they brought her belongings up from the inn.

Somehow they had let the barrette-camera slip by

them, but even that didn't matter since there were so many guards wandering around the place, she didn't anticipate having an opportunity to use it. In addition to Mike, Joe, Samson and Carl, she had spotted three others inside the fortress, and Kell had said there were half a dozen more patrolling the perimeter.

Still, her mission was proving to be a tremendous success. At the very least, she would walk away from this place with samples of the "power pills" Kell had developed for use by the Brigade's paramilitary forces. He was also giving her a steady stream of information about the Brigade. And last but not least, she might be able to get a picture of the Brigadier himself as he entered the premises on the weekend!

If she went home with all of that, she and Kristie would be heroes. They might catch a little flack about their methods, but SPIN and the CIA would still be impressed enough to allow them to become permanent members of the anti-Brigade team. Perhaps even to spearhead it.

"Are you upset, Jennifer?"

"What?"

"You're so quiet all of a sudden." Kell smiled apologetically. "Believe me, I wish I could invite you to stay longer—"

"Don't be silly. I have to get home and get kinky with Ray, right? I'll head back to Geneva tomorrow night—"

"You don't need to rush away. If you take the drug tomorrow, you'll have a helluva hangover when you wake up on Thursday. You should stay here until it subsides."

"We'll see," she murmured, concerned about having enough time to pick up the equipment she needed in

Geneva and then making it back in time to catch the Brigadier's arrival. If not, she might have to wait until he departed to photograph him, which would present additional complications.

"I'd rather just take the pill now, Jonathan. Please?"

"If you're a good girl and take your vitamins, *and* get a good night's sleep, I'll give it to you first thing in the morning.

"I have to admit," he added in a tone so guarded it momentarily alarmed her, "I can't wait to see the effect my power drug has on someone like you."

Chapter 9

By the time Kell escorted Miranda to his laboratory at the back of the fortress the next morning, she had spent so much time and effort masquerading as Ortega's girl-friend, she was almost beginning to believe it herself! It was "Ray this" and "Ray that"—tender stories and sexy ones, all culled from a montage of their one night together combined with their day at his mountain cabin. She had never before played an undercover role for this long, or with this intensity, and she was learning that it was true what other agents said—that after the first twenty-four hours or so, the difficulty wasn't so much maintaining the facade as reminding oneself that it wasn't really the truth.

"This is just what I expected," she told her host as she stood in the middle of a long, narrow room with spot-less white walls and gleaming stainless steel tables and equipment. Unlike the lab at BioGeniSystems, the place was spotlessly organized.

"Sorry about the lack of windows. I chose an interior room for my work for extra privacy. But it's such a large area, I never get claustrophobic in here."

"It helps that there are doors at both ends of the room," Miranda told him.

"The monks who built this place made sure there were always a minimum of two exits from any room. I suppose there was a certain amount of political intrigue in those days."

"Or they were claustrophobic like us." Miranda eyed her host hopefully. "Time for my pill?"

He chuckled. "Almost. I want to take your vital signs first. And I have a few questions if you don't mind."

"Shoot."

He wrapped a blood pressure cuff around her arm. "Think carefully. Is claustrophobia really your greatest fear?"

"Yes. Absolutely. I know, I know. Spiders and rats. I hate them, too, but it's the closed-in spaces that scare me the most."

"What about fear of the dark?"

"No." She hesitated, then admitted, "Pitch-black—with absolutely no hint of light—freaks me a little."

"Heights?" he asked, watching the meter on the dial as it recorded her pressure.

"No."

"Strange or novel situations?"

"Love 'em," she assured him.

He laughed. "Lucky you. Okay, so we'll go with claustrophobia. Next question: if you could change one event in your life—prevent it from happening—what would it be?"

Miranda bit her lip. The obvious answer—the night she became Ortega's dupe and ruined her career—was something she couldn't reveal to Kell. And in truth, while it was the first example to come to mind, she knew there was something else—another defining event—that haunted her even more completely.

"When I was fourteen, my father was thrown from a horse and ended up with both legs paralyzed. If I could change that, I would."

Kell seemed surprised. "That's very unselfish. He's lucky to have such a great daughter."

"It's not unselfish, Jonathan," she assured him sadly. "*My* life changed that day, too."

"Go on."

Miranda frowned. "I don't see why we need to go into this. But okay. Here goes. My dad was the proverbial best dad in the world when I was little. He was fun. Full of life. He adored me, even though he probably really wanted a son. Anyway, he was an active sportsman—rodeo, guns, archery, hunting, fast cars. He wasn't around much because he was always off with his buddies, having fun, or drinking, or whatever. But when he came home, he lit up the world for me.

"After the accident, obviously, his life changed and he was miserable. Bitter and mean and depressed. Everyone understood that, including me. Then one by one, people got fed up. His friends first. Then finally even his doctors. Even my mom. He said such hurtful things to her. To all of us."

"How long did this go on?"

"For me? Until the day he died, eight years later. But

Mom left after two years. She tried to get the court to give her custody of me, but I told the judge I wanted to stay with Dad. Not just out of guilt, but because I kept thinking the old Dad would return eventually. The guy who loved us. But he never did. He never again showed interest in anything I did. It was strange, because he had been so proud of my archery skills and my marksmanship. But after the accident, he didn't want to hear about any of that. It took me a while to understand that he was jealous, which makes sense, but still…"

"But still, you were his daughter."

She nodded. "He didn't come to my graduation because he said it would be too painful for him to see all the other parents walking around enjoying themselves. When one of my teachers came to see him, to suggest it would mean a lot to me if he showed up, he called me selfish. Through it all, I just kept remembering what a great guy he had been once. I kept waiting for that guy to come back. I don't think I really realized until after he died that…well…"

"That that great guy never really existed?"

She nodded.

Kell surprised her by grinning. "That's a great event. Just perfect for our purposes."

"Glad you like it," she muttered.

"You'll see." He set two paper cups in front of her, one containing a blue pill, the other, water. "Okay, Jennifer. Here we go. The drug works quickly. You'll feel good. Then you'll feel *great*. Euphoric. Powerful. One subject described it as getting rid of all your baggage, even the baggage you never knew you had. I think that's pretty accurate, judging from other responses."

"Are you saying you haven't tried it yourself?" she asked, honestly surprised.

"No. Not yet."

"Good grief, Jonathan! Isn't that the whole idea? You're the Phobia King, right? This is *your* drug."

He scowled. "My system is more sensitive than most people's. I have a lot of allergies, for example. It's complicated, and we're not talking about me at the moment. Do you want to take it or not?"

She gave him a sympathetic smile. He had grown so comfortable around her—behaving almost normally— she had nearly forgotten he was actually a bundle of nerves. How ironic that his fear of new situations—of the unknown—was so intense it actually prevented him from benefiting from his own miracle cure!

"How long will it last?"

"Four to six hours of intense relief, then it tapers off gradually. When you finally sleep, you'll sleep heavily. And as I warned you, there's a price—a painful headache when you wake up. But the vitamins and calcium should help with that." He touched her cheek. "I never tried this on a woman before, but the results shouldn't be too different than with a man. I think you're going to love it. And I *know* I'm going to love watching you on it."

She picked up the pill, her pulse racing with anticipation. Euphoria. Invincibility. No more baggage. It all sounded too good to be true. "It's not going to make me do anything crazy, is it? Like jump off a building because I think I can fly?"

He laughed. "No. It can affect your judgment to an extent, but not that way."

"My judgment?" She winced, wondering if the drug might make her feel so powerful, she might do something crazy, like reveal the truth to Kell about her real occupation or her nonrelationship with Ortega.

"Don't worry. You'll be rational. In fact, you'll probably be ultra-rational." Kell grinned. "You're getting cold feet?"

She returned the smile, then popped the pill in her mouth and washed it down without further hesitation. "Now what?"

"Walk around," he suggested. "We'll stay here for a few minutes, then move back to the drawing room if you'd like. Here," he added, jumping up and moving to a stainless steel cabinet, which he opened to reveal a bow and quiver. "You said you like archery? You can play with these later if you'd like. I have a target set up in the basement."

"Indoor archery? That's a new one," she said, teasing.

"For me, it was part of an experiment, not a sport."

"An experiment?" She stared in delight. "Are you talking about Night Arrow?"

Kell drew back, visibly shocked. "How did you know about that?"

"When Ortega told me about the torture, he mentioned that they were grilling you about something called Night Arrow." She winced and added lamely, "Listen to that. You've got me calling him Ortega instead of Ray! I already don't like this drug."

Get a grip, Miranda, she ordered herself. *Sixty seconds on this power trip and you're already blowing it! Talking about Night Arrow? Are you nuts?*

Fortunately, Kell seemed amused rather than suspicious. "I'll try to call him Ray from now on so I'm not such a bad influence."

"Thanks." She picked up the bow and tested it. "Nice. Ray said you didn't know anything about Night Arrow, or you definitely would have told them."

"That's true. But after I was released, I made it my business to find out what it was, and traced it back to a myth from deep in the jungle. About a race of warriors who hunted at night. According to the legend, they anointed their arrows with a magic potion that guided them to their victims. So they could shoot their enemies even when it was so dark they couldn't see them."

"Doesn't sound like something that can be tested in a lab."

"I agree. But Benito Carerra believed otherwise. He apparently thought I had re-created the red mixture that they used on their arrows. And my investigators confirmed that other researchers had made some inquiries. The natives who remembered hearing the stories insisted that the potion was made from the sap of the tree from which the arrow was made, mixed with the blood of the type of animal being hunted."

"Yuck." She grabbed the quiver, then smiled mischievously. "Let's go outside. I want to see what I can do with my new powers."

"You don't have new powers," he said, chuckling. "Just a *feeling* of power. I take it it's working?"

"Come on." She strode past him and into the hall, laughing as he trailed after her whining about his allergies, and UV rays, and assorted other reasons why they needed to stay indoors. She could see now that part of her mission was to get this guy a life!

"You're just scared, Jonathan," she said, grabbing him by the arm and dragging him out into the sunlight. "Don't worry. I'll protect you from humans and animals and bugs. Just remember that everything else—the sun, the air, even the wind—is *good* for you. You moved here for clean air, right? Let's get some."

One of the guards ran up to them, his hand on his pistol, apparently shocked to see his employer outside, much less dragged around by their houseguest.

Kell waved him away. "Go get my mask. And sunscreen. And my gray sweater. Jennifer? Don't you need a sweater?"

"Nope." She scanned the distance, looking for a target, finally settling on a group of trees far in the distance. "Which one of those do you want me to hit?"

"If you hit any of them, I'll be impressed. It's pretty far."

"The second one from the left, then. Two feet off the ground, dead center." She noticed that he was looking around and she glared. "Pay attention. I told you I'll protect you. Two feet off the ground, okay? Watch me."

Her movements were fluid as she drew an arrow, took careful aim, then sent it sailing through the air. The arrow hit the correct tree, but slightly off center, and almost three feet off the ground. "Damn."

Kell laughed. "Forget about the tree. Tell me how you're feeling."

She bit her lip, then admitted, "I feel so great. So free. So lighthearted. It's fun! Tell Carl to let the dogs loose so we can play with them." She held up her hand to stop any complaints. "They won't hurt you, right? You're their master. And dogs *love* me. I'll bet no one ever plays with the poor things, right?"

"Jennifer? Pay attention. I want to ask you some questions."

"Okay." She set the bow on the ground, then focused on him, her hands on her hips.

"You're not afraid of anything, correct?"

"Correct."

"Tell me why."

She shrugged. "There's nothing to be afraid of. Nothing's threatening us. And if something tries to, we'll deal with it. You need to relax, Jonathan. This is a fortress, remember? We're perfectly safe. In fact, I don't think this is a good test of your power drug. It's *too* safe here."

"Jennifer?"

"Yes?"

"If you could change one event in your life, what would it be?"

"I already told you. Dad's accident."

"How would that help you?"

She considered the question cautiously. "Well, obviously, my life would have been better. Because my father would have been happy. And he and my mom would have stayed together, although…"

She thought about the custody hearing and sighed. So much had come out that day, mostly about her father's infidelity. Not that that had really been a secret. Her mother had apparently always known about it, and accepted it as part of his nature. Even Miranda had begun to notice the way other women hung around him, too, although she hadn't been quite ready to accept the implications. Not at the age of fourteen. And then, after the accident, any opportunity for running around had been closed to him.

"I guess eventually, Mom would have left him. They had other problems besides the accident. You know what's strange?" she added wistfully. "I probably would have gone with her under *those* circumstances. I never thought about that before, but it's true."

She shook her head, then gave Kell another glare. "You know what, Jonathan? It doesn't matter what I'd change if I had the power. I *don't* have the power. I *can't* change the past."

"But if you could—"

"Pay attention! It's insane to dwell on it. Change one event? Or two? That's nuts. Changing the accident wouldn't change the fact that my father didn't care about anyone but himself. And even with Ortega…" She stopped herself, then muttered, "You talk too much, Jonathan."

"Even with Ortega, what?"

"There are things I would have done differently. But if I had, I might not be here right now. And I *like* being here. So thank God I don't have the power to change the past. I'd probably screw it up!" She grinned, proud that she had salvaged the situation, and also impressed with the truth. If she hadn't been duped by Ortega, she never would have gotten pulled into the Brigade operation— an operation that was going to make her famous!

Kell was clearly trying not to laugh out loud. "Shall we test your claustrophobia?"

"No. I've only got a few more hours before the drug starts wearing off. I want to accomplish something, Jonathan. I don't want to waste a minute of it." She grabbed both of his hands up in her own. "Let me take you into town. I'll protect you, I promise. We'll have lunch and shop."

"And if someone tried to bother us?"

"You have no idea who I really am," she told him solemnly. "I would kick their ass. And believe me, I know how to do it. You've never been safer than you are right here, right now, with me. Watch." She picked up the bow, drew a second arrow, and shot again at the tree. This time, the arrow hit—two feet from the ground, dead center. "See? I can do anything."

"And you're humble, too," he said with a chuckle. "I

know you're having fun. So am I. But I'd like to take your blood pressure again."

"You have *got* to be kidding. Do I look sick to you? I feel great. You need to try this, Jonathan Kell. I insist. Take a pill while I'm still under the influence, okay? So we can have fun together." Before he could object, she told him, "You've created a miracle here, Jonathan. Do you know how many lives you can improve with this? I'm talking *dramatic* improvement. Phobics, like you. But also people who are too submissive, right? Children who've been abused. Battered women. You can give them this taste of power...."

As her voice trailed into silence, Kell cocked his head to the side. "Jennifer?"

She turned away, not wanting him to see her expression, which she was certain was jubilant because she had just figured something out. Something amazing. Even more amazing than the revelation that she didn't want to change the past.

Battered women. The idea of empowering them. It had made her mind flash on Angelina Carerra. Hadn't Kristie said it? That victims like that didn't easily become powerful, self-confident women? But somehow Angelina had.

Angelina had stood in that laboratory, the picture of empowerment. Thinking clearly. Living in the moment, with no regrets. Zero baggage...

It was either the biggest coincidence in the world, or she had been taking the power drug that night. Except Jonathan believed Miranda was the first female to use it. So Jonathan didn't know about Angelina...

"Jennifer?"

"Shhh! Let me think."

Kell laughed. "Be my guest. Can we start walking back to the lab while you do so?"

She nodded, trying to keep her face expressionless as she sorted through the maze of half facts and suppositions that she was sure could lead her to the truth.

The next few hours were a strange mix for Miranda as she enjoyed her euphoria, entertained Jonathan Kell and slowly unraveled the mystery of Angelina Carerra's connection to the Brigade.

It had all started back there in the jungle, she surmised. Kell and Ortega and the Carerras. Under torture, Kell had talked—in fact, screamed—about his phobia research. And maybe he had talked about his political theories as well. Angelina had heard it all, either firsthand or afterwards. After Ortega's arrow freed her from her abusive husband, Benito, she had inherited their cocaine empire. She had slowly divested herself of the illegal elements, investing her millions in legitimate enterprises, becoming one of the world's wealthiest women.

But still afraid, deep down inside. So she kept her eye on Kell, thinking he might find a cure—a way to free her from her demons. But she wouldn't offer him money, because he didn't need or want any more than he already had. What he wanted was to vindicate his political theories—to see the system that had betrayed him collapse.

There was a piece of the puzzle missing. That was obvious. Still, Miranda was sure that somehow, when Kell had supplied samples of his power drug to the mysterious "Brigadier" who shared his political philosophy, Angelina had gotten her hands on the pills. Either she and the Brigadier were associated, or she herself was the leader of the Brigade, fueled by the power drug.

"Mr. Kell? We've got a serious problem."

Miranda snapped to attention at the sound of the guard's voice. A serious problem? Danger? Bring it on! The power drug, more inspiring than adrenaline any day, made her crave excitement in any form. She could almost taste it!

Kell's reaction was precisely the opposite. His face turned ash gray, and the tick under his eye began to beat as rhythmically as Miranda's metronome. "What's wrong? My God, I knew we shouldn't have come outside again."

"Don't worry, Jonathan. I'll protect you," Miranda reminded him. Then she gave the guard a hopeful grin. "What's wrong, monkey boy? You look so serious."

He gave her an annoyed look, then told his boss, "I need to speak to you alone, sir. Right away."

"You can talk freely in front of me," Miranda insisted.

Carl's voice took on a hint of panic. "It's about the visitor, sir. The special one. He's here."

"The visitor?" Kell's face went from gray to snow white. "What are you saying? He's here? Today?"

"Joe's driving him up right now, sir. I told them you'd meet him in the drawing room. And I told the other guys to go to their rooms and wait for further instructions." Carl's manner grew defensive. "It's not like I had a choice, Mr. Kell. I mean, it's *him*."

"Right, right. You did the right thing." Kell patted the guard's arm. "Give me a minute with Miss Aguilar. Then escort her to her room. The back way. Is that clear?" Without waiting for an answer, he turned to Miranda. "Jennifer? You need to listen to me carefully. I know you aren't afraid of anything. That's fine. But this is still my house. My rules. And I want you to go upstairs with Carl. Lock yourself in your room. Don't come out. Don't make any noise."

"Jonathan—"

"My visitor is a dangerous man. I gave him assurances that I would meet with him alone. If he knew you were here, he'd want to talk to you. I can't allow that for any number of reasons, most of them having to do with your safety."

"Jonathan—"

"I know," he said fondly. "You think you could kick his ass. You probably could. And then he would kill you. And me. Or Ortega would kill me for involving you in this enterprise. I'm begging you to just go to your room and stay there."

"Okay."

"What?"

She smiled sympathetically. "I'll go to my room as long as you promise to be careful. And come and talk to me as soon as you can."

Kell's eyes actually swam with tears as he grasped her by the shoulders. "Thank you. Thank you. I'll explain everything soon. But for now, I'd better get in there before he gets angry and comes looking for me."

"Go ahead." She kissed his cheek. "Take care, Jonathan."

Kell nodded, then hurried toward the house.

Carl took Miranda by the elbow. "Let's go. Up the back way."

"Okay." She kept pace with him, all the while plotting her next move. She had to consider the possibility, however remote, that Gresley had told the Brigadier about his altercation with an auburn-haired hooker. Or maybe Gresley himself was the Brigadier. He fit the profile, since he wasn't an American. And he had had all that literature at his house.

First Angelina's the Brigadier? Now Gresley? This drug is making you loopy! she told herself with a laugh. *It's going to be someone you'd never guess in a million years, so give it up. The good news is, he's in the drawing room! Just sneak down there and check it out. Then you'll take the intel to the CIA and be a hero, just like you planned. And way, way ahead of schedule.*

She cooperated completely with Carl, who was so distracted by the Brigadier situation that he didn't even bother to insult her. He barely seemed to notice her at all until the moment he ushered her into her bedroom and she turned on him, smiling sweetly, and asked him to help her move a rocking chair on the balcony. Once outside—and out of range of the video security cameras—she slammed her fist into his mouth while her knee connected with his groin. He went down in a heap of pain, and she kicked him full in the face, dazing him further. Then she yanked his pistol from its holster and cracked him over the head.

She wanted to be in position before the Brigadier reached the fortress, so she quickly bound Carl's hands and feet, then gagged him. Leaving him behind, she closed the balcony doors and slid a heavy velvet drape across them. After confirming that the pistol was loaded, she got the only other equipment she needed, the barrette from her suitcase, so that she could get a picture of the visitor. Then she hurried into the hall, where she edged toward the stairs, listening carefully for any sign of the other guards, but apparently they had followed Carl's orders and gone to the servants' quarters.

Perfect.

She impishly thanked the monks for making sure there were two entrances for every room in this monstrosity. The Brigadier would access the drawing room from the entry hall, so Miranda would sneak in from the back. She had noticed a narrow hallway there, with a door that was always partially ajar. No one would expect a claustrophobe to be lurking in so confined a space.

Again, everything was going *perfectly*. All she had to do was snap the picture, then return to her room and work on her exit strategy. Of course, she might not need to develop one. Jonathan was so anxious to get her out of the place, he'd probably have an escape plan mapped out for her.

Okay, reality check, she told herself as she tiptoed down the hall. *It's not going "perfectly" at all, so stop telling yourself it is. If you weren't high as a freaking kite you'd see you're in deep shit. You're stuck in this mausoleum with the Brigadier, when you were supposed to get out long before he arrived. Sure, you have a gun, but if you shoot him, then what? You think Jonathan Kell is going to save you? He'll hate you for ruining his political plans.*

She tried to listen to herself, but the power drug was doing its job too well. It had seemed to be tapering off a bit, but every time she thought of shooting the Brigadier, right between his beady little eyes, she felt a rush of excitement that made her doubt her own sanity. And of course, it hadn't even occurred to her that he might shoot back.

She was indestructible, so it didn't really matter.

And even if she got killed, wouldn't it be sensational to go out in a blaze of glory? At least the CIA would have to admit she had guts. And she'd be respected and

mourned by the best: Kristie Hennessy and Will Mc-
Gregor and maybe even Ray Ortega! That alone would
be worth dying over, wouldn't it?

The thought sobered her a little, and she decided that
as much fun as the power drug was, she probably ought
to get into position and then spend a few minutes doing
Ortega's breathing exercises. Power was great, but Ortega was right, it was also difficult to handle.

Balance was better. And thanks to him, she might
just be able to get it back in time to do a good job with
this op.

Sneaking up to the doorway, she listened intently
and was relieved to hear only silence. Apparently the
Brigadier hadn't yet arrived. She was fairly certain Kell
would be sitting at his desk, his eyes trained on the
entry doorway, and thus, wouldn't see her if she dared
to poke her head into the room from the back, just for
a second. And if she miscalculated, and Jonathan caught
a glimpse of her, he'd assume she was just pumped up
on power, and he'd shoo her away without suspecting
she was actually a CIA agent.

Taking a deep breath, she popped her head into the
room and saw that Kell was indeed staring at the doorway, but not sitting at his desk. He was standing, wring-
ing his hands, visibly scared to death, and her heart
went out to him. He was in over his head—*way* over his
head—just because he didn't have the tools to deal with
betrayal. Sure his employer and his country had let him
down, just the way Miranda's father, and to a lesser extent Ortega, had let *her* down. But she had been able to
overcome it. To function in society despite it.

Poor Jonathan Kell had never had that chance.

She wanted to go to him, to take him in her arms and

promise him everything would be okay. Of course, that would officially scare him to death, so she didn't dare. But she tried to send mental vibes his way, to remind him he wasn't alone, even though he was doing a good imitation of the world's most pitiful loser.

It was almost a relief when Joe's voice sounded in the entryway, saying, "Go right in, sir. Mr. Kell is waiting for you. I'll be outside if you need me."

Miranda drew back and listened as sounds of a man striding into the room reached her. She wasn't going to peek, even though she thought she could get away with it. She just didn't dare take that chance.

Then she heard Kell gasp *"You!"* as though he were standing face-to-face with Satan himself. And curiosity—mixed with the power pill—overcame her better judgment, allowing her to take a tiny step forward in time to see a man in military-style khakis glaring at Kell with eyes so furious, lips so curled into a snarl, contempt so unprecedented oozing from every pore of his commanding build, she almost didn't recognize him.

Except there was no mistaking the bronze flecks that flashed like fire in the irate man's eyes as he grabbed Jonathan Kell's quivering body and pressed the barrel of a black-handled pistol to his throat.

Chapter 10

Ortega...

The only thing that gave Miranda the strength not to blurt out his name was the power pill. She even suspected that without the drug in her system she might have come completely unglued at the sight of her despicable "boyfriend" manhandling a sweet, innocent angel like Jonathan Kell with such brutal disregard.

Kell's blue eyes were round with fear. "Ortega? How can this be? Wha—what's wrong with you?"

"Shut up," Ortega advised dryly. "You're the world's biggest fuckup, do you know that? You almost ruined everything. All our plans." Then he raised his voice to a rumbling bark. "Miranda! Get your ass out here. Now!"

She held her pistol tightly, wanting to step forward and shoot him, but forcing herself to think first. This was too unreal. Ortega was the Brigadier. She hadn't once considered such a crazy thing, even after she made the link with their captivity in South America. Nor had Kell made the connection, it seemed.

It's going to be someone you'd never guess in a million years....

Well, she had been right about that at least. But wrong—so wrong!—about everything else. And if she made one more mistake, she was going to get herself killed, and Jonathan Kell along with her.

"Th-there's no one here named Miranda," Kell dared to inform his assailant.

"You're a fucking idiot," Ortega replied. "She's CIA, and she's definitely here, playing footsie with you. That's her specialty, and like an idiot, you went for it."

Enraged, Miranda stepped into the open, steadying her weapon with both hands. "My specialty? You haven't *seen* my specialty yet, Ortega. Let Jonathan go or I'll fucking kill you."

"Jennifer, what are you doing?" Kell asked, sobbing.

"Jennifer?" Ortega howled with disrespectful laughter. "That's the best you and your spinner friend could come up with? You're as pathetic as Jonathan. At least *he* has an excuse."

"Kristie loves you, you creep," Miranda told him in disgust. "Let Jonathan go. I promise I'll put my gun down if you will. I want to kill you with my bare hands anyway, so no loss."

"She's on drugs, Ortega," Kell insisted tearfully. "I gave her a dose of the power pill. Don't take her seriously. Let's all just sit down and talk—"

"*Talk?*" Ortega roared. "How stupid *are* you? This bitch used me to get to you. Now she's using *you* to get to *me*. If you want to save her life, tell her to put down the weapon and slide it over here. Maybe then I'll be willing to sit down and talk."

Kell gave Miranda a desperate smile. "Do it, Jennifer. We can work this out. I don't want to die. But I don't want *you* to die, either."

"But if he has to make a choice," Ortega said, taunting them both, "he'll choose himself. Right, Jonathan?"

Miranda's heart broke for Kell, and she murmured, "That's enough." Leaning down, she carefully placed Carl's gun on the floor, then used her foot to send it sailing toward Ortega.

"Good girl." Ortega gave the weapon another kick so that it disappeared under the sofa. "Hands up, beautiful. Walk over here slowly. Jonathan? There's a set of handcuffs on my belt. Cuff her behind her back. Cooperate, Miranda, or he's a dead man."

She nodded, then walked over to them and turned her back, her hands behind herself. Once the cuffs had snapped closed, she turned again to face them, murmuring, "Now let Jonathan go. He deserves better treatment than this. He's been trying to do the right thing, Ortega. The honorable thing. You and I have both been manipulating that. Now it's over."

Ortega arched an eyebrow. "Over?"

"I'll do whatever you want. Just let Jonathan go. He didn't know I was CIA. He's loyal to you. I swear it."

Ortega eyed Kell coolly. "Is that true? Do I still have your loyalty?"

Kell nodded, whimpering. "Just don't hurt Jenn—I mean, Miranda."

"And what if I decide I need to kill her? Do I have your loyalty then?"

Miranda gave Kell an encouraging smile. "Go ahead, Jonathan. Don't let this creep ruin your vision of a wonderful new society. I'm dead either way."

"Maybe not," Ortega corrected her softly. Then he told Kell, "Miranda's not exactly the CIA's favorite daughter. She came here to salvage her career. Obviously, she fucked that up. But I don't particularly want to kill her. Let me talk to her, in private. Maybe she and I can come to an understanding."

"Go fuck yourself," Miranda told him in disgust.

"That's the drug talking, Ortega," Kell said quickly. "Wait a few hours. Once it's out of her system, she'll be more reasonable."

Ortega scowled but nodded. "We've come this far. We can wait a few more hours. Tell your men to stay in their quarters. I have troops positioned around the perimeter. They'll provide security. Maybe we can salvage this effort after all."

"I'm sure we can," Kell murmured. "Thanks."

Miranda looked up at Ortega defiantly. "It's not just the drug, you know. I hate you more than you can possibly imagine."

"Yeah, I know. But you're forgetting how persuasive I can be when I put my mind—and my training—to it." His eyes twinkled deviously. "Let's go to your room. We need to talk, and I don't think a wimp like Jonathan has the stomach for this particular brand of discussion."

They left Kell cowering in the middle of the drawing room, and in less than a minute, Ortega had herded Miranda into her room and slammed the door behind them. "Sit."

"Fuck you."

He laughed. "Sit down, Miranda. We're just going to talk." Pulling a small silver object from his vest pocket, he pushed a button and then set the device on a table. "Signal jammer," he explained.

"Fuck you."

"Yeah, I got that." He pulled a black cylinder from a second pocket, then strode to a corner and sprayed paint onto a tiny opening in the molding. Crossing to the opposite corner, he repeated the procedure. Then he murmured, "Did you realize Kell was watching you undress?"

"I'm used to starring in video porn, thanks to you."

He shook his head. "How much of this is the drug talking? Did you actually know about the cameras?"

"You're not the only one here who's CIA-trained, asshole. You're just the only one who uses it for evil." She glared contemptuously. "It doesn't bother me that you screwed *me*. But screwing Kristie? *And* your country? How the fuck do you sleep at night?"

"It's easy," he told her quietly. "I'm not really the Brigadier."

Miranda opened her mouth to respond, then closed it, completely speechless.

"I just pretended to be him," Ortega explained. "So I could get into this ridiculous stronghold and help you get out before you got yourself killed."

She winced, trying to understand his words despite the combination of power drug and adrenaline that was ordering her to kill him.

Ortega gave her a sympathetic smile, then walked over to her, spun her around, and took the cuffs off her wrists. Then he stepped a respectful distance away and said, "We can talk later. For now, we've got to move before Kell figures out what's really going on."

"Before *Kell* figures it out? How about letting *me* figure it out first?" She covered her eyes with her hands, then peeked through her fingers. "You're not the Brigadier?"

"It was the only way I could figure to get in here without making Kell suspicious. I'm just glad it worked."

"Yeah, I'm thrilled, too," she muttered. "I can't believe Kristie ratted me out."

"She didn't. I went looking for you. Checked your apartment, your family's ranch, then ended up at her place. She wouldn't tell me where you were, but I guessed."

Miranda eyed him curiously, noticing for the first time that his military outfit was sexy as hell, especially over his lean, muscled body. "You went looking for me? Why?"

He shrugged. "I didn't like the way we left things. I thought I must have said something to offend you. If I'd known you saw that stupid videotape, I would have come after you sooner. To explain—"

"Forget it." She looked him over again without bothering to hide her admiration. "I can't believe you bluffed your way in here. It's pretty amazing."

"It was easier than I thought. His guards have gone to seed over the years, protecting him from imaginary threats. I knew that if I could get to Kell, I could convince him—half by bullying, half because he would *want* it to be true. I'm his hero, after all," he added wryly. "But the guards were as terrified and convinced by my tantrum as Kell was."

"That's because you're the world's most persuasive guy," Miranda told him with a sigh. "And you make a great Brigadier, by the way."

He hesitated, then insisted, "We should get going. Kell's guards are supposedly in their quarters, so we should be able to sneak out—"

"We can't leave. Not yet. But…" She stepped up to him and ran her fingers over his chest. "I appreciate the rescue attempt. It wasn't necessary, but very cool. Did I mention how good you look in this uniform?"

Ortega winced. "I have a feeling that's the drug talking, but thanks. Get your things together. We've got to move."

"I haven't thanked you yet for charging to my rescue," she told him, sliding her hands behind his neck.

"Hey." He grabbed her wrists and pulled them to her sides, then assured her gently, "I took advantage of you once. I'm never going to do it again."

"I agree. It's *my* turn to take advantage of *you.*" Pressing her hands against his chest, she backed him over to the bed. Then she gave him a shove.

Rather than falling onto his back as she'd hoped he'd do, he sat down, his tone solemn. "Miranda…"

"My turn, Ortega. You've called all the shots up till now. Can't I have my way just once?"

He licked his lips, then nodded. "Sounds fair."

Amused, she tugged her dress over her head and threw it onto the floor. Then she straddled him and pushed him again, and this time, he cooperated fully, laying back and watching as she unbuckled the utility belt that held his gun and holster, then went to work on the buttons of his khaki shirt.

She ran her fingertips across his chest again, this time connecting with bare, tanned skin. Then she took off her bra and waited, and Ortega obliged her by stroking her breasts appreciatively.

"Oo, that's nice." She smiled. "Finish getting undressed while I get a condom." She crawled over to the nightstand and grabbed her purse, dumping it onto the comforter and rummaging through the multicolored packets.

"Expecting an army?" Ortega teased.

"I thought they were just props," she confessed with a laugh. "This is so much better. Let's try a blue one."

"Wait." He pulled her down alongside himself, then cupped her chin in his hand and gave her a long, lingering kiss.

Inspired, she slipped her arms around his neck and kissed him back, savoring the mint taste. His hands began to roam over her breasts, and her back, then inside her panties, tugging them down gently.

"It's time," she murmured, sitting up, then stretching and rolling the blue condom over him. Flashing a mischievous smile, she straddled him again, then slowly, luxuriantly, fit him into her.

The rush of sensation she felt was so intense, and so disorienting, she actually believed for the first time that the power pill was playing Cupid in this adventure. Forcing herself to exhale, she struggled to gain back a hint of spiritual balance in the midst of the heady physical pleasure.

"Miranda?" Ortega asked, his voice husky.

"I'm just trying to find my center," she explained without opening her eyes.

"I've got a better idea," he told her, rolling gently so that he was on top. "Why don't I find it for you?"

She laughed with delight, then wrapped her arms around his neck again, murmuring words of appreciation and encouragement as Ortega proceeded to make good on his offer.

* * *

"Mmm, Ortega…" Miranda stretched, then snuggled into her pillow when they had finished. "I forgot how good you were at that."

He propped himself up on his elbow and looked directly into her eyes. "Exactly how mad are you going to be at me when you finally sober up?"

She enjoyed the bronze glow for a moment before explaining, "It's not the drug. It's something else. Role-playing gone berserk, I think."

"What does that mean?"

She shrugged. "I needed to be convincing in the role of your mistress, so I spent hours fantasizing about you before I got here. I guess I got myself all lathered up."

"And I've been fantasizing about you for more than a year," he admitted, adding hastily, "but not with that stupid alibi video. I swear."

"Are you sure you want to bring that up now?" Miranda taunted him, then she sighed. "I was looking for an excuse to be disgusted with you that day. If it hadn't been the tape it would have been something else. I just wasn't quite ready to admit that you were an okay guy."

"And now you are?"

She sat up, pulling the sheet along with her to cover her breasts. "I guess so. And you can thank Jonathan Kell for that. You're such a hero in his eyes. So noble. Or at least—" she paused to glare "—you were until today. Did you have to be so rough on him?"

"I had to convince him—and you—that I was the Brigadier. A man with a ruthless agenda. And it worked, didn't it?"

"It worked for me," she agreed with a laugh. "But poor Jonathan is probably still shaking. We'd better get down there and reassure him a little. He's very sensitive, Ortega."

"Forget Kell. We've got to get out of here before he figures out the truth. He could get a communication from the real Brigadier at anytime. Then we'd be screwed."

"I don't think they communicate much. And the whole Brigade is scheduled to arrive this weekend, so I think we have some time." She smiled reassuringly. "We can't leave now. You've created a brilliant opportunity for us to get valuable intel. Dates, locations, names. We don't need the Brigadier's identity so much anymore. All we have to do is stake out the fortress this weekend and watch him arrive. But I get the impression their timetable is aggressive. The more we can find out, the better prepared the country can be when they make their move."

She could see he was listening, so she explained, "He only talked to me in generalities. Political theory, that sort of thing. But he thinks *you* know the specifics already. If you're clever—and we both know you are— you can get him talking. Really talking. Just get in touch with your inner spinner. I've seen what Kristie can do, and you trained her, so you might be even better."

He shook his head, laughing. "My inner spinner? That's a new one."

"You've got to try, Ortega. There's so much riding on this. More than we originally suspected, I think."

He pursed his lips, then spoke carefully. "If I agree to stay tonight—to try to get as much information out of him as possible—will you agree to leave with me tomorrow morning? No arguments?"

"I almost think we have to," she admitted. "I can't take a chance on being here when Alexander Gresley arrives. He'll recognize me, and he'd love to wring my neck."

"Because?"

She outlined her adventure in London, adding solemnly, "See? Wild horses couldn't keep me here any longer than absolutely necessary."

"Unbelievable." He rubbed his eyes. "Okay, we have a tentative deal. But if I sense the slightest hint of trouble, we leave right away. My call. Agreed?"

She nodded.

"Is there any chance we could turn Kell? Convince him to knowingly work with us against the Brigade?"

She shook her head. "He's so sweet. But he's obsessed with getting revenge against a system that abandoned him to torture and almost certain death. He hates America. Hates the establishment. And he craves being in a position of power, not for power's sake, but just so he can finally feel safe."

"I remember," Ortega murmured. "Sometimes when they'd bring him back from a really rough session with Benito Carerra, Kell would be delirious. Ranting about his vision for a safer world."

"Well, he found someone—or rather, a group of someones—that agree with him." She slipped out of the bed and reached for her dress. "We'd better get back to him."

"Don't wear the same clothes. I want him to know what happened between us. Wear something sexy. Lots of leg. Something you'd wear for a lover afterwards."

"Okay." She smiled ruefully as she watched him dress in his Brigadier uniform. "Want to do me a favor?"

"Sure. Anything."

"I had to overpower one of Kell's guards so I could get his gun. He's on the balcony, bound and gagged. And probably furious."

"I'll take care of it."

"His name is Carl. I had to act fast, or I never would have been so rough on him, even though he's a pain in the ass. Tell him I'm sorry, okay?"

"I'm the Brigadier," Ortega reminded her. "I'll tell him to suck it up."

"That works, too." She watched with wistful admiration as he strode onto the balcony. He was just what Jonathan Kell claimed him to be—a flawed man with heroic potential. Of course, she had seen the other side of him firsthand, and knew he wasn't perfect. Then again, who was?

Hurrying into the bathroom, she dressed in sexy pajamas consisting of white silk shorts and a matching sleeveless tank top. Bare feet. No jewelry. Just the glow from Ortega's lovemaking to adorn her.

When she returned to the room, Ortega was standing there, and from the look in his eyes she could see he approved of her outfit. But still she asked, "Is this what you had in mind?"

"Yeah." His voice was hoarse with regret. "I'll always wonder what would have happened if…"

"Me, too." She walked past him to the door, then smiled. "Showtime?"

"Yeah."

He surprised her by taking her hand and leading her to the stairs. Then she remembered that this was Ortega—the master. Hadn't he taught her to stay in character at all times, even when she didn't think anyone was watching? They were lovers again—publicly and privately. And in these roles, they were going to kick some serious ass, mission-wise.

She had attributed her amorous behavior to role-playing, too, but she suspected Ortega had also been right when he blamed some of her friskiness on the power pill. Jonathan had said it best, hadn't he? With the drug, there was no baggage. Just the here. The now. Forget about the past.

She had to admit, it had been amazing. Absolutely no regrets over making love with the man who had once been her nemesis.

But holding his hand? She wasn't sure what to think about *that*. But he was right about staying in character, so she went along with him, imagining how Jonathan would react when he saw the Brigadier in full uniform, including his pistol, and "Jennifer" in skimpy loungewear.

But when they reached the drawing room, Kell was nowhere in sight, despite the fact Ortega had ordered him to stay put. It worried her. And apparently, it *really* worried Ortega, because his voice was close to a growl when he asked, "What the fuck? Where is he?"

"We were gone a long time," she whispered soothingly. "He probably had to use the rest room. Or get a drink of water—"

"I *ordered* him to stay here," Ortega said between gritted teeth. "Not to move a muscle! This is fucked. *We're* fucked."

"Shh…the guards aren't around. That shows he isn't suspicious, right? Let's check his laboratory. And the bathroom. You scared him so bad, his stomach is probably twisted in a knot." She gave an encouraging smile. "He's ultraphobic, remember? And you're his hero. The last thing he'd do is cross you."

"Okay." Ortega nodded. "We'll check the lab and the bathroom. If we don't find him, we're outta here. Right? I mean it, Miranda."

"We can use the back passage to get to the lab." She waited until he had drawn his pistol, then she led him along the rear hall. "If he's in there, don't scare him again."

"Yeah, yeah," Ortega growled. "Worry about us, not him, will you?"

They reached the doorway to the lab, and Miranda scanned the room, which at first appeared to be empty. Then she saw a sight that sent a chill down her spine.

Jonathan Kell, curled in a fetal position in the far corner of the room, was so pale it bordered on lifelessness. On the floor in front of him were two paper cups, and she knew before she sprinted over to him what was in those stupid receptacles.

"Oh, Jonathan, no! You poor baby."

He stared at her through bloodshot eyes. "I w-wanted to save you, J-J-Jennifer. I tr-tr-tr—tried—"

"Shush." She cradled him against her chest, rocking him gently. "Oh, Jonathan. You did this for me? Oh, sweetie, I can't believe it. You're my hero, do you know that?"

"I d-didn't take the pill."

"But you tried to take it. With your delicate system, and all the possible side effects? You still tried to take it? To save *me*? Don't you know what that means to me? Ortega!" She gave the pseudo-Brigadier an accusatory glare. "Say something."

Ortega leaned down and said simply, "Pull yourself together, man."

"Ortega!" She stared in disbelief. "Have a heart."

"Come on, Jonathan," Ortega insisted, ignoring Miranda's criticism. "We've been through worse than this, haven't we? We survived then. We'll survive now."

Yanking Kell up by his shoulders, he reminded him firmly, "Breathe. In and out. Just like we did when Carerra had us.

"And don't worry about your precious Jennifer," he added with a wink. "She's got something I want, so she's safe. As long as she does what I tell her to do."

Kell grimaced but made eye contact with Miranda. "He didn't hurt you?"

"Actually..." She bit her lip, then managed a flirtatious smile—for Kell's sake. "Ortega and I came to an understanding, sweetie. So don't worry, okay? We're all in this together now."

Miranda could only imagine what Ortega was thinking as they sat with Kell in his drawing room enjoying an impromptu dinner of sandwiches, fruit salad, beer and tea. The former SPIN director had traveled across an ocean. Left the sanctity of his mountain retreat. Risked his life. All to save her. And she hadn't even said thank you? Instead, she was making a fuss over a lunatic who didn't have the guts to save himself let alone someone else!

"My hero," she crooned. "Have another sip of tea, Jonathan. Please? For me?"

Kell cuddled happily against her. "I'm fine. Just confused. I'm glad the Brigadier didn't hurt you, but... He said you're CIA—"

"She *was* CIA," Ortega interrupted. "I've convinced her to join us."

"Before you give your penis all the credit," Miranda told her lover with a sniff, "you should know it was Jonathan who really changed my mind. He told me all about your new political philosophy, and it make a lot of sense."

Ortega glared at Kell in disbelief. "You *told* her?"

"Nothing incriminating. Just philosophy, like she said."

Miranda nodded. "It's the lesson of history. Greece fell. Egypt fell. Rome really fell. Democracy had its day in the sun, but it can't protect us anymore. The big, lumbering countries take weeks to act on a threat. We need a system that uses modern technology—lightning speed communications—to protect us."

"That's all I told her, Ortega. I swear," Jonathan insisted.

Ortega nodded. "In a way, Miranda and women like her will benefit more from our new system than anyone. Look at her. The CIA used her as a whore. Do you know what her colleagues call her? The Sex Kitten. Because they use her to get information from horny guys."

Kell blanched. "Did they send you here to seduce me, Jennifer?"

"No," she muttered, annoyed at Ortega for portraying her so blatantly, even though she knew it was an effective tactic.

"The CIA sent her to *me,* not to you, Jonathan," Ortega explained. "I always knew they'd contact me once they found out you were involved with the Brigade. They wanted to use me to get to you. To find out who the Brigadier was. They never once suspected I was he. Miranda didn't, either. She came to my cabin and seduced me. Spent a week making love to me. Then she left without any information. Do you know what happened next?"

Miranda wanted to ask "what?" but left that to Kell, who quickly did the honors.

Ortega smiled. "She was tired of being the CIA's whore. She decided to come here herself, without authorization, and try to discover the Brigadier's identity. She hoped that if she could do that, they'd value her as something more than just a gorgeous piece of ass."

Miranda made a mental note to strangle Ortega, but didn't interrupt.

Kell gave her a wistful smile. "I don't blame you for trying to improve your situation." Turning to Ortega, he asked breathlessly, like a child hearing a bedtime story, "How did you find out she was here?"

Ortega shrugged. "She's a beautiful woman. And great in bed, thanks to the CIA's training. After a few days, I missed her, and tried to track her down. I found out she had disappeared, and I knew she must have come here. To solve the mystery of the Brigadier's identity. I was proud of her, but I couldn't allow it. I had to protect the Brigade. And I had to offer her a chance to join us. To save herself from the American hypocrisy that had stolen her dignity from her."

Give me a break... Miranda looked down at her hands, trying not to laugh out loud.

"Ortega's right," Kell told her softly. "Your own country made a prostitute out of you. You have more reason than anyone to join us."

She nodded. "Like I said, you've got me convinced that the era of huge, geographically limited governments is over. But still, you're talking about the United States of America, with its massive military strength, not to mention the strength of its allies around the world. They may be bloated, lumbering giants, but they've got the manpower. The Brigade is just five men and some small paramilitary groups, right? David against Goliath."

"That's the point. The next world war will be won quickly, with small, mobile forces using innovative technology. We will run circles around the giants." Kell gave Ortega an apologetic wince. "I should let you explain."

"You're doing fine."

Kell turned back to Miranda, his eyes sparkling. "We have twenty paramilitary groups ready to move in after the bombs go off. Combined with our networks in the social, financial and religious core of each major region, that will enable us to seize power by offering stability in the midst of chaos."

"The bombs?" she asked warily.

"They will provide our opening salvo. Strategically placed explosives in ten capitals, including Washington, New York, London and Beijing, timed to ensure that President Standish and comparable world leaders are home and will be instantly killed. We have the capability to immediately dominate global communications, and we will disseminate the message that fifty more bombs exist—in other capitals as well as dense population centers. If the Brigade encounters resistance, those will be set off as well. But we anticipate that negotiations will commence immediately, especially after we deploy the pharmaceutical weapon I developed."

Miranda shook her head. "That's pretty ambitious, Jonathan. Aren't you afraid the CIA and Interpol will stop you before you can get anywhere close to sixty bombs planted?"

"The last one was put into place yesterday. In Tokyo."

She shot Ortega a horrified glance, and was impressed when he nodded coolly. "As I told you upstairs, this is not a theoretical exercise. Our progress has been swift. More proof that the world is ready for this sort of takeover."

"Still…" She shook her head again. "Even with the power pill, your tiny forces can't overcome huge armies.

It's an amazing drug, Jonathan, but it only lasts a few hours, and it didn't really make me that much more powerful, mentally or physically. It cleared my head— that was amazing, I admit. But…"

"I agree," said Kell. "The power pill offers miraculous temporary relief for persons with severe phobias, but those people aren't likely to join the military in the first place. Most soldiers—whether in traditional armies or paramilitary forces—already have above-average ability to suppress their fear. Adrenaline works well for them." He cleared his throat, then admitted, "It is my other formula that will be vital to the takeover. I'm not proud of it, but it's a necessary evil."

"Your other formula?"

"Liquid fear," he told her softly. "We can easily introduce it into the water supply. As it turns out, it's much easier to turn normal people into phobics than to make phobics like myself normal."

"Oh, Jonathan," she whispered. "What have you done?"

"Miranda!" Ortega glared. "There's no room for sentimentality if we're to be successful. Change has a price. For global change, that price is high. But necessary. You'd better learn that lesson right now."

"But at some point, the price becomes too high," Kell countered softly. "That's the reason for our summit this weekend. Technically, we can make our move on Monday. And it would be dangerous to delay much longer, since suspicion is obviously growing. But I'm not comfortable with the anticipated civilian casualty projections, and neither is Chen." Turning away from Ortega, he explained to Miranda, "Originally, we projected a ceiling of ten thousand. Now Gresley tells us it will be ten times that. I have insisted that that number is unacceptable, and Victor Chen agrees. But Gresley and Tork disagree. Gresley, because he is uncaring. Tork—well, he's brutal by necessity. It's the reason he was chosen to head our paramilitary effort, but still, there must be a limit."

"Monday?" Miranda murmured.

Kell shrugged. "That's up to the Brigadier. It's the reason I insisted on a face-to-face meeting with him. This issue—civilian casualties—is critical. If something can't be done—if Ortega doesn't stand with Chen and me and demand that the effort be delayed until we can insure a lower figure—I will withdraw. I believe Chen will also. And without my drug, and Chen's communication network, the Brigade will have much less chance of success."

Almost speechless, Miranda looked to Ortega, and was again impressed by his ability to seem unsurprised, and also unconcerned.

His tone was firm yet had an inspirational ring to it befitting a true Brigadier. "We've come this far. I'm confident we'll reach a compromise this weekend that will satisfy everyone. But Jonathan, my old friend, you'll need to be reasonable. As will Gresley. I agree, one hundred thousand is too high. But ten thousand was unrealistic from the start."

Kell nodded. "I understand. As long as *you* understand I have my limit. This isn't just a power grab for me, and I hope not for you, either. It has a moral component. One that I'm proud of. One that I will insist we respect."

Ortega arched an eyebrow in Miranda's direction. "Obviously, our host and I need to talk. We don't want to bore you with meaningless details, so why don't you go up to bed. I'll join you in an hour or so."

"But—"

"Miranda? I don't want to argue."

"Do what he says," Kell warned, adding with a wistful smile, "you need a full night's sleep. It will lessen the hangover from the power pill."

She sighed. "Promise me you two won't argue? If it's true—if you're this close to succeeding—you shouldn't let anything come between you now."

"We won't," Kell promised. "But this discussion is long overdue. I agree with the Brigadier. It needs to take place in private."

"Good night, then." She leaned over and kissed Kell's cheek.

Then she stood and stepped over to where Ortega was sitting, but he waved her away, then began talking to Kell again as though she had already left the room.

Nice touch, she drawled silently. As much as she resented being sent away, and as anxious as she was to hear more details, she knew Ortega's behavior was reinforcing Kell's belief that Ortega was the Brigadier— a strong, maybe even omnipotent, leader.

As long as he doesn't overdo it, she decided, remembering how rough he had been on Kell when he first strode into the drawing room. It had been effective, but still difficult to watch. Would he browbeat the poor phobic again now? Or worse, get so impatient, he dropped the charade and interrogated him the way a former black ops specialist was trained to do?

Despite Kell's willingness to sacrifice thousands of civilians, Miranda still felt affection for him, which she chalked up to maternal instinct. He was like a child—

self-centered because he was so vulnerable, so weak—not because he was evil. If only he had been allowed to develop into a full-fledged adult, without the debilitating phobias, she was sure he wouldn't have gone along with the idea of civilian casualties at all.

Still, there was no question that they had to get the information they needed at almost any cost, even Kell's sanity, if necessary. If even one of the Brigade's bombs went off, the world would be plunged into chaos. Miranda didn't really believe the group had the global clout Kell thought they had, but if *they* thought they had it, and if their crazy faith in the Brigadier gave them the confidence to try anything—an assassination, interference with communication, or deployment of Kell's creepy Liquid Fear—

Yes, Ortega would be right to use any tactic at his disposal. She just prayed for Kell's sake that he wouldn't go overboard. If he did, wasn't it her place to intervene?

She lingered in the back hall and listened as Ortega began to speak, and almost immediately, she relaxed. Far from browbeating Kell, he was praising him for his vision. For his concern over civilian casualties. For his brilliance in the research laboratory. He assured Kell that he was an important—perhaps the *most* important—member of the Brigade, then suggested that they go through their plan, step-by-step, so that Kell could voice any misgivings, however slight. Ortega was determined, he said, to address them to Kell's satisfaction.

He's so inspiring. He can charm anything out of anyone, anytime he wants to, she told herself wistfully. *He made you trust him. Practically made you fall in love with him that night. Now he's going to get Kell to tell him every single detail of the Brigade's agenda, just like that.*

She didn't need to worry about Kell anymore. And now that the power pill had worn off completely, she had to admit she needed to get to bed. She'd be asleep before her head hit the pillow, which would help avoid the awkward moments that would have arisen if she and Ortega had hit the sack at the same time.

Especially with the way he's power-tripping, she thought with a rueful laugh. Then she sighed. Wasn't that exactly what he had been trying to avoid? The very reason he had sequestered himself in the mountains?

But his country needed him for one last op. In fact, the whole world was relying on him to play this part well.

She wondered if he would wake her up and give her an update when he finally came to bed. That would make sense strategically. He would want to get this vital information about the Brigade to the authorities as soon as possible. Perhaps he'd even want to leave in the middle of the night. But at least he'd want Miranda fully briefed so she'd be ready to leave at first light.

And when he woke her up, he'd still be heady with power from playing the Brigadier so masterfully. The bronze lights in his eyes would be flashing out of control. And Miranda would be warm, and sleepy, and eager to learn from him.

She winced, admitting that the power drug hadn't completely left her system after all. She was still fantasizing about Ortega, but it was harmless, and would pass without further incident.

But just to be on the safe side, she exchanged her silk pj's for a warm-up suit before doing an abbreviated version of her breathing exercises, then collapsing gratefully into bed.

Chapter 11

Miranda woke up to a throbbing pain that began at the top of her head and reverberated through every inch of her skull. And even though she suspected it was morning in the world outside her head, the thought of opening her eyes and allowing sunlight to invade them was more than she could bear, so she settled for stretching her hand out to the left, to see if Ortega was there.

When her fingers encountered a familiar wall of chest, she smiled through her misery. Apparently he was a gentleman, or at least enough of one to read the signal sent by her head-to-toe fleece clothing. Lucky for him, because if he had woken her in her present condition, she probably would have clobbered him, even if his only motive had been to brief her.

Briefing would hurt. She was almost sure of that. Her only hope was to keep her mind and stomach empty, and out of direct light, until these pesky waves of nausea subsided.

Sliding to the edge of the bed, she sat up, then buried her face in her hands, pressing on her eye sockets in hopes of numbing them.

"Hey," Ortega murmured. "How bad is it?"

"Too soon to tell."

"Jonathan predicted blinding spasms. He had some codeine stashed away. It's there on your nightstand. Next to the bottle of water."

"Thanks," Miranda said. "But I'm never putting a pill in my mouth again. Go back to sleep. My plan is to puke and die. I'll try not to make much noise."

His chuckle rumbled reassuringly through the air. "Don't be a hero. Take the codeine. Then come back to bed."

She struggled to her feet. "My sinuses are imploding. I need a shower. And absolute silence. If I live, I'll let you know."

She stumbled to the bathroom, stripping off her jogging suit and underwear along the way without worrying about the effect on Ortega. If she looked half as bad as she felt, his penis was shrinking in horror. And if by some chance he found pain arousing, he could be her guest. Nothing that happened to her from the neck down mattered at this point. She just needed to make her head stop doing this crazy rumba.

Cranking up the hot water, she waited until steam filled the room, then stepped into the shower, which she remembered from the previous morning, when she had been able to appreciate it, had a rich blend of terra cotta tile and delft-blue glass that lined the walls. Breathtaking. Unfortunately, to see it, she'd have to open her eyes beyond tentative slits, and she still wasn't ready for that.

"Hey," said Ortega softly from behind her.

She would have laughed out loud if she didn't know the vibrations would kill her. "You've *got* to be kidding. Go away."

"Come on, crazywoman. I've got the codeine. Take it. You'll feel better."

She sighed as he turned her around and pulled her against himself with one arm while pressing the tablet to her lips. His naked body felt pretty good, and she was about to congratulate him again on the excellent job he had done, converting a naturally great physique into a true work of art.

Then he ruined the mood by insisting, "Consider it an order, Cutler. Take the pill."

"Well, if you put it that way…." She pulled the pill into her mouth with her tongue, then spat it onto the floor of the shower, hoping she had fouled his bare feet.

"Damn!" He laughed with clear frustration. "You're nuts, do you know that? I'm trying to take care of you. As the senior agent on this stupid mission—"

"Since when? You resigned, remember? I'm the only agent on this mission at the moment."

"Don't kid yourself. Your pretty ass *must* have been canned by now." He pressed his lips to her ear. "Take the pill. I need you healthy."

"No more drugs," she told him. "The steam helps. Really. And so will the breathing exercises. I'll always be grateful to you for teaching me those, Ortega. They've changed my life."

"Come here." He cradled her with one arm, while

briskly massaging the top of her head with the fingers of his other, sending therapeutic waves through her skull.

"That feels so-oo good," she admitted. Then she grimaced as his less lofty, more carnal interest manifested itself against her with rock-hard insistence.

"Ignore him," Ortega muttered. "He still thinks he's the Brigadier."

She laughed out loud, then paid for it immediately with a stab behind her eyes. "Don't make jokes," she pleaded, leaning her face against his chest. "Just tell me the plan."

He massaged her head again. "It's all set. I told Jonathan I wanted to take you to Geneva. To seduce you into permanent submission with a night of clubbing, drinking and sex. I said we'd be back in time to meet with the others. As soon as we get away from this hell-hole we'll contact SPIN, and they can set up a meet with international authorities in Geneva, who can take it from there."

"We're leaving Jonathan behind?"

"I like the guy, too, but he's part of this conspiracy."

"He can't survive prison. He can't even survive normal life! And what if something goes wrong? If the Brigade finds out he gave us all this intel, they'll skin him alive." She pulled away and opened her eyes fully for the first time, just to fix her stare on Ortega. "Can't we bring him with us?"

"The guy was willing to murder ten thousand civilians to advance his cause," he reminded her. But when she just continued to glare, he scowled and nodded. "Yeah, okay. But we need to move quickly. Some of the stuff Jonathan told me is shocking. We've got to get the details to SPIN right away. I went for a walk outside last night, trying to get reception on my satellite phone, but Jonathan's system jammed it. We can't take the chance of allowing this intel to die with us if something goes wrong."

She backed out of the shower and wrapped herself in an oversized towel. "Hurry up, then. The sooner we do the exercises, the sooner we can get out of here."

"Go ahead by yourself. I'll head downstairs and see what's going on."

Miranda frowned. "I thought you did the routine religiously every morning. Dawn, noon and dusk. Remember?"

"For balance," he agreed. "But balance isn't what I need at the moment. The edge works for me. Keeps me focused. Sharp."

"Did it ever occur to you that this is where you make your fatal mistake? Choosing the edge over your instincts when the rubber meets the road?" She located the metronome and wound it up, then set it on a bureau, comforted immediately by its steady beat. "Come on, Ortega," she called out over her shoulder. "Get with the program. But put some underwear on first. I'm not ready for X-rated breathing. There's only so much this head of mine can take before it officially explodes."

The routine helped, but there was still a dull ache, enough so that the simple act of pulling a red tube top over her head made her wince. If only she had brought something cozier to wear with her favorite faded jeans and new red sneakers, but she had packed to support her call-girl image. Appearing attractive for the opposite sex was the last thing on her mind right now as she used all her concentration to tie her shoelaces.

"You were right, you know," Ortega told her.

She turned toward his voice, then smiled to see that he had dressed in jeans and tennis shoes, too—black ones, accompanied by a black V-necked T-shirt. "Right about what?"

"The exercises helped. Balance is always the answer, right?"

She nodded.

"Then take the painkiller." He held the container from her nightstand toward her.

"Codeine makes me sleepy," she told him with a sigh. "Bring it to Geneva, and you have my word. As soon as we're out of danger, I'll take the whole bottle."

He laughed and poured a pill into his palm, then broke it into halves. "How about a compromise?"

She knew he was right. She had to clear her head or she'd be no use to him, so she accepted the partial pill, washing it down with alpine spring water.

Then she continued to get ready, locating a rubber band in her suitcase and twisting her hair into a loose braid down her back and securing it. She wasn't about to blow it dry, or to put on makeup. Men were going to have to love her for her personality today. If not, she'd strangle them.

Another wave of nausea washed over her, and she cursed herself for ever having touched Kell's power pill. The euphoria and confidence, while nice, weren't worth the price.

Maybe not for you, she scolded herself. *But for men like Jonathan, who are scared of everything, it's a dream come true. Who knows what therapeutic uses it might have for fearful, timid people all over the world. Remember Angelina Carerra? A victim transformed into a powerful, confident female? Something did that for her. Education, or love, or drugs. Something. And it changed her life.*

She turned to Ortega. "Can I ask you something?"

"Sure. Anything."

"It's about Angelina Carerra."

Ortega winced. "That happened years ago. Long before I met you."

Miranda laughed, then paid for it with a stab to her sinuses. "I'm serious, Ortega. She was timid, right? Downtrodden?"

"Yeah. What about it?"

"I met her last week. She was confident. Radiant. In command. Men were jumping to obey her, and not out of lust. Out of fear and respect."

"Impossible." He cleared his throat, then admitted, "Radiant? Sure. She's a good-looking woman. And it's not all sex appeal. She's sweet. But no one fears her."

"It's been ten years."

"Doesn't matter. Unless she's had a complete personality transplant—"

"Or unless she was on drugs?"

He cocked his head to the side. "You said she seemed powerful, not high."

"Right." Miranda shrugged her shoulders. "I know it sounds crazy, but I also know how it feels to be on Jonathan's power drug. That feeling of invincibility. I swear, Ortega, Angelina had it. So I'm asking you, is there any way she could be the Brigadier?"

He barked in disbelief. *"Her?"*

"Okay, okay. Maybe she hooked up with someone after you killed Benito. Another powerful man. She told him about Jonathan's research. And about his political theories. The new boyfriend was so impressed, *he* set up the Brigade. Isn't *that* possible?"

Encouraged by the pensive expression on Ortega's face, she continued eagerly. "Jonathan told me he talked a lot about his theory while he was in that cage with you. He probably talked about it while they were torturing him, too. All of that information was available to Angelina, right?"

Ortega looked at her for a moment, his eyes narrowed, then he spoke carefully. "Something happened five years ago."

Miranda waited.

"I was just setting up SPIN. My operative days were behind me. But an old buddy sent me a copy of a report, just because he knew I'd want to see it. It registered, but seemed so nuts—and so completely unsubstantiated— I didn't pay much attention to it."

"What kind of report?"

"They were interrogating a drug dealer who swore that Carerra—Benito, not Angelina—was still alive and running the cartel. Everyone assumed the prisoner was just saying that to save his own neck. The CIA did some follow-up, but no one really took it seriously because…" He took a deep breath, then reminded her, "Because I put an arrow through Benito Carerra's throat. Pinned him to a fucking tree. You don't survive something like that."

Miranda walked over to him and looked deep into his eyes. "Did you check for a pulse?"

"A *pulse?*"

"Ow. Stop yelling."

"Sorry." He flashed an apologetic smile. "Carerra's men were everywhere. I needed to get Kell to safety. And it didn't matter—I didn't need to check for a fucking pulse—because the son of a bitch was pinned by his throat to a tree."

"Sure seems like he should have been dead," she agreed.

"Yeah. But you're saying Angelina somehow got her hands on Kell's power drug? Which means, Benito Carerra's alive? And he's the Brigadier? That's what you're saying?"

"No way. I never said that. I never even thought it." She gave him a weary smile and explained, as gently as she could, given her raging headache, "I think *you're* the one who's saying that."

She could see he needed a minute, so she flopped onto the bed and buried her face in a fluffy pillow, enjoying the fantasy that she might just go to sleep, and *stay* asleep, until the pain had subsided. But Ortega's theory had crept into her brain, and she found herself reviewing her conversation with Angelina.

Hadn't Miranda, a.k.a. Jennifer, said something like: *Ortega had his nerve saving you from your own husband?*

And hadn't Angelina said: *Ortega was so busy playing hero, he never once considered what would happen to me if Benito didn't die—if Benito found out I was unfaithful to him with Ortega, but Ortega was long gone, and I was left with that madman and his ruthless temper?*

Miranda was almost sure it had gone something like that. Of course, her brain was full of fuzz, so she knew she might just be making things up. Still…

"He's alive," she murmured finally, lifting her face from its cocoon to connect with Ortega.

"Yeah." He nodded. "Maybe so. He had the money. The information. The anti-American sentiment and megalomaniacal tendencies, not to mention, total confidence in Kell. He really thought the guy was another Einstein. Maybe so, Miranda. And if so..."

She waited again.

Then Ortega looked directly in her eyes, and to her surprise, he seemed almost jubilant. "If it's true, we've got it made."

Miranda sat at the breakfast table and listened to Ortega and Kell exchange tips about their reclusive lifestyles, and stories about "the old days," as though they were at a cocktail party. Meanwhile, her head, while improving thanks to the codeine, was still swimming, mostly because her thoughts themselves were a jumble.

Just play along with me, Ortega had instructed her. *We're gonna turn Kell. He'd never be a part of anything headed by the monster who tortured him. So all we have to do is present our theory about Carerra to him in a way that doesn't give him a goddammed heart attack.*

Relegated to the sidelines, she decided to use this opportunity to study Ortega's technique so that she could use it herself in future ops. There was a definite rhythm to his style of conversation. First he flattered Kell with outright compliments, then more subtly, by showing him he trusted him with secrets. Valued him as a sounding board. Then he raised the stakes by talking about their imprisonment and torture, reminding Kell of the reasons Ortega had been sent to assassinate Carerra in the first place—the drug dealer had been a true monster in virtually every sense, a danger to everyone around him. And as his sphere of dominance had widened from family to business associates to an entire region, the number of lives he ruined had grown exponentially.

Kell's voice was rich with fear and contempt as he confirmed the stories, explaining to Miranda that words like "cruel" and "ruthless" were inadequate to describe Carerra's depravity. It would have been bad enough if the man had simply been powerful and cunning, but he had been like an evil sponge, soaking up information from every source imaginable, then perverting it to his own uses.

Just as Kell's anxiety began to soar, Ortega artfully changed the subject, describing his Sierra sanctuary in great detail, a tactic that seemed to lull their host back to a feeling of safety. Then he complimented Kell's fortress, Kell's work, Kell's commitment to the future. And the cycle began again, always leading to Carerra, then retreating when Kell became too upset.

Miranda found herself realizing that of all Ortega's talents, patience was probably the most amazing. He was investing hours in this, confident that if he prepared Kell properly, he could get him to turn against the Brigade and cooperate with the CIA despite the scientist's strong hatred for his country and his commitment to the new political order he had helped to define. It was fascinating, especially given the fact that if Ortega failed, he had wasted valuable time that could have been spent getting away from the fortress and contacting the authorities, then rendezvousing with them in Geneva for an intelligence summit.

Finally, just before lunchtime, the moment of truth arrived. Ortega sent Miranda a warning glance, then said to Kell, "There's something we need to discuss, Jonathan. It's important. And I need you to hear me out before you react. Can you do that for me?"

Kell's eyelid began to twitch a little, but otherwise,

his trust in Ortega—the Brigadier—sustained him, and he nodded. "I'll do my best."

Miranda's heart sank. He was so vulnerable, and his world was about to come crashing down around his shoulders. He would have nothing left—not the Brigade, but also not his hero worship of Ortega, or his crush on Miranda. They had lied to him. Used him. He would never again be able to trust a human being. Even his life's work on phobias would be too tainted to offer him respite. That work had saved him after his ordeal in the jungle. Had given him a reason to live. Now his research would be as dead to him as everything else.

"Wait!" She held up her hand, suddenly inspired.

Ortega seemed too surprised to be annoyed, and settled for murmuring, "Is your headache worse?"

"It's gone. I can tell, because I just had a great idea." She gave him a hopeful smile. "Okay?"

He locked gazes with her, and was apparently satisfied with what he saw, because he nodded. "It's your show. Go ahead."

She stood, announcing, "I need to get something out of my suitcase. I'll meet you two in the lab, okay?"

"What's this about?" Kell asked her, more with curiosity than suspicion.

"You'll see," she told him. Then she gave him a quick hug and said, "I think you'll like it. I hope so."

She would have hugged Ortega, too, if it didn't seem so silly, so she settled for giving him another smile. Then she sprinted out of the drawing room and up the stairs, laughing as she heard the men discussing her with words that sounded a lot like "crazy" and "humor her."

The vial of Night Arrow was just where she had hidden it—inside an otherwise empty shampoo bottle, undetected by the search Kell's guards had conducted. She had regretted not being able to use it, but once she had decided to masquerade as Jennifer Aguilar, call girl, rather than Jennifer Aguilar, industrial spy, there had been no way to show it to Kell without totally confusing things.

But as Miranda Cutler, CIA operative, she could offer it up, both as a lead-in to Ortega's horrifying revelation about Carerra, and as a consolation prize—a new project for Kell to explore after the Brigade fantasy was ripped from him.

Hurrying back downstairs, she found the men waiting for her in the lab as directed. Kell's expression showed anticipation, while Ortega was looking a little annoyed around the edges. She gave him a quick, confident wink, then placed the vial on the stainless steel workbench at which they were seated. "There," she announced mischievously. "Three guesses what that is."

Kell picked up the vial and examined it. "Is it safe to open? Remember my allergies."

"Come on, Jonathan." She rolled her eyes for emphasis. "Live a little."

He frowned, but twisted the cap, then carefully sniffed the vial's contents. "Some sort of resin?"

"Be more specific."

"Miranda," Ortega said with a growl. "What's going on?"

"Let Jonathan guess. I'll give you a hint," she added, her voice softening as she smiled at the scientist. "I got it in South America. Last week. When I went to Bio-GeniSystems to sneak a peek at your old personnel files."

"What?"

Ortega leaned back and folded his arms across his

chest, finally seeing where she was going, although she imagined he still didn't quite understand where the vial fit in. But at least she could see he approved of the way she was handling this, breaking it to Kell so gently.

She took a deep breath, then explained. "Like Ortega said, I wanted to move my career out of the sex kitten business and into something a little more valuable. The CIA sent me to his cabin for information about you, and when he didn't tell me anything we didn't already know, I decided to do some more snooping on my own. Your old files seemed like a good place to start. With my training, breaking into a drug company wasn't much of a challenge. I got what I needed, but decided to poke around a little more. That's when I found this."

Kell sniffed the vial again. "What is it? A new drug?"

"Not a drug. A weapon."

"Huh?"

"They call it HeetSeek. But you and I call it Night Arrow."

Kell stared at her in disbelief, while Ortega muttered, "What the hell...?"

"I know," she said, pleased with their reactions. "Isn't it amazing? I was interrupted before I could steal their research, but at least I got this sample. You can analyze it, right, Jonathan? Duplicate it, test it, improve on it. At least we finally know it exists."

"Night Arrow? Those bastards actually *were* developing it? Do you have any idea...?" Kell shook his head in disgust. "They almost got me killed, withholding this from me."

"No, no, Jonathan. I don't think they were researching it back then. According to the files I saw, the experiments have only been running over the last five years or so. They probably did the same thing you did, looked into it *after* Carerra raised the issue during your, well, your ordeal."

Ortega cleared his throat. "Speaking of your ordeal—"

"Wait!" Miranda smiled to downplay the interruption. "My point is, Jonathan, that you can use this sample to re-invigorate your own research. BioGeniSystems got some interesting results. Inconclusive, but still interesting."

"It isn't even red," Kell observed, shrugging. "Probably a dead end."

"They locked it in a safe. Doesn't that mean they thought they were on to something?"

"Miranda?" Ortega eyed her sternly. "You said you were interrupted before you could steal the research. Tell Jonathan who interrupted you."

She sighed, knowing he was correct. It was time to break the news, so she walked around the table and took Kell's hand. "It was Angelina Carerra and a bunch of armed guards. And a doctor of some sort."

Kell gave her a blank stare. "Carerra's widow? What was *she* doing there?"

"That's a good question. I assumed they were doing some sort of research for her. Maybe about cocaine purity or whatever. But now that I've talked to Ortega, I don't think that was it." She squeezed Kell's hand. "Angelina was so confident. So in control. Like she thought she was invincible."

"Invincible? Her? People always said she was timid."

"I think maybe she is. I think maybe that night, she was testing out your power pill."

Kell licked his lips, visibly confused. "How would she get her hands on it? Only one sample ever left my control. The one I gave Ortega."

"No," Ortega told him quietly. "The one you gave the Brigadier."

Kell frowned, still confused, and Miranda was about to offer further explanation, but Ortega held up his hand, silencing her. And because she trusted his instincts on such things, she decided to wait. And watch. And hope their sensitive friend was going to work this through on his own without getting too upset.

"I don't understand," Kell said finally.

"I think you do," Ortega told him. "Deep inside, you know I'm not the Brigadier. Isn't that so?"

Kell stared.

"It was the only way I could get in here. To rescue Miranda, who clearly didn't need rescuing. It was an act, Jonathan. I apologize, but at the time, I thought it was necessary."

"He did it for me," Miranda agreed. "And then I convinced him we should stay."

"To get information from me?" Kell whispered. "To bring down the Brigade? And I was so *stupid*. I *trusted* you. Now I'm a dead man. The real Brigadier will kill me for betraying him."

"The real Brigadier." Ortega nodded. "The one who used the sample on his own wife, transforming her from a battered woman to a confident, independent female for a few hours."

Kell's hand went to his throat, and Miranda knew he thought it was closing up. And maybe it was! She had felt that way for a few seconds on the airplane, and she didn't scare easily. For Kell, this nightmare had to be unbearable.

"Jonathan—"

"Don't!" He pushed her away, then took a few steps

backward. "You lied to me. You were never my friend. Don't touch me! Get out of my house!"

"Jonathan," Ortega told him. "You need to breathe."

"Shut up! I don't take orders from you! You're not the fucking Brigadier, remember?" He gasped for air, but managed to insist, "And neither is Benito Carerra. You *killed* him, Ortega. I *saw* you. We left his dead carcass nailed to a tree in the jungle like the animal he was."

"Actually, my old friend," said a voice from the narrow doorway that led to the back hallway. "That's not entirely accurate."

Chapter 12

As a dozen guards poured into the room from doorways at either end, the distinctive sounds of semiautomatic rifles being readied for firing filled the air. Hammers being cocked, bolts being slid, cartridges being fed into chambers—metal slamming metal—all executed with absolute precision.

There was no point in contesting them. Not yet at least. So Miranda and Ortega raised their hands without protest, allowing the guards to step forward, cuff their wrists behind them, and then pull Ortega's pistol from his holster, before stepping back so that Benito Carerra's view of his prisoners was once again unobstructed.

As for Kell, it clearly didn't matter to him if there was one guard or a thousand. He leaned against a work table, the blood draining from his complexion as though life itself were leaving his body, and stared into the hypnotic eyes of the man who had kept him in a cage and tortured him mercilessly.

Miranda could only imagine what was going on in her lonely friend's fear-wracked brain, so she tried to reassure him by whispering, "It's going to be okay, Jonathan. You're on *his* side this time, remember? Go and stand with your friends."

"Your pretty visitor is correct, Jonathan," Carerra told him. "It's time to choose sides. I suggest you choose wisely, as Carl here did when he alerted me to the CIA's presence."

Tears streamed down Kell's face as he edged past his tormentor then sunk to the ground in the corner where Miranda and Ortega had found him the previous evening. Except this time, he didn't have a power pill in front of him. And he was shaking so violently, he probably couldn't have steadied his hand enough to take one even if it were available.

There was nothing Miranda could do for him, so she turned her full attention to Carerra, trying to make eye contact without seeming to either challenge or submit.

He looked right past her, as though smiling at someone else. "You were right, Alexander. She's very attractive."

Alexander?

Miranda felt a wave of dread similar to what she assumed Kell was experiencing. Still, she didn't want her captors to know what was going on in her mind, so she calmly turned in time to see Gresley enter the laboratory from the other door, along with two other men she recognized from the Brigade files: Victor Chen, a middle-aged, serious-looking fellow who was tall and slender; and the giant Tork, whose brawny build and scarred face confirmed his reputation as a street fighter turned paramilitary leader.

Gresley walked up to her and without missing a beat, slammed his fist into her gut so hard, she doubled over and almost vomited.

"Bastard!" Ortega sprang forward and head-butted Gresley before four guards intervened, wrestling him to the ground. Miranda sent her sometimes-lover a grateful smile, then looked up at Gresley, noticing with satisfaction that Ortega had caused a gash in the bully's forehead almost as pleasing as the greenish bruise that ran along the side of his jaw, courtesy of Miranda's blow three days earlier.

"Stand her up again!" Gresley directed the guards with a roar.

Victor Chen surprised Miranda by stepping between her and her assailant. "They're no use to us unconscious. The Brigadier wants to question them, remember?"

"At least don't hit her in the mouth," Tork agreed cheerfully.

"I have other plans for her mouth that have nothing to do with questioning," Gresley assured him, causing the giant man to burst into laughter.

As alarmed as she was by the Englishman, the giant Tork concerned her more. If *he* had been the one to hit her with that huge fist of his, powered by those Atlas-like shoulders, she wouldn't just be gasping for air. She'd be dead.

Carerra waved his hand, and the guards stood her on her feet, then did the same with Ortega, with two of them keeping a grip on him just in case he decided to go berserk again.

Then the Brigadier stood in front of her and asked, "Do you know who I am?"

She nodded.

"So the question is, who are you? Jennifer Aguilar? Miranda Duncan? Jennifer Duncan?"

"I'm Miranda Cutler. I work for the CIA, but they didn't send me on this op. They don't even know I'm here." She licked her lips, then admitted, "They use me exclusively for seduction ops. It's a waste of my talents and training. So when I heard about the Brigade, I decided to try and impress my superiors by doing what everyone else had failed to do—learn your identity and agenda."

"Interesting." Carerra flashed Ortega a wide grin. "For a spy, she's quite chatty, don't you think?"

Ortega growled in agreement, but she suspected he knew exactly what she was doing.

She was protecting Kell, pure and simple. If she didn't tell them what they wanted to hear, they'd question the scientist, and it would destroy him. Even if they didn't raise a hand to him, the flashbacks from being questioned by this monster again would scare him to death.

So Miranda would cooperate, hopefully not sharing anything with Carerra he hadn't already figured out from talking to Angelina, Gresley and that sniveling little Carl. It wasn't as if she knew much, anyway, since Ortega had sent her to bed before the real intel began to flow.

She hoped this maneuver would buy them some time, despite the slim hope of rescue. But Victor Chen had shown a tendency to be reasonable, and he might object to the hasty killing of two American agents. She also wanted to minimize Carerra's excuse to brutalize them. Assuming a chance for escape would eventually present itself, they needed to be conscious and able to take a few steps without screaming in pain.

So she asked him softly, "Do you want to hear more?"

"Absolutely. Go on."

"Okay." She took a deep breath, then continued spilling her guts. "I went to South America to get some information about Jonathan Kell. So that I could seduce him. I figured there would be psych profiles and personnel reports in his employment file at BioGeniSystems, and I was right. I photographed the file, using a camera hidden in a barrette. I also stole a sample of HeetSeek, but your wife interrupted me before I could photograph those files, too. She was there getting her blood tested by that doctor, right? Because she had just taken the power pill? I didn't figure that out until this morning."

Carerra laughed again, and again Ortega appeared to be disgusted by her willingness to confess before any real torture had been applied.

Or at least, she *hoped* he was pretending to be disgusted.

"After that," she continued, "I went to London to seduce Gresley. And then I came here. I was making progress, then suddenly Ortega showed up to quote-unquote rescue me. He posed as the Brigadier."

Carerra glared toward Kell's quivering form. "Sniveling idiot. You almost ruined everything, falling for that."

"Don't blame Jonathan," Miranda interrupted. "Your buddy Gresley had already given me the information I needed about the Brigade. I only came here to get a sample of the drug."

"I beg your pardon?"

"She's lying!" Gresley shouted.

The Brigadier silenced him with a wave of his hand, then asked Miranda to continue.

"Gresley had a briefcase at his town house that was filled with information about the Brigade. If you don't believe me, check my barrette. I photographed the whole thing. It's in the front zippered pocket of my overnight case."

Carerra inclined his head toward Carl, who disappeared into the hall.

Gresley was trembling with anger. "That file didn't have specifics, Carerra. I swear that. Just philosophy—"

"Shut up, imbecile." To Miranda, he said simply, "Anything else?"

"I think that's about it. Unless you have any questions."

"I have two. The first is, have you communicated any of this to your government?"

She smiled, glad to have a chance to send a compliment in Chen's direction, just as she had been delighted to get Gresley into trouble. "Jonathan's system is too tight. We couldn't get a message out. Our plan was to call the CIA as soon as we got off these grounds, then rendezvous with international authorities in Geneva."

"Shit," Ortega muttered. "Why don't you just draw him a fucking map?"

"If I could, I would," she assured him. Then she reminded Carerra, "You said you had two questions?"

"Yes, thank you. I—" He stopped when Carl returned with the barrette in his hand. Examining it quickly, he said, "I see the camera. Very clever. Angelina, do you recognize this?"

To Miranda's shock, Angelina Carerra stepped out of the hallway and into view for the first time, her movements tentative and unassuming. Accepting the accessory from her husband, she nodded. "It's true, Benito. She was wearing this at BGS."

"Hey." Miranda gave the woman a hesitant smile, uncertain of the reception she would receive. In South America, they had been kindred spirits. But this Angelina was nothing like that one. If Miranda had seen her on the street, she would not have recognized her.

The wife's posture was submissive, almost to an extreme. There was none of the bravado that had made her so memorable during their last encounter. But this Angelina was special, too—quiet, lovely, graceful. She was visibly making an effort not to look at Ortega, as though the handsome agent might be able to seduce her again, right in front of her maniac husband. And she didn't seem all that wild about making eye contact with Miranda, either.

The thought that Angelina had gotten in trouble for letting Miranda escape in South America was a concern, but she decided she had enough to do just saving Kell and Ortega. She simply couldn't handle anyone else. So she settled for giving the wife a smile and saying, "Nice to see you again."

Angelina grimaced. "I do not know what to think of you. You lied to me. Especially about *him*," she added, gesturing unhappily in Ortega's direction.

"I lied about a lot of things. But not about him. He really did screw me over." Miranda paused while Carerra and Tork laughed. Then she insisted, "I just wanted to get out of there without being arrested. It never occurred to me that you were part of this."

The Brigadier stepped up to Ortega. "I'm curious. What is this Miranda woman to you?"

"At the moment, a pain in the ass," he muttered. Then

he added firmly, "She's just a rookie, Carerra. Let her go. I'm the guy who shot you in the neck. Not Miranda. And not Kell, either. Jonathan's been religiously loyal to your fucking Brigade."

"Enough." Carerra turned to Carl. "Is there a dungeon on these premises?"

The guard nodded. "In the basement."

"Transfer the prisoners. We will continue the interrogation down there."

"Why?" Miranda demanded. "I've told you everything you need to know."

Carerra flashed a wide grin. "Haven't you heard? There are many reasons to torture a person. To get information, certainly. But it is also underrated as a sport. Just ask Jonathan. And speaking of simpering traitors—" He touched Carl's shoulder and suggested coldly, "Take Kell to the dungeon as well."

"No!" Miranda's heart almost stopped. "He's been so loyal. And you need him to succeed with your plan."

"All I ever needed from him was the fear drug. Which reminds me. Tork? Find it. It has to be in this lab somewhere." A smile flitted across his lips. "I believe we have found the perfect subjects upon whom to test it."

Under the supervision of the hulking Tork, the guards forced Miranda and Ortega down a steep set of stairs that led to the dungeon, relying on the cuffs on their wrists and the weapons at their throats to control them. Meanwhile, Jonathan Kell, while unbound, was so miserably unnerved—so tormented by fears gone amuck— that he had to be flung over Carl's shoulder and carried.

Even in midafternoon the dungeon was dark, with its only illumination coming from the open door at the top of the stairwell and a narrow one-foot-long window near the ceiling that afforded a glimpse of the ground outside and not much more. Miranda knew that even if she stood on Ortega's shoulders to reach it, she couldn't possibly slip through, although she'd be more than willing to try, assuming the opportunity ever presented itself.

The stone walls were damp, a fact the prisoners learned firsthand when they were pinned against one so that their handcuffs could be replaced with manacles imbedded in the stone. Their wrists were fastened to the wall above their heads, while individual leg irons at the ends of short chains kept their ankles from moving more than a foot or so in any direction. Miranda's position was less than a yard from Ortega on one side, with Kell on the other side of her, but they might as well have been separated by miles for all the good they could do one another beyond moral support.

Carerra paced back and forth in front of them, enjoying his role as captor, regaling them with stories from his ten years of clandestine life. It had taken three of those years, along with four surgeries, he told them, before he had regained his voice. During that time, he had hidden himself away, running the business through Angelina with great success while also "elevating" himself into "enlightenment," as he called it, by immersing himself in great works of philosophy. He claimed that Kell's political ramblings about small, mobile powerhouses with no geographic limits had inspired him, and eventually, he had decided to assemble a team to mount a global coup.

He had needed Kell on that team, he admitted without hesitation, not so much for refinement of the concept, since Carerra had already honed it to perfection, but for the antiphobia drug he was sure the scientist had discovered in the time since his captivity. Proceeding through a complicated web of intermediaries, he had finally made contact with his old victim, and the Brigade had been formed. The other elements of the plan—finance, military, and communications—had fallen into place thereafter with such ease, Carerra considered it a sign from heaven that he was destined to be the father of this new political institution.

Originally he had kept his identity a secret for practical purposes, certain that Kell would never knowingly work for him. But the mystique had done wonders for the group dynamic in other ways, and had distracted and confounded the intelligence community when they had finally become aware that something new was in the air.

"The only small disappointment," Carerra admitted, "was Jonathan's antifear drug. I had hoped it would usher in a new era of combat, arming the Brigade with superhuman forces. But his power drug worked best on phobics, not soldiers. There was a silver lining, however. One of the early formulae backfired, intensifying rather than alleviating fear. When I heard about that, I knew we had found our new era of combat, not by strengthening Brigade forces, but by weakening our enemy."

Miranda winced. She had been studying Carerra closely, reluctantly fascinated by his egomaniacal ramblings. But this new mention of the fear drug reminded her that their ordeal had only just begun. Carerra planned to administer it to them, and then to torture them, knowing that their reactions would be intensified by the drug.

For Kell, the man of many fears, it would be unbearable. For Miranda, perhaps it would be survivable. After all, she didn't have that many actual phobias. Kell had identified most of them, with closed-in spaces and the corresponding lack of perceptible air being the only one that was abnormally intense. The others—the dark, bugs, snakes, rodents—would be manageable, given the fact that the dungeon, like the rest of Kell's home, was relatively spotless.

There were certainly no snakes, although theoretically some could slither in through the window. The walls were old enough to hide holes that rodents could inhabit, but without a source of food, she imagined they had long since abandoned those old nests. She also hadn't spotted a single spider or web, or any other bug for that matter, during her entire stay at the fortress.

That left claustrophobia, accentuated by the relative darkness. That would definitely freak her out, so she started reassuring herself now that the window, while little, had no glass in it, but rather just a simple screen that would let plenty of air into the dungeon, even if the Brigadier closed the stairwell door. And it would give them light for a few more hours at least. After that, if Carerra wanted to continue torturing them, he'd have to bring in some artificial light for his own uses, so darkness wouldn't present an overwhelming issue.

She had no clue what kind of phobias Ortega might have, although his success in black ops suggested he had few, if any. He had survived Carerra's torture before, which was a good sign. Of course, Kell had survived, too, so perhaps Carerra's tactics included pushing his victims up to, but not over, the edge.

She certainly hoped so for all their sakes.

"Tell your friends here about the effects of the Liquid Fear," Carerra suggested, moving to stand directly in front of Kell. "It is your most brilliant discovery. And your last. Take a few moments to brag about it."

Kell looked at him through eyes red from sobbing, and just shook his head, clearly exhausted.

Carerra laughed. "We haven't even begun yet, and already you're defeated? Do I frighten you that much, old friend?"

Kell nodded.

"So many memories." Carerra pulled out a gold-cased lighter and flipped it open, then took a slim cigar from his vest pocket and lit it. Blowing on the tip until it glowed red, he asked Kell playfully, "Remember this?"

The scientist whimpered and drew back against the stone wall.

"Leave him alone!" Miranda shouted.

Carerra turned to her, his expression twisted. "You're giving me orders? That's not too intelligent, is it?"

"Intelligent?" She glared. "You spend an hour telling us how hard you studied and how much you quote-unquote elevated yourself? Then you turn around and pick on someone defenseless? I don't think you really grasp the whole enlightenment concept, Carerra. Enlightened men aren't bullies."

"Miranda, shut up," Ortega whispered.

Carerra walked over to her and said with a sneer, "Enlightened men are scientists. They conduct experiments. That's the only reason you're still alive, Miss Cutler. So that I can test Jonathan's miracle drug on you and your friends. You'll be a *particularly* interesting subject for us, isn't that true, Gresley?"

"I am quite looking forward to it," the Englishman agreed.

"Let's get started then, shall we?" Carerra motioned

to Carl, who had been standing nearby with a tray containing three cups. Setting his cigar down, he picked up one cup. "Is the dosage correct?"

"I don't know, sir," Carl told him. "Kell never let anyone in the lab when he was working."

"Too much will k-kill us instantly," Kell insisted.

"We'll start with you first then, since you're the least entertaining." Carerra strode over to him and put a cup to his lips. "Drink!"

Kell gulped it down without protest, and Miranda wondered if that meant he could see the dosage was safe, or knew it was lethal and welcomed the prospect of death compared to torture.

She exchanged looks with Ortega, and she knew he was thinking the same thing she was—that perhaps a quick death for Kell was the most they could wish for their friend.

Then the scientist started screaming, his high-pitched shrieks filling the air, his words incomprehensible.

"Jonathan!" she called to him unhappily.

"Kell!" Ortega ordered. "*Breathe*, goddammit."

"It's filling my lungs!" the scientist wailed. "My throat's closing. The mold! It's everywhere. And the snakes—"

"There *aren't* any snakes!" Miranda told him. "Open your eyes, Jonathan. There aren't any snakes."

"Help me! Ortega, help me!"

His shrieks stopped abruptly as Carerra pulled out a pistol and cracked the hysterical man on the back of the head, rendering him unconscious. Then he calmly holstered the weapon and turned to Miranda. "Your turn."

Oh, God...

She tried for a defiant stare, but already she was

scared to death, mostly because Kell's reaction had been so extreme, even for him. Enhance his phobias? It was more like the drug had fed actual images into his brain. Images of the things he feared most.

"What kind of drug *is* this?" she asked, speaking aloud, but not to anyone in particular.

"Don't you know?" Carerra grinned. "It accentuates your fears. Our friend Jonathan has so many, it didn't take long to drive him insane. I hope you give us a longer show."

"He *saw* snakes."

"Ah, yes." The megalomaniac paused for the desired effect. "The original formula had intriguing results—a quick burst of abject fear, followed by waves of phobia and paranoia. Just the thing to undermine enemy forces. But something was missing. Something concrete to be afraid of. So I asked Jonathan to add a mild hallucinogen to the drug, on the theory that a picture is worth a thousand words."

Miranda inhaled sharply, then began cataloguing the room.

No snakes, no rats, no bugs. No snakes, no rats, no bugs. Keep it together, Miranda. There's nothing scary here except this creep.

"Drink up now," Carerra murmured, holding a cup to her lips as though she were a fevered child and he a caring parent.

She clamped her lips together, determined to let as little of the green liquid into her system as possible.

Rather than force her mouth open, Carerra simply turned to a guard and said, "Shoot Ortega in the kneecap if she doesn't cooperate."

"No!" She opened her mouth and gulped down the entire dose, which seemed to be about a teaspoon full.

It had a sweet and sour taste to it, burning a little, but not altogether unpleasant. And to her relief, it didn't seem to have the instant effect it had had with Kell.

Carerra grinned. Then he stepped aside and motioned to Gresley. "Would you like to play with her now?"

Miranda's throat tightened at the thought of those disgusting hands on her, and she tried to squirm away despite the futility of it.

"Perhaps we should allow Carl to do the honors," Gresley murmured. "As a reward for alerting us before these two could do any damage."

"You're sure?"

"As Miss Cutler knows, I enjoy watching as well as participating. Carl? Is there anything you'd like to do to our little slut?"

The guard grinned, setting down the tray.

"Carerra!" Ortega's voice boomed. "You want to test your drug? Test it on *me*. You never broke me, remember? I know how that bugged you. But here's your chance. Let's see how creative you've gotten."

"An excellent reminder. You will enjoy her ordeal much more fully with the drug in your system." Carerra picked up the last cup and carried it to Ortega, adding over his shoulder, "The same insurance as before. If he struggles or resists, cripple Miss Cutler."

Miranda cringed, certain her kneecap was about to explode into bits. And the most hideous part was, she knew it wouldn't stop Carl. His face was already contorted by lust and depravity, as was Gresley's. Ortega's antics, while providing a momentary reprieve, were useless. Unspeakable acts were about to take place, probably by each of these monsters in turn, their hands and mouths defiling her with sickening, uninterrupted, unending thoroughness.

And she had only herself to blame. She had wanted this, hadn't she? She had been so stupidly, *stupidly* intent on being a spy. Her father had warned her, hadn't he? He had known from the start where this would lead. What they would want from her. The deviant uses they'd find for her.

Her chest was so tight, she imagined she was having a heart attack, then she realized that her heart wasn't the problem at all. It was her lungs! There was no air in this room! Her captors had used it all up with their lustful panting. And they hadn't even touched her yet!

"Miranda?" Ortega murmured. "Take a deep breath."

"With what? There's no air," she told him unhappily. "I think that's how we're going to die. I just hope it happens soon."

"Fascinating," Carerra said. "Ortega, are you feeling the effects yet?"

"Do you mean, am I afraid? Of *you?* Don't make me laugh. You're pathetic," he declared. "You and your friends claim to represent the future, but you only want to destroy everything you touch."

"He's right." Chen's voice from the background was soft but insistent. "This is getting out of hand. We need to prioritize. If you want to kill them, fine. Kill them. Then let's move on. We need to finalize our plans. Then we can call the plane, blow this place, and move on. Am I the only one who's still committed to our agenda?"

"I'm testing the drug," Carerra muttered.

"What more proof do you need? Look at the girl. She's disintegrating right before our eyes. Look at Kell, for God's sake. I don't even think he's still alive. And Ortega..." Chen walked right up to the ex-agent and said coolly, "He's starting to panic. I can see it in his eyes. The drug's a success, Carerra. Shoot them and move on."

Tears were streaming down Miranda's cheeks as she tried to focus on Chen's words. But all she could see was Carl, unbuckling his belt, licking his lips. She *was* disintegrating, but not quickly enough. She wanted to die, and couldn't figure out why she hadn't already. Her lungs were so thick from lack of air—and probably mold, too, just like Kell had warned—she couldn't breathe enough to sob.

"If you want the girl, be quick about it," Carerra said to Gresley.

"No...please..." Miranda despised herself for whimpering, but couldn't stop. "Please don't."

"Leave her alone," Ortega warned, but his voice sounded unfamiliar, and Miranda's last hope was crushed. He was panicking, just like Chen had said. Even Ray Ortega, the superagent, knew this was hopeless. Knew Miranda was going to be defiled, and then they were all going to be shot in the kneecaps—

"Benito!" Angelina's voice rang out from the stairwell like a ricochet. "I don't want them to touch her."

Carerra turned toward his wife, his expression more confused than angry. "What did you say?"

"Gresley's a pig. I don't want any part of his depravity. I agree with Chen. Kill them so we can leave this ugly place."

Through her haze of misery, Miranda heard Carerra laugh. Then he said, "I was wondering where you were, my love. Now I understand. You've taken the power pill again."

Angelina walked up to him and curled her arms around his neck. "Do you remember how much fun we had the last time?"

"I like you this way." He kissed her roughly, then gave her a challenging grin. "Do you really want to save your new friend's dignity? Then shoot her."

Angelina shrugged. "Gladly. I don't care about her, Benito. I just don't want to be part of senseless cruelty. Ortega's correct about that. We are the future. We should behave with dignity."

Carerra hesitated, then nodded. "Go upstairs. All of you. I will take care of the prisoners myself."

Chen and Angelina filed up the stairs, followed by Gresley, Tork and the guards.

Shocked by the reprieve, Miranda gulped for air. The men weren't going to touch her. And Carerra wasn't going to shoot them in the kneecaps. That was good. Very good. He was just going to kill them, which didn't matter, since she couldn't breathe anyway.

When the Brigadier was alone with his captives, he said quietly, "My wife wishes a quick death for you, but you will not be so fortunate. You should not have interfered with my plans this way. And Ortega? You should never have touched my bride."

Miranda glanced at Ortega, and saw that he was looking directly into Carerra's eyes, not with defiance, but with resignation as he said, "You're right. I made love to her. Do what you want to me, but leave Miranda and Jonathan alone."

"I intend to leave you *all* alone," Carerra promised with a laugh. "Miss Cutler? Carl tells us you are claustrophobic. That is why your lungs are hurting. It will be worse when we cover the window from the outside. And then, when we are ready to leave for the plane, we will set off explosives at the top of the stairs, sealing the entrance to this place and burying it under tons of rubble. If your heart hasn't given out from fear by then, your lungs truly will explode."

"Just go then," she whispered. "And thank Angelina for me."

"You would be better to thank *me* than my wife. I made the decision, not her. I am the one showing you mercy."

She nodded, too weak to argue, and too terrified to provoke him.

"You agree then? I am enlightened?"

"You've changed," Ortega interrupted. "We all agree about that."

"I want to hear it from *her,*" Carerra insisted.

Miranda could feel Ortega staring at her, willing her to placate Carerra. She knew he was right, so she forced herself to nod again, this time saying softly, "You're not as much of an animal as Gresley."

"I'm the Brigadier. The future." He squared his shoulders proudly, then turned away from her and strode to the stairway. As he disappeared from view, he threw one last taunt at them, saying, "Once the explosives seal the doorway, this will become your tomb. I will enjoy imagining your slow, torturous death."

When the door slammed, the amount of light in the dungeon was cut by more than half, the shadows now predominating. Miranda had a feeling the rats would be coming out now, emboldened by the dark, and enticed by the fresh meat hanging on the walls.

"Miranda? Are you okay?"

"For now. But we can't survive without air."

"We've got plenty of air."

"But once they set off the explosives—"

"Fuck that. We'll be out of here before then." Ortega's tone grew brisk. "Is Kell still alive?"

"I don't know. He hasn't moved—"

"I'm alive," a groggy voice informed them. "I wish I wasn't. My lungs are filled with mold and my skin's crawling. When the rats come out—"

"There *are* no rats," Ortega said with a growl. "Check your shackles. One of mine is loose. On my foot, unfortunately, not my hand. But I'm going to try to work it out of the wall. Miranda, do the same."

"If you make holes in the wall, the rats will pour out," Kell objected. "I can already hear them squeaking—"

"Shut up, Jonathan. Miranda? Any luck?"

She tested each of her manacles, but they were securely affixed in the stone. "Mine are solid. You keep trying. But don't use too much oxygen. We're already running low. Oh, no…" She stared up at the window, where booted feet had appeared, casting more shadows. Then a board was shoved over the opening, and the entire dungeon was plunged into inky, unrelenting darkness.

"Oh, no. The rats…" Miranda cringed as scratching sounds began to fill the air. "I hear them now, too."

"Keep it together, dammit!" Ortega exploded. "You're our only hope."

"Me?"

"You think *I* can do it?" he asked, his tone mocking. "I fucked this up every step of the way. We should have left this morning, but thanks to me—thanks to my goddammed, fucked-up rivalry with Carerra—we're all dead."

Miranda started to respond, but a gnawing on her tennis shoe made her shriek instead. Swinging her foot as hard as she could, she told Ortega, "I've got bigger problems! I can barely move, and my lungs are killing me. If you can get one of your goddammed feet free, then *do it!* Be glad the rats aren't feeding on your toes."

"The rats are all in your head. Didn't you hear Carerra? You think you see them, hear them, feel them, but you don't."

"I *get* it! They're in my head. Try telling that to my foot, jackass." His attitude infuriated her. "What about *your* demons, Ortega? They're just as imaginary as ours, so stop lording it over us. You don't want to lead us out of here because you think you can't handle power? Boohoo! You didn't fuck this up any more than I did, so get over yourself. Yank that manacle out of the wall and save us. Now!"

Her order was punctuated by an explosion that started at the top of the stairs, then reverberated through the ceiling. Dust poured down, coating the prisoners, and Kell began screaming hysterically, "We're buried alive! We're going to die!"

"Shut *up!*" Miranda and Ortega shouted in unison.

There was a short silence, then Kell muttered, "Well at least the explosion scared the rats away for now."

Miranda laughed out loud at the ridiculous statement, then realized that the commotion had cleared her head, at least for the moment. It had helped Kell, too, apparently.

But Ortega was silent, so she prodded him warily. "Ortega? Are you okay?"

"I should have gotten you out of here when I had the chance. I'm sorry, Miranda. I got caught up in the game. I swore I'd never make that mistake again—never let my judgment get clouded by the thrill of the chase. But that's who I am. I'll never change. I'm just sorry you had to get mixed up in it."

"Sheesh! Get over yourself," she told him dryly. "I got into this mess all by myself, remember? You're halluci-

nating worse than Jonathan if you think *you've* been calling all the shots." She paused to kick viciously at the rat
that had returned to gnaw on her shoe. "Get off me, goddammit! Jonathan, how long does this stupid drug last?"

"We'll be dead long before it wears off," the scientist assured her. "I'm covered with welts and my throat's
just about swollen shut. We're running out of air, and
even if Ortega manages to get free, we can't dig out in
time. I think we should all just stay quiet and still. Try
not to breathe too much."

"Actually, we need to breathe more, not less," Miranda corrected him, suddenly inspired. "Your exercises combat fear, right? So we're gonna do them.
Ortega? You're the one with the best chance, so I'll
count for you. Let's go—Ow! Dammit! Something bit
me on the neck! Something real this time. Ugh."

"A spider?"

"Probably a bat," Kell announced glumly. "I was
wondering when they'd come out."

A chill shot through Miranda's spine, but she forced
herself to laugh it off. Bats? How many more secret
phobias did she have? Her own imagination was bad
enough, but Kell's was going to land her in the loony bin!

"Ortega? You said I was our only hope, so do what I
say. I'll count, you breathe. Ready? Inhale. One…two…
three…four…five…six…seven… Ow! Little bugger!
Sorry. Exhale, one…two…three…four…five…six…
seven…eight."

She repeated the pattern, and was surprised to find
that the simple act of counting, even without the long,
deep breaths, was calming her a little. She could only
hope that for Ortega, who could actually cleanse his
body as well as his mind, the effects were even stronger.

More steadying. Giving him the balance he so sorely craved, yet didn't trust himself to find on his own.

As she counted, she decided he had the worst of it. Rats, darkness, even bats—the external enemies at least could be hated. But Ortega hated himself, or rather, something he was convinced was lurking inside himself. How could he hope to combat that? Add the fear drug into the mix, and he was probably in more danger than any of them if he didn't get it under control.

She started counting more softly, just to be sure he was cooperating, and to her relief she could hear the powerful sound of his lungs, drawing the air in. Refusing to consider the fact that the dungeon was running out of oxygen more quickly now because of Ortega's deep breathing, she forced herself to keep counting.

Kell hadn't made a whimper for almost two minutes, and she assumed he had passed out. Then he surprised her by saying, "I'll count, Miranda. You breathe with Ortega."

There was something in his voice—not exactly courage, but at least, a hint of hope—and she realized that even *he* had benefited from the rhythmic counting.

He did a good job of it thereafter, speaking the sequence of numbers like a prayer. And in a way it was. For her part, she began breathing with Ortega, and by the time she reached her first sixteen-beat breath, she finally believed there was plenty of oxygen left in the room, because her lungs felt rejuvenated—as though they were drinking in the fresh alpine air outside the window rather than the musty fumes of the dungeon.

When Ortega finally spoke, his tone was confident and inspiring. "You two keep counting and breathing. I'm gonna get this goddammed foot free." His chains began to rattle, but Miranda and Kell ignored all that, concentrating on their exercises, until the sound of mortar shattering made them squeal with delight and they lost count completely.

She wished she could see Ortega's triumphant expression, but the room was too dark for that, so she settled for saying, "My hero! What now?"

"Honestly? I have no idea," he admitted. "I'm trying to kick the pin out of the cuff on my other foot, but even if I get that one free, my hands don't have any give."

"Mine, either." She pursed her lips. "Can you lift your leg up here enough to kick the pin out of one of *my* manacles?"

"I doubt it. I can't even see you. I'd probably break your hand trying."

"Try anyway."

"Yeah, okay." She heard him swing his foot, then she felt the blow on her shoulder and exclaimed, "Ow! I didn't realize you were still wearing the stupid leg iron." She laughed off his apology and insisted, "Try again. That was a little low. Aim higher."

"I might hit you in the head with the chain. This isn't working."

She pursed her lips. "That metal is pretty sharp. Can you use it to dig out some of the stone near my foot? I'm pretty flexible. If my legs were free, I think I could get to your hands."

"Worth a try. Tell me when I'm close." He began thumping his foot against the wall, inching toward her.

"Stop! There, that's perfect." She gritted her teeth as he repeatedly plunged the sharp edge of his shackle into the rock beside her foot. Any miscalculation and he could shatter her ankle with one blow.

"Okay. Try it now," he instructed, and she began tugging with her foot, pleased to feel mortar giving way. "It's working! It's—there!" The chain pulled completely free of the wall, and she immediately began to use that foot to pound the stone beside her other one.

Then she admitted, "You can do it faster, Ortega."

She lifted her free leg out of the way, and he repeated his original process until she was able to dislodge her other shackle. Then she warned him, "When I swing my legs up to your shoulders, these chains will hit you, so keep your eyes closed. And I'm sorry in advance, because I think it's going to hurt."

"Just do it."

She swung her body like a pendulum, higher and higher, until she made contact with his chest, then she "climbed" him to his shoulder, where she rested both ankles, while prying one tennis shoe off with the other one. Then she used her toes to feel her way up to the manacles on his wrists.

"The pin had a head at the top," Ortega told her. "I'll try to take the pressure off my left wrist so you'll have a little more play in it. It's rusty, so I'm hoping it'll be loose."

"Actually, it's pretty tight," she muttered, wedging her big toe under the head of the iron pin, prying carefully. When she had finally managed to edge it up a bit, she was able to grab it between her toes and slowly but surely worked it free.

"Unbelievable." Ortega used his now free hand to lower her legs gently back down to the ground. Then she heard him unpin his other hand and foot.

"Hey." His hands made tentative contact with her through the darkness, followed by a hearty, full-body embrace. "Man, you feel good."

"So do you." She laid her head against his chest for a moment, then insisted, "Free my hands. We don't have much time. And at some point, we really will run out of air."

"Agreed." He unlocked her wrists, then moved toward Kell. "Jonathan? You awake?"

"Here." The scientist's voice was weary. "You two are amazing. But it's all pointless. We'll run out of air before we can dig out."

"Maybe so," Ortega said. "But we have to try. At least we won't die in chains."

"And you're forgetting about our secret allies," Miranda reminded them. "The monks. Remember, Jonathan? They made sure there were at least two ways out of every room."

"This isn't a room. It's a dungeon. The whole point is to keep people in," Kell reminded her.

Ortega's hand found Miranda's in the dark and he grasped it firmly. "If you're right, then we need to start checking the walls. I didn't see anything that looked like another door. Damn, I wish we had a light."

"Let me climb on your shoulders. Maybe I can push that board away from the window."

A tiny thread of light, otherwise useless, showed them where the opening was, and Ortega gave her a leg up, then held her ankles firmly while she pounded at the board until it gave way and fell into the flower bed.

"Yay!" Kell clapped his hands, as giddy as a toddler at a birthday party.

"Shhh! Jonathan, quiet." Miranda held her breath as two limousines pulled up alongside the house twenty feet from the window. If Benito Carerra or the other Brigade members noticed that the board had been dislodged, they'd realize the prisoners had somehow gotten out of the shackles. Knowing Carerra, he'd probably lob a grenade through the window, just for "sport."

As she watched, the Brigadier and his wife exited the fortress and approached the first limousine, getting in without even glancing toward the dungeon window, so certain were they that the prisoners were sealed for all eternity under tons of rubble. Then Carl and another guard climbed into the front seat and the vehicle sped away. Gresley, Chen and Tork got into the other car, again with several guards, and they followed Carerra down a dirt road that led to the back of Kell's property rather than back into the village.

"Whew, that was close." She smiled down at the men. "Alone at last."

Although the sun had begun to set, and the window was small, the difference between some light in the dungeon and none at all was astonishing, especially when Ortega lowered Miranda to her feet, then grasped her chin in his hand and stared into her eyes. "You look even better than you feel. If we don't get out of this, I hope you know how sorry I am. For everything."

"That's the drug talking," she scolded him. "Don't let it get to you, Ortega. I need your help. Jonathan? How bad off are you? I mean, I'm okay with the air and the rats now, but I'm still pretty shaky. That's the drug, right?"

He nodded. "The breathing helped. As does the light and the air. But panic will set in again. I'm almost sure of it. When night falls, if we're still in here, I predict another round of hallucinations. Maybe worse, because we'll be exhausted by then."

"Then let's hurry." She appraised the room quickly.

"In the lab, the doors were at opposite ends. It's that way in the drawing room, too. So…" She strode over to the corner opposite the stairway. It looked solid, but she kicked it anyway, then winced when only her ankle showed any weakness.

"Here, allow me." Ortega scooped up one of the manacles and began pounding the stone and mortar, chipping away at it bit by bit. "What's on the other side of this wall, Jonathan?"

"As far as I know, dirt."

Ortega stopped his activity and turned his attention overhead. "What's up there?"

"The kitchen," said Kell. "The guards' quarters were right above the stairwell. All of that is rubble by now, I assume. But right over this spot? I'd say it's the pantry, and probably still intact."

"The pantry? Sounds like women's work," Ortega said with a grin.

Laughing at the pseudo-sexist remark, Miranda grabbed a manacle, then scrambled up onto his shoulders and began hacking cheerfully at the ceiling.

Chapter 13

"I still don't understand why we can't just let the CIA handle this," Kell was complaining as he watched Ortega kick through the debris that had once been the guards' quarters.

"I *am* the CIA," Miranda reminded him, still giddy from her victory in uncovering the trapdoor and pull-down ladder in the ceiling of the dungeon.

"They didn't leave one goddammed rifle behind," Ortega announced. "Did you find any weapons in the lab, Miranda?"

"Only this." She held up the bow and quiver, then pulled the vial of Night Arrow from her pocket. "And this."

Ortega seemed unimpressed, but didn't argue. "I got through to SPIN. Sounds like Kristie was miles ahead of us. She had a team standing by in Geneva—don't ask me how. They'll meet us at an airstrip about thirty minutes from here. Jonathan tells me Gresley landed a small plane there once before, so we're assuming that's where Carerra's headed." Jingling a set of keys, he added, "The Land Rover I rented is still outside, so we're good to go."

"It will take Carerra thirty minutes by road," Miranda mused. "But *we* can save time cutting across the meadow, right? So maybe we can make it in time." She flashed Kell a sympathetic smile. "Stay here and get some rest. We'll be back for you as quick as we can."

"No! I don't want to be alone."

"Okay. Then swallow this." She held one of the power pills out in her palm. "No arguments."

Kell's eyes widened. "I thought Carerra took all the drugs."

"These were in an envelope in the archery cabinet. I'm guessing they're the ones you set aside for me to take home. For my elevator rendezvous with Ortega."

Ortega arched an eyebrow. "Your what?"

"Never mind. The good news is, there are three pills. One for each of us. Hopefully they'll counteract the fear drug, and maybe even give us a little extra edge."

"None for me," Ortega told her. "But Jonathan, I agree with Miranda. We can't have you falling apart out there. Either take the pill or stay behind. Case closed."

Kell grimaced, but placed the capsule in his mouth, muttering, "If my throat swells up—"

"Just shut up and take it."

Miranda bit back a laugh as she watched the nervous man gulp it down. "Thanks, Jonathan. That's very brave of you. Now…" She eyed Ortega. "Your turn."

"I'm fine." He cleared his throat, then reminded her, "The last thing I need is an artificial infusion of power.

I don't even handle the natural stuff well, remember? It fucks with my judgment. We don't need that right now."

She ran her fingertips lightly along his jaw. "I've got news for you, handsome. That wasn't power fucking with your judgment last year. It was pride."

He scowled. "What?"

"You had a lot to be proud of," she assured him with a fond smile. "You were the best. Everyone raved about you. The CIA, the FBI, the president of the United States. New recruits like me whispered your name in awe. You *earned* that adulation. Then just when you were about to be recognized publicly—to be given a prestigious appointment—some jackass in L.A. took a swing at you and jeopardized everything. *That's* what you couldn't handle. The blow to your hard-earned image."

He cleared his throat again, but didn't respond.

"If this were a pride pill, yeah. I'd be flushing it as we speak," she continued with a teasing smile. "But power? That's exactly what we need to kick Carerra's ass. Plus, we've got Jonathan's fear drug in our systems. We have to counteract it so we can do our jobs. Right?"

"You're pretty persuasive," he murmured.

"I learned from the master," she responded, enjoying the flashes of bronze in his warm, admiring gaze.

"Miranda's right, Ortega," Kell interrupted coolly. "You're wasting precious time. Just take the pill and let's go get those bastards."

They turned to look at the scientist, flabbergasted by the change in his attitude. He was standing straighter than usual, his chin high, his eyes brilliant with confidence.

Ortega gave a rueful chuckle. "If that's what the power pill does for a guy, then absolutely." He held out his hand with his palm turned upward toward Miranda. "Let's go get 'em."

The plan was simple. They'd stop a safe distance from the landing strip, sneak up on the Brigade through cover of darkness and protection of scattered pine trees, and try to quietly overpower two of the guards, confiscating their weapons. Jonathan would stay out of the fray, but with an important assignment, to build a small stash of explosive cocktails that could be lobbed at the limousines and eventually at the plane itself if necessary.

They knew that they would be facing ten adversaries at a minimum: four Brigade members, including Carerra, four guards, Angelina, and at some point, the pilot. Under the worst case scenario, the rest of the guards had headed for the airstrip in other vehicles. More likely, they had been sent into town to board the train for Geneva. With luck, the plane was the one Gresley had used before, which had seated only ten, meaning that it wouldn't be bringing reinforcements.

There had been no sign of a plane landing or taking off, so Miranda was confident that they still had time, especially with Ortega at the wheel, driving at breakneck speed. He pulled up behind a grove of trees at the far edge of the strip, then pointed to a group of stationary headlights in the distance. "The two limos. No other vehicles."

Miranda nodded.

"Jonathan?" Ortega touched him on the shoulder. "Bring the supplies. We'll find a safe spot for you, as close to the vehicles as possible. Miranda? When we get there, stick with the plan. No deviations. You need to take down one of the guards and get his weapon, then retreat. Don't proceed further unless absolutely necessary. Clear?"

She nodded again.

"We'll take out as many guards as possible, one by one, but not at the cost of attracting attention or giving away our position. If we screw up, Tork will be our main problem. Or should I say, *my* main problem, because I'll handle him personally. I'll also take Carerra and Gresley. You take Chen and Angelina."

"Get over yourself," she advised dryly. "You can have Tork with my blessing. He'd kill me for sure. But if you take him and Carerra, you'll have more than your share. Plus, I *want* Gresley. So that's how it'll go. I'll handle him and Chen. I don't think Angelina's going to be a problem for either of us, even with the power drug. So we'll just play that part by ear. Agreed?"

They crept toward their prey, encouraged that there were still no sounds of engines approaching. Four guards were visible in the woods at four corners of a perimeter twenty-five yards or so from the limousines, which were parked together. Tork and Gresley stood alongside, chatting and smoking. Chen and the Carerras were presumably still sitting in the vehicles.

If the plane arrived before the SPIN team, Ortega hoped to use Jonathan's homemade weapons to prevent escape by the Brigade. Until that time, their main goal was to keep from attracting attention, even if they remained unarmed except for Miranda's arrows. But taking out a few guards to arm themselves while keeping their own positions a secret appeared to be their best hope of complete success, assuming Tork didn't catch on and retaliate before they had confiscated at least two firearms.

As Ortega studied the enemies' activity, waiting for the perfect time to make a move, Miranda enjoyed herself watching Jonathan Kell, who was so happy he was practically glowing as he concocted incendiary devices. It was clear that for once, he was reveling in his talents without focusing on some doomsday scenario like allergies, bugs or lightning. The irony, of course, was that this endeavor had significant doomsday overtones. Yet Kell was too pumped to let those deter him. In that sense, his mood mirrored that of the trained agents, who also couldn't wait to get the operation officially underway.

"Miranda?" Ortega whispered. "Ready?"

She nodded.

"Be careful. If it feels wrong, retreat."

She nodded again, then they crept away from one another and toward their respective prey. Concentrating on her own target as well as the movements of the other two guards and the Brigade, she still allowed herself to keep an eye on Ortega, who reached his man first, jumped him, then felled him in one amazing motion before disappearing back into the shadows.

"Wow." Inspired, even though she knew her own effort would probably not go so quickly, she took a deep breath, gripped her supplies—a length of rope and a rock—then scrambled to her feet and rushed the guard, looping the rope around his neck and jerking him backward to the ground, where she pressed her knee to his throat and clobbered the top of his skull with the rock.

Not bad, she told herself, unbuckling the guard's holster and looping it over her shoulder, then picking up his rifle, checking to ensure that the safety was on. Then she scampered low to the ground, from tree to tree, until she had rejoined Kell and Ortega.

A commotion started in the vicinity of the vehicles, accompanied by extinguishment of the limousine headlights, and Ortega grimaced. "They know."

"But we're armed now," Miranda whispered. "I'll bet we could take them."

"Unless the plane gets here, or they get a fix on us, we're sitting tight."

"I can blow those limos sky-high," Kell boasted, his voice hoarse with excitement. "The blast will kill everyone in them, *plus* Tork and Gresley. Then the two other guards will probably just surrender."

As Miranda bit back a laugh, Ortega groaned and told him, "You're flying a little high there, buddy. Settle down. That's an order."

Without the glow of the headlights, it was impossible to detect the exact positions of the guards and Brigade members. Meanwhile, the faint sound of an approaching plane could finally be heard overhead.

"Now we *have* to do something," Kell insisted.

"Yeah, yeah." Ortega pounded his shoulder. "Just have those cocktails ready, okay? Miranda, I'll need to get up closer so I can be sure to hit the plane. You'll cover me. Got it? Once I light the match, I'll be a heckuva target, so you'll have to keep them busy."

"I'm with Jonathan. Now that we have to make our move anyway, let's blow the limos first. Keep them busy so you can get closer to the plane."

"Just humor me for once," he muttered. Then his voice dropped to a growl. "They're fanning out. Approaching. Hear that? Keep still."

Miranda looked at Kell, and was amazed to see that he still wasn't caving, although his boyish enthusiasm was now tinged with concern. She could relate to that, since this was her first operation under fire aside from live training exercises, and she, too, was beginning to wonder if she was up to the challenge, bravado notwithstanding.

Without warning, a spray of bullets erupted, strafing their entire area, coming perilously close to them. Ortega crouched, aimed, and took out the shooter with two quick rounds.

Kell punched the air with his fist. "Excellent!"

"Lie flat!" Ortega ordered under his breath. "Tork has our location now. Miranda? Go up and around."

She nodded, then pressed the rifle she had taken from the guard into Kell's hands. "See this? It's the safety. It works like this. Otherwise, this weapon is ready to fire. If anyone comes near you, take the safety off, then shoot him right between the eyes." She hesitated, then gave the scientist an urgent embrace. "See you soon."

She moved slowly through the darkness, aware of the approaching plane that would soon shed some light upon the runway. Meanwhile, she heard the unmistakable sounds of footsteps on either side of her, and while she could have avoided them, she realized that someone was moving directly toward Kell. The thought of the scientist actually having to defend himself was unpalatable, so she changed course, then lunged forward, wrestling the target to the ground, trying to make as little noise as possible so as not to betray her location.

But her opponent had other ideas, shouting, "I've got the bitch!"

It was Carl, and Miranda took great pleasure in throttling him while insisting, "Shut up, big mouth."

He was strong enough to flip her onto her back, knocking the wind out of her lungs momentarily, but she instinctively kneed him in the groin, then rolled free as he yelped in pain. Now that they had made so much noise, shooting him was a definite option, but he attacked again before she could aim her pistol. His fist struck out, glancing across her jaw, and she staggered backward, then fired.

Her vision was blurry for a few seconds, but she kept the weapon trained on him as he slumped, first to his knees, then into a ball, holding his chest, his expression one of complete disbelief. She remembered his rude, dismissive treatment that first day, and realized he had never updated his prejudicial view of her, despite hearing she was with the CIA.

"That's right," she told him in disgust. "A girl shot you. Live with it. Oh, right, you *can't*."

Then she heard a weapon being cocked behind her, and Alexander Gresley called out, just as Carl had done, "I've got her!"

She turned to look at him, feeling disappointed rather than scared. She had wanted so much to kick his ass! Now he was going to fill her full of bullets instead.

Then a shot rang out, and Gresley's skull literally exploded in front of her eyes. She turned toward the source, prepared to thank Ortega, but her savior was Jonathan Kell, looking like an incongruous version of Rambo with the bow and quiver slung over one slender shoulder, and the rifle held tightly in his hands—hands that were shaking so violently, she was afraid he'd shoot *her* next.

"Lower the rifle," she murmured, and when he had done so, she ran to him and gave him a huge hug. "My hero! You saved me, Jonathan."

His voice was so hushed it was almost nonexistent as he told her, "He was going to kill you."

"Believe it!" She laughed and hugged him again. "Have you seen Ortega? Look! The plane's landing. He's going to need your cocktails now. Are they ready?"

Kell nodded.

She could see that the scientist was beginning to wear down, so she kissed his cheek and reminded him, "It's almost over. We've gotten four out of ten that we know of, and you can bet Ortega has taken out at least one more."

"There could be dozens more on the plane."

"Or it could be empty except for the pilot. Go back and wait for Ortega. I'm going to scout around some more."

"Wait, Miranda. Take this." Kell handed her the bow and quiver. "Use the red arrow. It's good luck."

"The red one?"

"I put some of your Night Arrow potion on it. It turned red on contact. That's a good omen, right?"

She nodded. "Go on now. Take the rifle. Try not to shoot yourself. Or Ortega," she added with a teasing smile.

Surprised that no one had come to avenge Gresley, she darted quickly to the edge of the treeline and saw that all eyes were on Ortega and Tork squaring off at the other side of the strip. Two motionless bodies lay nearby—one in uniform, one in a suit. She could only assume the latter was Chen, killed by Ortega.

It seemed crazy that Carerra hadn't simply taken a shot at Ortega by now, but the Brigadier was standing by the limousines, holding a knife to his wife's throat, his rapt attention focused on the fight, and she realized he was just bloodthirsty enough to want to see his old nemesis torn limb from limb by a giant.

And it certainly looked like Tork was the man for the job. He was a full foot taller than Ortega, and Miranda guessed he had fifty pounds of muscle on him, at least.

Not that Ortega was a lightweight himself, but compared to Tork, his broad shoulders and powerful build were dwarfed.

Miranda raised her pistol and steadied it with both hands, not willing to take a chance on the outcome despite her confidence in Ortega. But before she could fire a clean shot at Tork, the two men charged one another and began exchanging vicious blows. She didn't dare shoot now, for fear of missing Tork and hitting the man she practically loved.

The plane was taxiing to a stop, but no one seemed to care. The battle between Tork and Ortega was the only game in town. Then the sound of a helicopter in the distance brought everyone back to their senses, and Carerra began dragging Angelina toward the plane, the knife still held to her throat.

Miranda shook her head, amazed that Carerra thought she'd refrain from shooting at them just because Angelina had intervened for her. As much as she had appreciated the wife's gesture, she wasn't going to let the husband get away. Plus, to be fair, Angelina had been more than comfortable with Miranda's death. She had only drawn the line at molestation. Admirable, yes. But not quite admirable enough to earn herself a complete pass.

Apparently Jonathan Kell was having the same thought, because a fiery bottle suddenly sailed through the air, landing between Carerra and the plane, exploding into a wall of dancing flames.

Dropping the knife, Carerra sprinted into the darkness, with Angelina running after him, calling his name. Frustrated, Miranda took a quick glance toward Ortega, who was being pummeled, but was still fighting back.

In a minute, the chopper would land. She knew the smart thing to do would be run and help Ortega defeat Tork. The SPIN team would find Carerra soon enough.

Then the plane door slid open, stairs were unfolded onto the runway, and three uniformed men, armed with rifles and a rocket launcher, appeared in the doorway.

She groaned aloud. They were going to take down the chopper, which meant she had to kill them before they could set up. Carerra had known exactly what he was doing, getting out of the line of fire, hiding in the dark, waiting until his troops had succeeded before coming back, with or without Angelina in tow.

Forget Carerra, she told herself, but for reasons she couldn't understand, she was fixated on him to the point where she could swear she heard the sound of his running feet pounding the strip, even though he had disappeared in the darkness. She could even hear his labored, frantic breathing! He was too far away for her to shoot at him with any degree of accuracy, but still she could hear him. Almost *smell* him!

And she knew she could hit him with an arrow. The *red* arrow—for luck, just like Jonathan had suggested. Pulling it from the quiver, she notched it, then aimed toward the sound of Carerra's feet.

Then she gasped aloud, realizing that someway, somehow, she could now see him as well as hear him. Or at least, she could perceive him—the heat from him—as though she were wearing night vision goggles.

There was no time to analyze the phenomenon, so she embraced the infusion of confidence it gave her, then she released the string, and the arrow shot forward. In her mind, she could follow its progress easily as it cut through the night, and she knew the precise instant when it penetrated Carerra's back and sliced through his evil heart.

She couldn't pause to savor the victory. Instead, she began to run, closing the distance between herself and the new troops, who were just hitting the ground. Then another fiery bottle flew past her, landing on the wing of the airplane, exploding on impact, and the three armed men went sailing through the air as a spark-filled concussion blast assaulted them.

Jonathan!

Laughing out loud, Miranda looked over at Ortega, who was standing, his hands on his hips, staring at the conflagration. At his feet lay the lifeless body of Tork.

"Good riddance," she murmured, aiming her pistol steadily as she began to walk toward the guards that had been stunned by the blast. Ortega did likewise, until the chopper touched down, and six men in black uniforms rushed onto the strip to take over.

Miranda scanned the edge of the woods for Kell, finally locating him. He was kneeling, clearly exhausted. Running to him, she pulled him into an embrace. "You were incredible, Jonathan. Just incredible."

"I'm tired," he confessed. "Is it over?"

"Yes. Thanks to you." She hugged him again, then stood to greet one of the SPIN team, who approached cautiously, asking, "Are you okay, ma'am?"

"I'm fine. This man saved our lives. Can you get him a blanket and some water?"

"Sure." The man leaned down and helped Jonathan to his feet. "Let's go, buddy. We'll get you squared away."

Kell sent Miranda a dazed smile, then limped away, leaning heavily on the soldier.

Ortega walked over to where Miranda was standing and announced, "That freak of nature almost fucking killed me." Then he grinned. "You okay?"

She nodded.

He motioned toward the helicopter, where Kell was being greeted by what appeared to be a team of medics. "How's the man of the hour?"

"Exhausted, the poor baby," she said with a fond smile. "Can you believe how great he was?"

"We couldn't have done it without him."

"Make sure you tell him that. It'll mean so much, coming from his hero."

"There's something I want to tell *you* first."

She bit her lip. "Right now?"

"Yeah, right now." He stepped up to her, pulled her into his arms and kissed her passionately.

"Agent Ortega?" a booming male voice demanded from a few yards away.

Miranda wriggled out of Ortega's embrace in time to see him scowl and demand, "Russo? What the hell are *you* doing here?"

"Nice to see you again, too," the newcomer said, winking in Miranda's direction. "Agent Cutler, I presume? I'm Special Agent Justin Russo, at your service."

Ortega snorted. "Has SPIN lost its mind, sending an FBI agent on an international op? And is that a Red Cross on that chopper? You used a nonmilitary carrier for this mission?"

"We pulled it together pretty fast," Russo explained, giving Miranda a dazzling smile. "S-3 knew I was vacationing in Lyons, so she recruited me. Luckily, I'm friends with a girl who works for the Red Cross in Geneva. The rest just fell into place."

"You just happened to know a girl in Geneva? Big surprise. You never change, Russo."

"Right back at you, Ortega," the agent said with a chuckle. "I just wanted to report that we've rounded up all your strays. Found Benito Carerra shot through the heart with an arrow. And this time," he reported with a sly grin, "he's actually dead. I'm guessing there's a story there, huh?"

Ortega looked at Miranda, who murmured, "Lucky shot."

"*You* did it?" Russo whistled. "Maybe you can give Ortega here some lessons. He aims a little high, right?" Before Ortega could answer, the agent insisted, "That's all I wanted to say. Things are under control, so you two can get back to debriefing each other."

Ortega glared. But Miranda insisted warmly, "You got here just in time. Thanks, Agent Russo. We really appreciate it."

"If I'd known how good-looking you were, I'd have been here sooner," he assured her. "Let us know what you need. I'll be over there, wrapping up."

Miranda waited until the handsome agent was out of earshot, then she teased Ortega. "You weren't very nice to him, considering he saved our lives."

"*He* didn't save our lives. Jonathan did. Plus, that guy aggravates the hell out of me. Always has."

"I noticed," she said with a laugh. "He seems nice enough."

"He thinks he's James Bond. Running around with women, breaking rules, making flashy entrances like he did just now. It's all a big joke to him. Kristie's got a soft spot where he's concerned, but to me, he's a menace."

"Well, *I* like him."

"Big surprise. Women *always* like him. That's how he gets away with as much as he does. If I were his boss…" He caught himself and laughed. "I almost was. That would have been a nightmare for him. I guess he's the only one who really benefited from that mess. Speaking of which…" He reached for her again.

"Can we check on Jonathan first? Then—" She slipped her hands behind his head and pulled it forward, gently kissing his lips. "Then you'll have my undivided attention. I need to talk to you, too," she admitted.

"Okay. I want to see your handiwork on Carerra anyway."

She hesitated, then said, "It was such a weird sensation. Even though it was too dark to see him, and he was so far away, I swear I could hear him breathing. I knew just where he was. It was like all of my senses were sharpened. Because of the Night Arrow potion," she added warily.

"Right," Ortega drawled. "It was the Night Arrow. Not the hallucinogen in Jonathan's fear drug."

"Oh." She grimaced. "Good point. I forgot about that." Then she laughed and insisted, "I like my explanation better."

He laughed, too, then took her by the arm and they strolled over to the helicopter, where Carerra's body was on display, the arrow still imbedded in his chest. Ortega stopped to admire it, while Miranda walked over to Angelina, who was sitting on the ground, wrapped in a blanket. "Hi."

The widow looked up, her bloodshot eyes vacant.

"We had to sedate her pretty heavily," a medic whispered. "But she'll be fine."

Miranda sighed, knowing that Angelina wouldn't be "fine" at all. She'd be charged with conspiracy. And she'd be all alone, a nightmare in itself for a woman accustomed to depending on men. Touching her arm, Miranda told her, "I'll make sure they know what you did. In your own way, you tried to help."

Angelina nodded, then pulled the blanket high so that it covered her face.

Miranda sighed, then asked the attendant, "How's Mr. Kell doing? Did you sedate him, too?"

"We made him as comfortable as we could," the medic murmured. "There was only so much we could do. He lost a lot of blood."

A chill flashed up her spine. "What are you talking about? What blood?"

Not waiting for an answer, she strode over to the stretchers that were being readied for loading onto the chopper. On the first lay Victor Chen, sound asleep, his face bruised and swollen but his color otherwise good.

Then she saw Kell, his eyes closed, his face pale, an intravenous tube in his arm.

"Oh, my God. Jonathan?" She knelt beside him and took his hand in her own. "Are you okay?"

"I'm fine," he said, his breathing labored.

She noted a streak of blood on the otherwise pure white sheet covering him, and she steeled herself before taking a peek underneath, where bandages were already seeping, unable to completely stem the flow from two wounds, one under his arm, the other below his throat. To her shock she realized that a single bullet must have gone through him, wreaking havoc with lungs and arteries.

She jumped up and shouted, *"Ortega!"* Then she knelt again and patted Kell's cheek. "Don't worry, Jonathan. It's going to be okay."

"I didn't even feel it," Kell murmured. "I still don't.

So don't be upset. Just remember that because of you, I had the best day of my life today."

"Shh...don't talk like that. You'll be fine."

"You mean, I'll be my old self?" He shook his head. "I can't go back to that. Being miserable...terrified..." His eyelids fluttered as he insisted, "Not again. Not after this. I'm finally free of fear...."

"Jonathan?" Miranda sighed, her heart aching for him. He was dipping in and out of consciousness, and she told herself he needed his rest to get strong again, so she held his hand but didn't wake him. Instead, she looked up at Ortega, who was towering over them, his expression stricken.

"I just heard," he told her hoarsely. "They said he's not in any pain. But he's not going to make it, Miranda."

"Don't say that!" She sandwiched Kell's face gently between her palms and whispered, "You're going to be fine, sweetie."

Kell's eyes opened, glazed but shining.

"He's pretty tough," the medic said. "Most guys would have gone down in a heap."

"Hear that?" Kell gave Ortega a sheepish smile. "I'm tough."

"I knew that from the jungle," Ortega told him, his voice choked. "You've survived worse than this, buddy. Just hang in there."

"The best day of my life," Kell repeated as he gazed up at Miranda. "For once, I wasn't afraid."

"Oh, Jonathan..."

"Back at the house, when Gresley punched you, I wanted to kill him. But I couldn't. I was shaking. Scared. Useless."

"It's okay. When it counted, you saved me. You shot him, Jonathan. I'm alive because of you."

"Remember me that way," he begged her. "Saving you. Loving you. Protecting...strong...love you..."

Tears began to stream down her Miranda's cheeks.

"Be happy for me," Kell told her. "I'll never be afraid again. Be happy..."

"Jonathan?" Miranda bit her lip. "Oh, no."

Ortega knelt beside her, wrapping an arm around her shoulders. After a long, silent moment, he closed Kell's eyelids, murmuring, "So long, buddy. You did great. You saved the woman you loved. That's every guy's dream, and you lived it."

When Miranda sobbed Kell's name, Ortega cradled her against himself, then helped her to her feet. "It's true, you know. He went out a hero. Something he could never have dreamed possible. Then you came along, and *made* it possible."

"It was his power pill, not me."

"Don't kid yourself. You made his last hour a perfect one." Ortega brushed a tear from her cheek. "Come on. Let's get you into the chopper. We can have our talk later."

"No." She stepped back and gave him a shaky smile. "I don't want to waste another minute. Isn't that what Jonathan just taught us?"

He nodded. Then with a last mournful look at Kell's lifeless form, he took Miranda by the hand and led her away from the helicopter.

They strolled back to the Land Rover in silence. After Ortega turned on the headlights, Miranda leaned against the vehicle and looked him straight in the eyes. "Let's hear it."

He nodded, then spoke in a solemn voice. "You can't

imagine how sorry I am about that night. The alibi tape. Everything that happened. If things had only been different between us—"

"Things *are* different between us."

"What?"

Miranda enjoyed the hint of hope in his eyes before explaining. "We had a rocky start. That's undeniable. I mean, you lied to me. You ruined my life. Made a mockery of my career and generally acted like a selfish bastard." She smiled sadly. "But there are a few things in the plus column I just can't ignore."

"Such as?"

"Such as, you never blame anyone else for your mistakes. If anything, you're too hard on yourself. I like that. Plus, you're brave and patriotic, and you taught me to find balance. You came halfway around the world and posed as the Brigadier to rescue me—we're gonna be reenacting *that* little fantasy for months. And I love being with you. It gives me such a thrill. Your eyes, your voice, your way—just standing here with you now, I'm literally drowning in sensation. And hope. And love." She bit her lip, closer to tears than she had ever imagined she'd get over romance. "Just don't ever lie to me again, and we'll be fine. It's as simple as that, Ortega."

"You can let the rest go?" He stepped forward, resting his hands on her shoulders. "Everything I did? My God, Miranda, I've wanted that. Every day since I first met you. Every time I watched that tape and saw you looking up at me like, well, like *this*." The bronze flecks in his eyes were bursting with light. "I swear I'll be completely honest from now on. No more secrets, no more lies. That's a promise." He started to lean his mouth down to hers, but an insistent ring from his satellite phone broke the spell.

"Go ahead," Miranda told him with a sigh.

He barked his name into the phone, then murmured, "Hey, Kris. Nice work getting a team together so fast. But next time, send a real man, okay? Huh?" He scowled, then told Miranda, "She wants to know what you thought of Russo."

"I'll tell her later. In private."

"Unbelievable." He chuckled and asked Kristie, "Did you hear that? Yeah, she's hilarious. Yeah." He flushed. "She's that, too. What about you? Did McGregor fire your ass?"

He laughed again, and Miranda smiled in relief. Even though she couldn't hear what Kristie was saying, it was clear she was still employed by SPIN, a fact that was further confirmed when Ortega shook his head, then said to Miranda, "You won't believe this. She wants us to go to South America and retrieve the Night Arrow research from Carerra's hacienda before it falls into the wrong hands."

"She's right. It's too valuable to lose."

He gave a frustrated laugh. "Since I promised to always be honest, I'll tell you I think it's nuts. But whatever you want. We'll rest up, then head down there."

"We need to go right away. We can't take any chances."

He held the phone back up to his ear. "Okay, set it up. Yeah, I figured that. We'll call from the airport. Yeah, you too."

He disconnected the call, then explained. "This operation is strictly off the books. Big surprise. But she's as nuts as you on the subject. Russo filled her head with crap about that shot you made, I guess."

"Just because my arrow killed Benito and yours didn't, don't be bitter." She smiled hopefully. "Kristie and McGregor are okay?"

"He's putting her on some kind of strict monitoring program. I tried that once. Doesn't work."

"I meant, are they okay romantically?"

"She said to tell you the make-up sex was worth it," he admitted with a grin. "I can't believe those two aren't married yet. What the hell are they waiting for?"

"I think she was waiting for you to get together with me," Miranda murmured. "Somehow she knew. Isn't that…well, romantic?"

He nodded, then pulled her into his arms again, asking carefully, "So what are we saying here exactly? We'll what? Date? Live together?"

"Don't worry, Ortega. You didn't accidentally propose," she assured him.

"Are you kidding? I'd marry you in a minute."

She stared, knowing she should say something, but feeling completely speechless.

"You don't have to say anything," he assured her quickly. "I'm just being honest. No secrets, remember?"

When Miranda moistened her lips, still searching for just the right thing to say, Ortega insisted, "You're the woman I want. The woman I need. I've known that since the night we met. I've thought about it—about you—for more than a year. The question is, what do *you* want? What do *you* need? You should take some time to think about that, then—"

"Ortega?"

"What?"

She looped her arms around his neck and suggested

with a loving smile, "Shut up and marry me. But first…"
Her pulse began to race with anticipation. "Let's go get
the Night Arrow."

* * * * *

"Santa Bella is the biggest mall in the South, and on Christmas Eve, about 20,000 last-minute shoppers will be rotating through, keeping the facility packed to its three-story rafters."

Twenty thousand. Oh, man. Major challenges trying to defend in that situation. Major challenges. Maggie chewed her lip. "Are post-attack projections in yet?"

"Some. Two to four thousand fatalities and a minimum additional two thousand permanently disabled. I didn't get dollar cost projections on contamination losses. Bean counters are still working on them."

Good God, two to four *thousand* fatalities? Maggie broke into a cold sweat. "Are the projections as dire for all potential targets?"

Darcy nodded. "I'm told some are worse."

Maggie expected it, but hearing it confirmed curdled

her blood and she regretted choking down that donut earlier. This kind of news was best digested on an empty stomach.

Kate curled her fingers, gripped the table. "What are we likely looking at with the infiltrators?"

"We don't know." Darcy grimaced. "Intel can't project which specific GRID operatives will launch the attack, though they believe that Kunz will use his own subject-matter experts and not outside forces to release the virus. For tighter control and lower odds of leaks. We have no idea how many GRID operatives will work the launch, or in what part or parts of the mall they'll cut it loose—if, of course, Santa Bella is their target."

"This is a nightmare from hell." Maggie looked at the colonel.

"It gets worse," Colonel Drake said. "We can't forget the body-double factor."

"What body-double factor?" Justin Crowe asked, looking baffled.

Colonel Drake responded. "A lot of high-powered, influential people hire body doubles, Dr. Crowe."

He nodded, familiar with the concept. "And that relates to this…how?"

Colonel Drake didn't dodge. "Our experience has revealed that Kunz has a number of body doubles for himself and for key business associates on high-impact, lucrative black-market deals. He has a nasty habit of inserting them when he knows, or senses, we're closing in on him."

"I see." Justin leaned forward on the table and rubbed at his temple, clearly distressed by this added complication. "Is there a way to know whether we're dealing with a double or the real McCoy?"

"DNA," the colonel said. "Though we have noted a three-month absence trend."

"Three-month absence?"

The colonel's gaze slid to Amanda, and she responded. "Kunz kidnaps the person he wants to double, keeps them drugged and learns all he can about them. During that time, his surgeons and shrinks are creating a body double. One who looks, acts and learns to think like the real person. It's an intensive training program to become that person, and it's very effective."

Justin's expression sobered. He'd intuited that Amanda had been one of Kunz's victims; Maggie was certain of it.

"Anyway," the colonel resumed her briefing, "we obviously must be on our guard and expect that he's made insertions of body doubles on this mission as well."

Maggie nodded. "He has a one-hundred percent track record, Colonel. Every attack, every mission…"

"So who would he be likely to double?" Justin asked, still seeking a firm grip on this new complication to an already complicated mission.

"Anyone in authority or with the power to countermand our actions," Maggie said. "Anyone who might be able to relay our actions and defenses to him."

Justin paled. "But that's pretty much everybody."

"Yes, it is."

Amanda turned the topic back to the attack location. "Why doesn't Intel recommend a total shutdown of all potential locations?"

"Can't. The administration wouldn't consider it, much less go for it. Makes us appear too fearful and vulnerable, which emboldens all of those against us." Darcy blew out a slow breath. "Listen, the truth is Intel isn't certain enough that the attack will be at any of the identified targets to request Homeland Security order shutdowns."

"True," Colonel Drake cut in. "But local First Responders are on heightened alert, advisory status. They are not, at this point, activated. If at any time we discover hard evidence Santa Bella is the target and conditions warrant activation, we can call them up to assist us."

"By then," Maggie said, "it'll be too late for them to successfully intercede or be much help, Colonel. And knowing Kunz, he'll keep things ambiguous until the very end. He always has, to prevent us from being able to go after him with full force."

Colonel Drake's level look proved she didn't like this circumstance a damn bit better than Maggie, but her hands were tied. "I'm aware of that, which is why I'm telling you, Maggie, if the rules get in the way on this mission, you break them."

Maggie frowned. Often in the S.A.S.S., rules had to be broken, but that didn't mean Maggie had to like breaking them. Actually, she hated it, and the colonel well knew it. Hence, the reason for the direct order—and there was no mistaking by anyone at the table, except maybe for Crowe, that this remark had been a direct order. "Yes, ma'am."

"Right now, we work with what we've got," Colonel Drake said. "And what we've got is Intel, Homeland Security, the Pentagon and the president all stating their belief that this threat is credible. In our post-9/11 world, that compels everyone responsible for defending the public to act. The S.A.S.S. unit has been activated, and we will defend Santa Bella—whether or not it wants to be defended."

Justin Crowe frowned. "What if one of the other targets Intel identified is attacked? Will this S.A.S.S. unit then stand down?"

"No." Colonel Drake sent him a regretful look. "We can't assume Kunz and GRID intend to attack only one target. He could launch simultaneous strikes at all identified targets."

"Or none of them," Maggie said.

"Or none of them," Colonel Drake agreed. "Which is why we must be on-site and prepared to intervene if Santa Bella comes under biological attack." She let her gaze slide down the table. "Maggie, you're primary."

"But, Colonel, " Kate called out, no doubt to oppose Maggie being given primary rather than Kate, who also had bio-expertise and was senior in experience.

"Yes, Kate?" There was steel in Colonel Drake's eyes, and if Kate was half as smart as her dossier and records stated, she'd shut up now.

Evidently, she noted it. "I, um, will be happy to provide backup, ma'am."

Naturally, she wouldn't object this one time when Maggie wouldn't mind. The last person in the world Maggie wanted to work closely with was Dr. Justin Crowe. He was too disturbing. Kunz had infiltrated high-level government positions before. Crowe could be a body double.

HOMICIDE DETECTIVE
MERRI WALTERS IS BACK IN

Silent Reckoning
by **Debra Webb**

December 2005

A serial killer was on the loose,
hunting the city's country singers.
Could deaf detective Merri Walters turn
her hearing loss to advantage and crack
the case before the music died?

Available at your favorite retail outlet.

Silhouette®

BOMBSHELL™

COMING NEXT MONTH

#69 DOUBLE DARE—Vicki Hinze
War Games
For U.S. Air Force Captain Maggie Holt, Christmas had always been about eggnog, mistletoe and holiday cheer...until the biowarfare expert discovered a plot to unleash the deadly DR-27 supervirus at a crowded mall on Christmas Eve. Now Maggie needed a double dose of daring—and the help of the DR-27 antidote's handsome inventor—to defuse certain tragedy.

#70 MS. LONGSHOT—Sylvie Kurtz
The It Girls
After the suspicious deaths of several top show horses, the Gotham Rose spies called on socialite Alexa Cheltingham to go undercover as a grubby groom. Her riches-to-rags transition wasn't easy—mucking stables was a far cry from partying on Park Avenue. She had to protect the mayor's show-jumping daughter, hunt for the horse killer, even dodge a murder rap— all while resisting her chief suspect's undeniable charms....

#71 THE CARDINAL RULE—Cate Dermody
The Strongbox Chronicles
Talk about mixed allegiances! Agent Alisha McAleer's latest assignment involved stealing the prototype of an artificial intelligence combat drone from her CIA handler's own son. And others wanted the drone—including a clandestine organization called the Sciarri and her former partner-turned-mercenary. With even her bosses proving untrustworthy, Alicia was on her own. Again.

#72 SILENT RECKONING—Debra Webb
Going deaf hadn't stopped Merri Walters from rising to the rank of homicide detective. But she had a new set of problems. Her old flame was now her boss, her new partner didn't want to work with a woman and a serial killer was on the loose, targeting country-music starlets. Posing as killer bait seemed suicidal, but Merri marched to her own tune, and wouldn't let anything—or anyone—stand in the way of nabbing her man....

SBCNM1105